A fter the mannequin won
   He'd eaten up some s
in his time, but he had never, e̶v̶e̶r̶ ̶r̶u̶n̶ ̶l̶i̶k̶e̶ ̶t̶h̶i̶s̶. but never before
had he run out of complete irrational fear either. He had known
fear once or twice in his life, but it was usually mild and fleeting.
The time he thought he had knocked-up Megan Mundy in high
school was a good example.
　　This was different.
　　This was Grade-A USDA prime fucking terror.
　　This was animal terror.
　　This was what rabbits knew when owls swooped overhead
or gazelles felt out on the savannah as lions stalked them. Yes,
animal terror. The fear of the hunted, the terror of prey.
　　Don't-don't-don't think about it, he told himself in the vast
emptiness of his skull. *Worry about explanations and stuff later. For
now…for now…just-just worry about getting out of here.*
　　Jesus, his thoughts were stuttering. Was that even possible?
　　He didn't seem to know anything anymore. He was crouched
in the shadows in the backyard of a looming dark house. Every
house on the block was looming and dark. None of them had
any lights on. There had to be people in them, though. And cars
in garages. Yet, he had not seen a single one since they arrived.
　　And that was weird.
　　No cars, no people…what did that mean?
　　He waited there, chewing at his nails until they bled.

DOLL FACE

BY TIM CURRAN

1

It wasn't until later that Ramona realized how neatly it all fit together. Like pieces of a die-cut puzzle, everything simply fit into place in that purely seamless and smooth sort of way that fate managed when it wanted something to happen. Or it wanted people to suffer.

Chazz was too drunk to drive by the time they hit Highway 8, only no one was saying so because although he was a real mellow, easy cat when he was sober, when he was drunk, he was mean as skunk piss and if you didn't want *that* spraying into your eyes; you learned to keep your mouth shut and go with the flow like a turd being sucked down a toilet.

Ramona knew all about that.

"You missed the turn-off," Creep pointed out, getting nervous because he had to cover the morning shift at Donut Den back in the city and five a.m. came real early once you passed the midnight hour.

"I'm taking a shortcut," Chazz told him, an edge to his voice cutting beneath his words like a razor. "So fuck off."

Lex giggled in the backseat and Soo-Lee did, too, because if Lex thought it was funny, then surely it was.

Ramona reserved judgment. She was having trouble finding the humor in a situation where the drunken idiot behind the wheel didn't have the good sense to hand over his keys or admit he was lost.

"This'll cut twenty minutes off the drive," Chazz explained, taking the next right and almost putting the van in the ditch as the road curved sharply down a low hill. The rain was coming down in sheets and the pavement was greasy like it had been oiled with cooking spray.

"You never mentioned a shortcut," Ramona said.

"I just thought of it."

"But you've taken it before?"

"Of course I have."

Which was bullshit of course, Ramona knew. Chazz's sense of direction was seriously challenged when he was sober let alone after ten beers and half-a-dozen Jager Bombs. He had no idea where he was going and with all that alcohol in his system, he couldn't have pissed in a straight line let alone walked one. Any moment now, some hotshot sheriff's deputy was going to come screaming out of the williwags with both flashers going and siren screaming.

And I hope it happens soon, she thought, *before he fucking kills us. Jail time and a suspended license is exactly what he deserves. Some time in a cage will do wonders for him.*

She lit a cigarette and mainly because she knew it would annoy Chazz, who was virulently anti-smoking inside his van. She could feel him tensing behind the wheel, but he didn't say anything. He didn't dare because once he did, she was going to start riding him about the shortcut and exposing his inadequacies behind the wheel.

"My old man's gonna kill me if I lose another job," Creep said.

"You won't lose your job," Lex assured him. "The corporate gods of Donut Den will spare you because of your sheer wizardry with custard and powdered sugar."

"Piss off," Creep said.

Ramona sighed. Why Creep bothered opening his mouth at all was a mystery. Every time he did, Chazz got irritable and Lex got smart-assed. It was strictly a lose-lose situation.

Chazz was leaning forward now, trying to see through the windshield as the rain fell harder and the wipers pumped back and forth manically.

"Can't see shit," he said.

In the back, Danielle said, "We were in this storm once and it was really bad and the next day my sister and I went looking around. The water was really deep and we saw this rat float by. And we were both like, *OMG, that's a rat, a fucking rat.* Who knew we even had rats?"

Ramona had to bite down on her lip because Danielle was such an incurable, inveterate airhead. She could almost hear everyone rolling their eyes.

"Well, if we see any, we'll let you know," Lex said.

Soo-Lee giggled.

Ramona was leaning forward, too. She squinted her eyes as the van came down a hill and into a wooded valley. A green day-glo road sign passed in the murk. "Stokes," she said. "We're coming into some place called Stokes." She turned to Chazz. "What sort place is it? You must have visited it the last time you took this shortcut."

Chazz gritted his teeth. "I don't know. There's lots of little fucking towns out here."

She was getting worried about a little more than Chazz's denial or inebriation by that point, because the twisting road leading down into the valley had an easy two inches of rain covering it and it seemed to be getting deeper. Chazz brought them across a bridge that spanned a swollen river, cut down another curving hill, and the town opened up before them.

Things happened in rapid succession then.

They came in way too fast. It seemed like one moment the town was not even there and the next it opened like a flower, spreading its petals and engulfing them. Chazz hit the brakes, and the van skidded on the greasy pavement. It went to the left, then the right as he fought the wheel and worked the brake pedal.

About the time it seemed like maybe he was going to get it under control, a shape stepped out in front.

Ramona only saw it for a split-second: a vague, man-like shape with raised arms.   ·

Then the van hit it.

They were only doing about thirty-miles-an-hour. Under ordinary circumstances, it was hardly a deadly speed, but certainly enough to break bones and cause concussions and all manner of nasty injuries. Purely from the sound of the impact— something that made Danielle scream like a little girl—Ramona was certain it was going to be ugly.

And particularly when they rolled right over what they had hit with both sets of tires. *Thump-thump, thump-thump.*

2

"*Fuck, fuck, fuck, fuck,*" Chazz was saying, bumping his head repeatedly against the steering wheel. "*I just killed a guy...I just fucking killed a guy.*"

In the back of his mind, he supposed he was waiting for one of them to disagree with him, but nobody was saying a thing. That made it worse. That made him practically want to scream.

You could have listened to Ramona. Just for once you could have listened to her and let her drive.

But he hadn't.

Hell, something in him just *couldn't*. Admitting he couldn't drive because he was fucked-up was like admitting he wasn't a man. It would have been like handing her his balls. *Here, you take these. I'm no good with them.* And there was a dark, macho truth to that, he knew, and one that now sounded unbelievably childish and unbelievably stupid. They wouldn't much care for it in court.

Because he would be going to court.

Drunk driving. Manslaughter. It meant doing time. If he only got five years, he'd be lucky. Five years in a goddamn state hole filled with animals that would all want something from him, if it wasn't his ass, it would be money.

"Maybe you should just drive away before someone comes," Creep said.

Which was exactly the sort of dumbass thing you expected Creep to say...but it was exactly what Chazz was thinking. Drive off, pretend it didn't happen. He was actually considering it. As dangerous and reckless as it was, it made a certain amount of sense.

He looked out through the windshield.

Stokes was dead. He didn't see so much as a single light on. Apparently, they were all sleeping. Nobody had been roused, and that was a good thing. If he drove off and drove off now, who'd be the wiser? Really, who'd be the wiser?

"There's no other way," he said.

The van had died when it skidded to a halt. He turned it over and the starter whined, but it did not catch. He tried it again, and that's when Ramona grabbed his hand. "What the hell are you doing?" she asked him.

God, he could feel her dark eyes boring into him.

"I'm saving my ass," he told her, trying to turn over the van again. "I'm trying to save *all* our asses."

"We're not going anywhere," she said.

He knocked her hand aside. "Oh yes, we are."

She stared at him. "You're going to leave the scene of an accident? Aren't you in enough trouble as it is?"

"Shut up," he said.

"You might want to listen to her," Soo-Lee said. "If you leave the scene of an accident—"

"Zip it," Chazz told her.

Lex sighed. "He won't listen to reason. It's like trying to get a monkey to stop eating its own shit."

"Oh God," Danielle moaned.

"All of you shut the fuck up!" Chazz told them.

"Please, Chazz," Ramona said. "Please, just listen for once, okay? Don't make matters worse."

"Shut up, Ramona. I won't tell you again."

"You won't have to," she said, opening her door and stepping out.

"FUCK ARE YOU DOING, YOU STUPID BITCH?"

"Here we go," Creep said.

Chazz beat his fists against the dashboard. "GET THE FUCK BACK IN HERE OR YOU'RE STAYING BEHIND!"

Ramona didn't bother justifying that with a reply, she slammed her door shut.

Chazz unrolled his window. "Ramona! Get back in here! We have to go."

"I'm not going."

"Get in here or I'll leave you behind! I swear to God I will!"

"Then go," she said. "And when the cops arrive, I'll give them your name and address and the license of your van. Go ahead, Chazz, run from your fucking mistakes like you always do. Just see how far you get."

His jaw hung open. "I can't believe you. After all we've been through."

The truth was, he *did* believe her. This is exactly what he'd expected her to do when he needed her to stand with him. It wasn't that she had high morals or steadfast ethics. No, it wasn't that at all. She had been waiting for something like this. Waiting for a time when he needed her like never before so she could shit all over his parade.

I told her I loved her, too. I actually told the bitch that.

"Fuck you then," he said.

Even though he knew that she had him, he kept trying to start the van but it wasn't happening. The distributor must have gotten wet and all he was doing now was wearing down the battery. The only thing to do was wait, but he couldn't do that. He didn't have the time to wait.

He heard the side door of the van slide open.

"What the fuck are you people doing?"

What they were doing was apparent: they were getting out. Lex got out followed by Soo-Lee, Creep and Danielle. Fucking herd mentality. They were all just like Ramona; they couldn't wait to hang him out to dry. Well, that was fine. They would need him, too, some day. That's what he was going to wait for.

As Creep walked by the open window, Chazz seized him by the arm. "I said, *what the fuck are you doing?*"

Creep, with uncharacteristic defiance, yanked his arm away. "You ran somebody down. Don't you think we should check and see if that somebody's all right?"

But the idea of that made Chazz practically deflate inside.

3

As he followed Ramona over to where the body lay in a crumpled heap, Lex knew that was what he loved about guys like Chazz: the bigger the muscles, the smaller the balls. He was a real force of nature out on the field—Christ, the guy had rushed for three touchdowns against those animals from Cardinal Sprague and that was beyond belief—but when it came down to it, he was a gutless coward. Things had always been too easy for him. He got by on his natural prowess, his athleticism and dark good looks. But none of that was going to buy him beans this time.

Not that Lex was going to tell him that.

Chazz was big. Chazz was powerful. Maybe he had a peanut for a brain, but he could kick serious ass and Lex had no interest in being on the wrong side of *that*. There would be no physical contest between them, because Chazz would have stomped him flat. Mentally, Lex knew he could have pared him down to shavings in a matter of moments, but physically, hah, forget it.

Chazz was back by the van, grumbling.

Soo-Lee was right behind Lex. Creep and Danielle were following her, but hesitantly, like they weren't moving of their own volition, but being towed along by a string.

When they got to the body, Lex said, "Is he…is he alive?"

Ramona shrugged. "I'm not sure."

"Well, is he breathing?" Creep asked.

But nobody could really say.

It appeared to be a man, and he was facedown in the wet street. One arm was stretched out, the other tucked beneath him. One of his legs looked like it was broken at the knee, the foot turned nearly around on the ankle. If he was alive, then he was pretty broken up.

Ramona jogged off and, after a few seconds of arguing with Chazz, returned with a flashlight.

She shined it on the body.

And immediately gasped.

The guy was wearing a dark coat, gray woolen pants, and dirty brown shoes. He was hardly a fashion plate. Lex figured from the way he was dressed he might be a bum or a homeless person or something. His clothes were ragged, his shoes badly scuffed. It looked like he'd grabbed what he could find from a dumpster out back of St. Vinnie's.

Beyond that, he didn't look so good.

His body was terribly distorted—hips twisted, back hunched, head bent to the side at an unnatural angle. There was a rut in his lower back where he had been run over. One of his hands was smashed, marked by a clear tire tread.

Lex didn't know much about medicine, but even he knew that if this guy survived, he would never walk right again or even stand up.

"Well?" Creep said. "Aren't you going to check him?"

The tone of his voice suggested that Lex would have to do it because there was no way in hell he was going to. The revulsion was thick under his words. Danielle wasn't much better. She was mumbling nonsensical things and Lex was certain they were a jumbled version of the *Lord's Prayer.*

"Is he fucking dead or what?" Chazz said, coming up behind them.

He was looking around nervously to see if any of the good folks of Stokes had come out to investigate yet. Lex figured that he was still planning on running.

"Let's just get out of here. I ain't going to prison over this guy. No fucking way."

"Just calm down, you idiot," Ramona told him. "I'll tell them I was driving."

"You...*hey*, that might work," Chazz said, brightening considerably. "It just might."

"Good idea," Lex said. "Let your girlfriend do the time for you."

"You better shut up," Chazz told him.

Lex shrugged. "I wonder if it's true what they say."

Chazz narrowed his eyes. "What?"

"All that stuff about prison rape."

"You motherfucker—"

Lex knew he'd pushed it too far with that one. Chazz came right at him and he would have had him, too, if Ramona hadn't gotten between them and told them both to knock it the fuck off. She was a petite thing, but when she got pissed, she was filled with black, seeping venom.

"Lex?" she said. "Check his pulse."

He kneeled down next to the body. In the beam of the flashlight he couldn't see any blood or other fluids leaking from it. The pavement was wet but only with rain. The others were all watching him, pressing in, eyes wide, mouths hanging open. Christ, he felt like he was about to be lynched.

They trust me to do this. An engineering major for chrissake. Why not Danielle? She's studying nursing.

But he knew the answer to that.

Danielle was a basket case on a good day and today was not a good day. Sighing, he reached down to the guy's extended, smashed hand. It looked like a withered funeral lily. Very pale, almost white as if it was fake or something. Remembering how they did such things on TV, Lex placed his fore- and middle fingers together and reached them beneath the guy's wrist.

And yanked them back.

"What?" Chazz said.

But he wasn't even sure himself. The guy's wrist did not feel like skin at all, more like rubber. Cool rubber. It wasn't right. Lex had never touched a corpse before, but he had a pretty good idea that they did not feel like that.

Swallowing, he touched the wrist with an extended finger.

No, that wasn't right. It was *like* rubber, but it was definitely not rubber. It felt like some kind of plastic...soft, yielding, doughy. He had the feeling that if he jabbed his finger into this guy, it would leave an indentation that would not push itself back out.

"I don't know what the hell's going on here," he said. "But that ain't skin."

4

Soo-Lee reached down and took Lex by the arm, pulling him away from the body and to his feet. It was an impulsive action and she was not even conscious of doing so. The only thing she was aware of was the fact that there was something very wrong here.

"Well, somebody's gotta check him," Creep said.

"How about *you*?" Lex suggested.

"Fuck that."

Soo-Lee looked from the body to the houses and buildings, all of which were black and silent. No, none of this was right. The whole damn town looked like a set from a movie. That was insane and it made no sense whatever, but that's what she was thinking.

Everything's artificial here. Nothing's real.

A creeping dread had gotten beneath her skin now and she started to tremble minutely. She badly wanted to take Lex by the arm and run as fast and far away from this place as they possibly could. She tried to speak, but her mouth was dry as sand.

"Listen," she said when she finally got her voice working. "I think Chazz is right. I think we need to drive out of here right now."

"At last, some common sense," Chazz said.

"We can't leave the scene of an accident," Ramona reminded them. "Now let's just figure out if this guy is okay or not. Can we all agree on that?"

Lex nodded. "Of course, but I'm telling you right now there's something weird about that body. I'm not touching it."

Soo-Lee held on to him tightly as if to guarantee that.

Everyone stood there a moment. Nobody said a thing. They all waited around like mourners, staring at what was sprawled at their feet as if what Lex had said was not perfectly ridiculous, but made a certain amount of sense. In fact, they all backed away a bit in case the body moved.

"Well, somebody needs to do something," Creep said.

"Let's just go," Danielle suggested.

"Oh, you people," Ramona sighed.

She stepped away from them and whipped out her iPhone. She dialed 911. Soo-Lee held her breath. She was certain it wouldn't work, certain they wouldn't get a signal way out here. That's how things worked in horror movies and she was nearly convinced that they had stepped into one, somehow and someway.

But it worked.

Ramona told the operator that they had a man down in the street. He had been hit by a car and they weren't sure if he was alive or not, just unconscious. She answered a series of questions and then she told them where they were.

"Stokes," she said. "Just off Highway Eight. S-T-O-K-E-S. Yes, Stokes."

Here it comes, Soo-Lee thought. *Here comes the bad part.*

Ramona was clearly getting agitated. "Listen, I'm not an idiot. The sign said Stokes." She held the iPhone away from her ear, looking at the others. "Didn't it say Stokes?"

But nobody was sure. She had been the one who'd seen it.

"That's what you said. *Stokes*," Lex told her.

Everyone was standing there in a little knot, pressed together out of some nameless anxiety as Ramona argued with the 911 operator. Soo-Lee had nearly relaxed, thinking Ramona was bringing civilization and safety to them in the form of cops and paramedics.

But that wasn't the case.

"They're saying there is no fucking Stokes," Ramona said, more than a little exasperated. "They never heard of a town called Stokes."

Lex shrugged. "Fuck it. They should be able to track your signal with GPS."

"Yeah," Creep said. "They should be triangulating you right now."

They won't find this place, Soo-Lee thought.

Ramona finally lost it. "Just fucking get here, will you?"

Chazz laughed nervously. "See? They don't give a fuck, so why should we?"

"Somebody's still got to check that body," Lex said.

5

"Oh, for godsake," Ramona sighed. She stepped forward and crouched down. She mumbled something under her breath about the poor guy being hurt and how she couldn't believe everyone was acting like this. But despite her common sense, concern, and daring, they all sensed the hesitation in her words and the hesitation in her movements when she reached out to touch the body. It was like she was sticking her fingers under a shelf where an especially large spider had crawled.

She grasped the wrist and pulled her hand away.

"See?" Lex said. "Maybe it's an artificial limb or something."

"Get it over with already," Chazz snapped, getting frustrated and more than a little pissed-off—two of his most common moods—but not daring to come any closer.

Ramona felt like a kid on a dare.

The others were waiting for her to touch the body again as if it was some dead thing they'd found stuffed in a sewer pipe. Sucking in a breath between clenched teeth, she touched the wrist again. Lex was right: it wasn't skin. It was more like rubber or vinyl, oddly smooth and soft to the touch. She had an insane idea that she could have kneaded it in her fingers, pressed it into any shape she wanted.

She felt around, feeling ill in the pit of her belly, trying to find a pulse.

The skin of the wrist, if skin it was, felt cold before but now it was feeling warm, practically hot with life. Then she found something else. Something that made her yank her hand away.

There was a clear seam between the hand and wrist.

It wasn't a cut or an injury, it was a seam as if the hand

and arm were some kind of prosthetics, artificial parts joined together. She turned to tell the others about it, but something happened that sealed her lips shut.

A siren.

She heard a siren.

But it wasn't from any ambulance or police car. No, this was loud and cutting, a constant droning that rose and fell like a World War II-era air raid siren. It was a shocking, unnerving sound as it reverberated through the streets, echoing across the dark little town, bouncing off rooftops and down narrow alleyways.

Danielle sobbed, but nobody accused her of being a drama queen or a wimp; everyone was as scared as she was. They were rooted to the spot. Hands went up to ears as the droning grew louder and louder, but nobody bolted or ran because there was nowhere to bolt or run *to*.

Ramona herself was shaking.

The siren had a very primeval sound to it like the roaring of some prehistoric beast. Her mind vainly searched for an explanation, but there simply wasn't one. It wasn't a shift whistle or a fire siren. It was bigger than that, louder than that, more menacing than that.

"What the fuck?" Chazz cried out, but they could barely even hear him.

Then it cut out and the only indication that it had even been, was the constant ringing in their ears like they'd just sat through a set with Metallica.

All of them were looking up toward the sky, the rooftops, maybe expecting something big, something *really* big to come ghosting down like a mother ship and abduct them in a beam of light.

Ramona heard a clicking.

Click-click, clicka-clicka-click.

It was coming from the man Chazz had run down. There was a weird clicking sound coming from him, coming from *inside* him. He started to tremble, then shake, thumping and thrashing on the pavement. He reminded her of one of the dummies from that old Herbie Hancock "Rockit" video...it was like his brain was going haywire. His legs were kicking, his hands slapping, his body twisting, his face hammering against the pavement.

She pulled away from him, her guts white with fear.

Then he started to rise.

Still making that weird clicking noise, he got to his knees. His head was bent over to his right shoulder, the hair hanging off to the side as if his scalp had been nearly peeled free. His spine was horribly twisted, his hips nearly sideways, one arm obviously broken as was one leg.

He stood up.

He was facing away from them, balancing himself on his good leg, the other horribly crippled, broken in several places, the foot jutting out at an unnatural angle. As he stood, Ramona heard those clicking sounds. And as freakish as they were, they were nothing in comparison to the series of creaking and cracking noises as he pulled himself up uneasily.

Lex said, "Listen, mister, you better stay down. The ambulance is coming and—"

That's when the guy turned his head and looked at them.

His back was to them…but his head swiveled completely around on his neck until it was facing backward. His face was a contorted thing of some white puttylike material, not a face at all but a mask. It had no eyes, only empty sockets where they might be placed.

Danielle screamed, and she wasn't the only one.

Creep, Lex, and Soo-Lee nearly went over in a heap as they tried to backpedal away and got tangled in each other's legs. Danielle folded-up and went to her knees. Chazz slowly backed away.

Ramona fought to her feet. The flashlight shook in her hand, creating a strobing image of the broken man as he looked back at them. With more groanings and minute snappings, he turned completely around to face them, bringing his head around.

It had to be a mask.

It was some guy wearing a mask, she thought, but it rang hollow. *He turned his fucking head completely around.* He started in her direction, dragging himself forward, his head bouncing on his broken neck. His face was no mask because masks could not grin and he was grinning at her with a lewd, puppetlike smile, making a grating sound in his throat as he tried to speak.

He held out one hand to her, the smashed one, and it looked like a bloodless, crushed starfish.

In all the commotion, no one heard the door of the van slam shut.

6

Everyone scattered.

Chazz shouted out to them to get in the damn van, but they were horrified and something inside them demanded that they run, that they run like hell. There was no thought behind it. There was only instinct, cool and unreasoning survival instinct.

"HEY!" Chazz called out again. "OVER HERE! WHERE THE HELL ARE YOU GOING?"

Lex and Soo-Lee led the charge, Creep pulling Danielle along with him. All of them ran flat out to the end of the street and darted around the corner, disappearing.

Ramona was slowly backing away from the thing that was bearing down on her with its painful, damaged stride. Its body was wrenched to the side, one shoulder humped up higher than the other, its head bouncing around. It was making some awful scraping sound that might have been a voice.

"Ramona!" Chazz cried. "Over here! C'mon! C'mon! Over here!"

In the back of his mind, he knew that this was one of those defining moments in life where a man either proved himself a man or he spent the rest of his years squatting to pee. The freak bearing down on Ramona was not a big guy…but he was weird and fucked-up and disturbed. Chazz figured he could have flattened him, but he wasn't about to do that.

No way in hell.

If that *thing* got its hands on him and put that white grinning face in his own, it would be too much. He would faint. He would go right down. He would crawl under the van and start sucking his fucking thumb and even all his muscles and machismo on the gridiron could not change that fact.

"C'mon!" he cried again.

Ramona was keeping her distance from the broken man, but if she tripped and fell, he would have her. And Chazz had the worst feeling that he would not be able to help her. That he would scream and run. He would not be able to stop himself from doing so.

"Get over here! Get in the fucking van, you dumb bitch!"

Sometimes, he figured, a good insult got somebody's attention all that much quicker. And it worked. She turned away from the thing stalking her and jogged over to him. Chazz, feeling chivalrous, grabbed the passenger-side door and opened it for her.

She was nearly to him.

Then, not four feet away, she skidded to a halt and backed away, tripping and falling on her ass. Chazz, grumbling under his breath, made to go help her up—actually, he was thinking of grabbing her by the hair and *throwing* her into the van—but then something touched his arm.

Something soft and warm.

With a cry, he turned and saw another one of those things sitting in the passenger seat. In the glow of the dome light, he saw it was a woman…or a grim mockery of the same. Her face was white like the man's, set with tiny cracks like an antique vase. She was bald like a mannequin without a wig and had no eyebrows. She had blank white eyes like boiled eggs. She was naked, her breasts—lacking nipples—were pert and artificial looking.

He screamed.

He wasn't even aware that he had until it came ripping out of him with considerable volume and force. She had his arm. She was gripping it with considerable pressure, her sharp little fingers digging in deep. As he tried to pull clear of her, he saw one thing that nearly put him to his knees.

Her hand.

It wasn't real.

It wasn't flesh-and-blood.

Dear God, the fingers were perfectly white and perfectly smooth, tapering and feminine, though mottled as if they had been stored away in some moldering trunk for many years. But for all that, he saw that each finger was segmented—in place of the knuckles there were glassy ball joints.

It took him maybe a split second to realize that.

And by then, she had turned in the passenger seat. She only had one arm. Some kind of armature protruded from her shoulder where another might have been attached. Her breasts and belly were mottled like her fingers. Her cracked, white doll-like face was smiling at him, one corner of her mouth pulled up in a crooked grin of defilement.

But the worst thing was that she had spread her legs to show him the hairless slit between her thighs.

Chazz, vaguely aware that Ramona was crying out behind him, lost all control. The horror of the situation bottomed him right out. Everything inside him seemed to get sucked into some massive spiraling black hole and he screamed and went wild with rage. With every bit of strength he had, which was considerable, he yanked his arm away and the mannequin woman came with it, holding on tight. He flailed his arm around, trying to throw her and her body made a horrible clacking sound as if she was a jointed wooden doll. Her mouth was open in a wide toothless grin by that point and she was trying to wrap her legs around him. He saw all of this in ghosting, blurring images as he swung her back and forth.

Finally, he threw her.

She hit the ground and broke apart on impact, her arm clattering away from her body, one leg broken free beneath the knee. Her head rolled across the pavement like a ball, the jaws still opening and closing.

Her hand was still clenching his forearm.

Even divorced of her body, the fingers were still moving, squeezing and kneading his arm. He screamed again and tore it free, leaving four bleeding ruts in his flesh. Not only that, but a single white finger that still trembled like a dying insect.

He was out of it by then.

He was drenched with a cold/hot sweat, shaking and hysterical, making shrill moaning sounds in his throat. When Ramona tried to reach out for him, he knocked her aside, sent her sprawling to the pavement with his animal fury.

Then he ran in a wild, blind flight.

Because the pieces of the mannequin woman were not as dead as they should have been...they were still moving. And he was sure her decapitated head was calling his name.

7

When she hit the ground, Ramona was knocked unconscious. She was out of it no more than two or three minutes, but when she opened her eyes and looked around, Chazz was nowhere to be seen. A voice in the back of her head, the same one that had warned her away from him in the first place, said to her, *he cold-cocked you. He knocked you on your ass so he could make his getaway. That's the kind of person he is. I hope you're really fucking happy with your choice in men.*

But she wasn't.

She never had been.

Ever since she was fourteen, unfortunately, she seemed to choose the same type again and again, fulfilling some puerile fantasy of the perfect guy with the perfect body and the perfect face. But if there was one thing she'd learned again and again the hard way, it was that the better something looked on the outside, the less there was on the inside.

This all passed through her mind upon waking, upon realizing that she had been abandoned.

Get your ass moving, Ramona! You're in danger!

And oh yes, she was, she certainly was at that. It didn't take her long to remember why. She got up, sitting there on her ass, a throbbing in the back of her head. Her fingers brushed over a knob of flesh that had risen almost cartoonlike under her long dark hair, which was matted with blood.

I swear to God, Chazz, you're going to regret this. One way or another, you're really going to regret this, you asshole.

And it was as that passed through her mind that reality inserted itself and she realized exactly *why* she was in terrible danger. The broken man. He had been after her…but she saw no sign of him now. But there was more than just him to contend with.

The mannequin woman.

She had still been alive, been animate, whatever you wanted to call it, after Chazz had knocked her to the ground in pieces.

Very alert suddenly, Ramona looked around.

Yes, the woman's parts were still scattered, but they weren't moving.

Her torso was about ten feet away, her leg off to the side, her arm off near her head, which lay there dead and sightless on the ground, jaws sprung. Her hand was over near the curb.

Breathing hard, Ramona crouched there on all fours looking at the remains.

A very rational voice in her head told her that the very idea of this doll-like thing actually being alive, actually moving after it was broken apart, was ludicrous. It wasn't a person. It was some sort of machine and now it was broken. Like the man, it was broken.

Oh, what kind of fucked-up nightmare is this anyway?

And why the hell weren't the police here by now? What the hell were they doing for godsake? Didn't they realize this was a fucking emergency?

She stood up, feeling dizzy and disoriented.

She dug in the pocket of her leather coat and pulled out a pack of Marlboros and a lighter. The cigarette tasted good. Besides, Chazz wasn't here to chide her about smoking and when she saw that piece of shit again, she was going to flick her ash at him and butt her cigarette right in his fucking eye.

Where the hell were the others?

Christ, the idea of being alone in this place was just too much.

She stepped away from the shadow of the van and got up on the sidewalk. She took out her iPhone and called 911 again. It took her precious seconds to get through and all the while, she felt nervous. She had the most awful feeling she was not alone.

"Listen, I don't know what's going on, but I called for an ambulance, for the police, over here in Stokes, and nobody has shown up. Yes, I know you don't know where it is. Can't you track my signal or something?"

"Ma'am," the operator said. "We're having trouble with our equipment."

"So what am I supposed to do?"

"You're sure you haven't made a mistake?"

"Yes, I'm sure!"

There was silence for a moment or two. "Ma'am, could you give me your exact whereabouts again?"

Un-fucking-believable. "Stokes. S-T-O-K-E-S. I'm not from here and I don't see any street signs. I'm just inside the town, just off Highway 8. If they come in on Highway 8, they'll be right on top of me."

More silence. "Ma'am, there must be some kind of mistake."

"There's no mistake! I can see the highway from where I'm standing and—"

What the fuck?

The highway was not there.

She knew they had come in on it. They had just entered the outskirts of Stokes when Chazz hit that guy or whatever the hell he was. There was no doubt of that. She had seen the highway leading out when she was backing away from the broken man.

But now there was no highway.

The road led off to a dead end, two streets intersecting it. She saw nothing but a solid wall of houses down there. It was impossible. Her knees felt weak and her heart skipped in her chest. This couldn't be happening. It wasn't possible. The van was still there. She could see the skid marks. Everything was the same except the highway had disappeared.

"Ma'am? Ma'am?" the operator was saying over the line.

"Please…please hurry," Ramona said. "I'm in Stokes and I'm in danger, I'm in terrible danger."

"Ma'am, please listen to me, okay? The only Stokes on Highway 8 burned to the ground back in the 1960s, I'm told," the operator said with a curious dread beneath her words. "So you must be mistaken."

Ramona found that she could barely breathe. "Please… please just come after me. Oh, dear God…I know I'm in danger."

And she was. This was a nightmare. The highway brought them in, now it was gone. Mannequins walked. Reality was turned upside down and inside out. It would have been extremely easy to have a nervous breakdown and give up. Far too easy.

She heard a clattering sound behind her.

Her skin went cold, a needling fear spreading in waves from her belly to her chest. She turned around, breathless with terror.

The mannequin woman…or her parts…were moving.

The torso stood up, hovering there in midair, swinging back and forth as if it was connected to fine invisible wires high overhead. It balanced on one leg. As Ramona watched, the rest of it began to come together. The broken hand crawled over to the torso. The other leg followed suit, inching its way along as did the arm. The head rolled like a ball. And when they were near, they were drawn in place, again, as if unseen wires manipulated them.

But even so, the mannequin woman was not whole.

Not entirely.

Her broken arm hung from its socket by cords as did her hand and leg, her head slumped forward on her neck.

Ramona screamed.

She wasn't and had never been a screamer, but what she saw was like ice water thrown in her face and everything inside her vented itself.

The mannequin woman dangled there, loose and boneless like some limp marionette…and then she jumped away into the darkness above. Or was towed away.

Regardless, she was gone.

That's when Ramona heard the van start up.

Chazz?

The headlights came on, spearing into her. They were so bright that she had to squint her eyes and hold her hand up. The engine was revved again and again. Slowly, cautiously, she walked over in its direction, stepping very carefully and expecting trouble. She could see a shape in the driver's seat.

A shape with a broken neck, head drooping limply to one shoulder.

Shit!

The van roared forward, laying rubber. It came right at her, picking up momentum. It was going to run her down. As it vaulted forward, jumping the curb, she threw herself to the side and it missed her by inches, plowing right through the plate glass windows of a little barbershop in a spray of glass. The engine revved again. The driver—and she knew very fucking well who or *what* that was—was trying to pull back out. The rear wheels were spinning and smoking. The van was lodged on something.

She broke into a run, heading in the direction she thought Lex and the others had gone.

Behind her, the van pulled free and squealed out into the street.

Headlights framed her again as it bore down on her.

8

"Now what?" Creep said when they finally came to a stop and caught their breath. "Now what the hell do we do?"

"We just try and mellow out," Lex told him.

"Oh, wonderful plan."

Soo-Lee shook her head. "Just shut up. We need to get a grip here and quit panicking so we can figure things out."

"I just want to go home," Danielle said.

Which was about the tenth time now that she had said that. The sound of her voice was starting to go right up Creep's spine. He had a mad desire to slap her right across the face. He would never do such a thing, at least he didn't think so, but he wanted to really bad. And that was partially out of rage, frustration, and annoyance, but mostly because her insipid weakness reminded him so much of his own.

They had taken off in a blind run after that shit came down with the crazy man. Creep still wasn't sure what to make of that. Had he really seen it? Yes, yes, of course he had. It had taken something real ugly to get them all running in the first place and it had been ugly all right. But where were they now? He wasn't even sure. They had run down the street and around the corner and kept running. They were two or three streets away from the van now.

Away from Chazz. No loss there.

But also away from Ramona and Creep had a real thing for her. He hadn't known her before tonight. He knew Chazz. Christ, he was the guy who fixed Chazz's laptop after the idiot locked it up downloading porn. Creep did a lot of work for the boys on the team and that's how he had hooked up with Chazz. Ramona was Chazz's squeeze, but they barely tolerated each other and he knew for a fact that Chazz was sleeping with at least three other girls. And he was sure that Ramona knew it, too.

What was her thing? Did she dig abusive relationships? Maybe. Some girls were like that.

Chazz had thrown the whole thing together. Lex and Soo-Lee, he and Ramona, and Creep. They caught Green Day at the Garden. Danielle was some chick Ramona knew, so they brought her along as Creep's blind date. It hadn't worked so well. She gave him the cold shoulder and he thought she was an idiot. She was strictly the girly cheerleader type that you had to treat like a princess just to get a freaking handjob on the fifth date.

Not like Ramona.

Ramona was petite with long black hair, great cheekbones and big dark eyes. Kind of olive-skinned like a Native American. And fierce. God, she was fierce and smart and in-charge. She made his blood boil.

"Let's just wait here a bit," Lex said. "If things are cool, we'll go back and look for Ramona and Chazz. My guess is that they're hiding out, though. They probably won't come up for air until the police get here."

"Shouldn't they have been here by now?" Danielle said.

Score one for the dizzy blonde, Creep thought.

"Soon," Lex said.

"Sure," Soo-Lee agreed, although it was obvious she didn't believe it for a minute.

"They're not here because they don't know where *here* is," Creep said, which only got him stony silence.

He peered down the street and saw only darkness.

The glass fronts of shops reflected back cool moonlight. Shadows spilled out over the walk in murky puddles. He had no reason to believe there was any immediate danger down there, hiding and waiting to leap out at them...yet, he was certain of it. He could feel that dread certainty crawling inside his guts like looping worms.

They were in danger.

Incredible danger.

He could feel it moving around them in the darkness like the cold coils of a snake. It was circling them, pressing in ever closer, grinning with long white teeth and watching them with hungry, ebon eyes.

Just stop it. Just stop that shit.

He swallowed it down before he lost it, before he really lost it, and did something stupid like running again.

But Christ, whatever was out there—and he figured the broken man was but a finger of it—it was like he could feel it reaching out for him, wanting to wrap bony digits around his throat.

"I don't like this shit," he said. "We're like sitting targets or something."

Soo-Lee sighed. "Calm down. We called 911. The police and ambulance should be here soon. We should be hearing their sirens anytime now."

Creep rolled his eyes.

He didn't like this shit.

Soo-Lee was easy on the eyes, exotic and Asian and all that, but she was like some extension of Lex and he didn't like that at all. They could pretend there wasn't something very messed-up about this situation, but they were wrong. They could try and rationalize it all they wanted, but Creep's fucking Spidey-Sense was tingling. In fact, it felt positively electrical. His stomach was hollow and his scalp felt like it wanted to crawl right off the back of his head. He had the most disturbing feeling that they had now entered the Twilight Zone.

And if he needed more evidence, then that man...that mannequin...that *thing* they had run down pretty much clinched it.

Danielle was pressed up against the plate glass windows of a coffee shop now like a spider flattening itself on a brick to suck up some heat.

Her entire body was shaking.

She isn't goddamn well helping, he thought. *She isn't helping at all.*

And again, he knew it was because she was acting on the outside the way he was feeling on the inside.

"Danielle," Soo-Lee said in a very relaxed, calming voice. "It's going to be okay. The police will be coming soon. Then we can get out of here. Just try to take it easy."

But she wasn't taking it easy.

She was shaking so bad she was rattling the window.

"It's gonna come for us. It's gonna find us. It's gonna kill us," she said, her voice high and squeaking like she was eight years old again. And maybe she was at that.

Lex walked down to the corner and Creep followed him. Soo-Lee made to join them, but Danielle gripped her arm like a little girl who was afraid of the dark.

Creep looked down the street. "I think someone should go take a look for Ramona and Chazz. What if they're hurt or something?"

Lex nodded. "I'll flip you for it. I don't want us both going. I want one of us to stay with the girls."

Creep liked that. It was the kind of thing a hero said in an old movie. One of those silly Hollywood clichés. But he was okay with it. He swallowed down his fear. "You stay, Lex. I'll go. You're a cooler head than I am. I'll just make them more nervous."

Lex didn't argue the fact; it was obvious.

"I'll take a quick run down there and run right back."

"Okay. Be careful."

Creep took off. He was surprised he had the guts to do it at all. Was it Ramona? Yeah, he figured it was. He had an adolescent fantasy brewing in the back of his mind where he rescued her and she was grateful.

Very, *very* grateful.

He went down to the block where they'd turned the corner. God, the shadows were everywhere, so black, so reaching. They were strung like knitted yarn. He got to the last storefront, a bank with gold leaf lettering in the windows. Nice and archaic. He peered around the corner.

His heart was pounding and his knees felt weak.

He could see the van down there. Moonlight glimmered off the windshield. One of the doors was open. There was nothing between it and he but glistening wet pavement.

No sign of Chazz or Ramona.

Nothing at all moved down there.

He pulled out his Nokia and called Chazz's cell, got his voice mail and texted him, but got nothing in reply. Either he didn't have his phone with him or it was dead or he was—

Don't get going with that shit.

They could have been behind the van, he supposed. That was possible.

No. He wasn't going to go down there. Too risky. He'd checked on them and that's all he'd intended on doing. Lex was probably right: they were hiding. Yet…his stomach felt light and fluttery. If it had wings, it could have flown right out of his belly.

The doll man was nowhere to be seen.

Weird. It was all so damn weird.

He peered back around the corner to make sure Lex and the others were still there, they were, then looked back toward the van…except there was no van. It was gone. The moonlight was shining off the pavement where it had been.

Creep blinked his eyes like they did in movies when they couldn't trust what they were seeing, but the van was still gone. He was confused, disoriented. Reality seemed to be unwinding like a ball of twine. He peered back around the corner, thinking of calling out to Lex, then turned and looked again.

The van was there.

What kind of fucked-up shit is this?

He ran back down until he reached Lex. He leaned up against a building, panting. "They're not down there. I don't see anything but the van."

And maybe I don't even see that.

Lex sighed. "Well, we can't wait for 'em. We have to find some place to hide or a vehicle to get us out of here…unless we chance the van."

Creep swallowed. "I don't like that idea."

"Then we need a car."

"Man, have you *seen* a single car? A truck? A bicycle for that matter?"

"No."

Creep was going to elaborate further on that but Soo-Lee called, *"Lex!"*

They ran back to her, expecting trouble. Expecting at the very least that Danielle was really losing it or having a breakdown or something. But that wasn't it at all.

"Look," Soo-Lee said.

At the end of the block across the street, lights had come on.

9

It took Chazz a good twenty minutes to calm down, to get his heart to stop racing and his skin to stop crawling and that god-awful clamminess out of his bones. But even so, he wasn't in the best of shape. He was still shaking, his eyes still darting about madly, and his teeth given to strange bouts of chattering. He felt feverish and sick in his belly, and he was certain he was crazy.

After the mannequin woman, he had run and run and run.

He'd eaten up some serious yardage out on the gridiron in his time, but he had never, ever run like this. But never before had he run out of complete irrational fear either. He had known fear once or twice in his life, but it was usually mild and fleeting. The time he thought he had knocked-up Megan Mundy in high school was a good example.

This was different.

This was Grade-A USDA prime fucking terror.

This was animal terror.

This was what rabbits knew when owls swooped overhead or gazelles felt out on the savannah as lions stalked them. Yes, animal terror. The fear of the hunted, the terror of prey.

Don't-don't-don't think about it, he told himself in the vast emptiness of his skull. *Worry about explanations and stuff later. For now...for now...just-just worry about getting out of here.*

Jesus, his thoughts were stuttering. Was that even possible?

He didn't seem to know anything anymore. He was crouched in the shadows in the backyard of a looming dark house. Every house on the block was looming and dark. None of them had any lights on. There had to be people in them, though. And cars in garages. Yet, he had not seen a single one since they arrived.

And that was weird.

No cars, no people…what did that mean?

He waited there, chewing at his nails until they bled.

Knowing he had to come up with some sort of plan but, God, he was afraid to move. He wished Ramona was here. She would know what to do. She always seemed to know what to do.

But you left her out there.

No, he didn't leave her. It wasn't like that. He'd run, and he thought maybe she was running with him. The fear had gotten the best of him. He knew part of that was true and part of it was a dirty lie, but it went down easier that way because cowardice was something he despised in other people and could not tolerate in himself. That's why it was better not to think about it, to shove it aside where he didn't have to look at it or think about it or consider the kind of person he truly was now that his black roots were showing.

The thing was to think about how to get out of this.

He breathed in and out deeply until he calmed. He often used breathing exercises before a big game when his nerves were a little on edge. Coach had taught him that. God, he wished Coach were here now. Like Ramona, he would know what to do.

"Just stop being a pussy," he whispered there in the darkness.

Yeah, that was the thing. On the good side, he hadn't really run anyone down, just some kind of dummy that looked like a man but wasn't really a man, maybe a robot or some kind of big windup toy. The idea of that made him want to giggle, but he was afraid to giggle. He had the most awful feeling that once he started he would not be able to stop.

Regardless, it hadn't been a man he had hit…just a thing.

And there were more than one of them in this damn town so he had to be careful. The way he saw it, there were really only a couple things he could do. He either backtracked—if such a thing was even possible by this point—and found the others or he tried to find the van. Other than that, he could knock on some doors and try to find some help.

Or keys. If I can find some keys and a car, I'll fucking steal it.

Either way, he wasn't going to accomplish anything sitting here shaking in his shoes.

Carefully, he stood up.

He took inventory of himself head to toe. He was a big, fast, strong guy. He felt his own power and it calmed him, gave him strength, brought some of that old arrogance back. If anybody could get this done, it was him, because he had the tools.

Letting out a breath, he moved through the shadows of the yard.

Everything was so unbelievably silent out there. There was not so much as the sound of a truck in the distance or a dog barking. It wasn't fucking natural. The moon had come up now, big and bright, frosting rooftops and lawns. But for all the light it brought, it also increased the shadows.

He walked around to the front of the house, still staying in the shadows of a big old oak in the sideyard. He was tense and expectant. Looking down the street, he saw the direction he had come from. Either he retraced his steps or he'd have to start knocking on doors.

And why did the very idea of that terrify him?

But he knew. If he made noise, he could be heard and he was afraid of being heard. If there were more of those things out there, they'd know exactly where he was.

As he edged nearer to the sidewalk, he retreated back under the tree.

Something, instinct maybe, made him go back. He didn't like the idea of being out on the sidewalk or in the street where he could be seen. It was better to sneak through backyards. That made him feel more relaxed. He liked the idea of camouflage.

He vaulted hedges and fences, dropping into yards, hiding in pockets of shadow until he felt it was safe to move again. The farther he went, the more confident he became.

He slipped over another fence, scanning the yard between the house and the garage that flanked the alley. It looked all right. In fact, it—

Shit.

He heard a sound and everything inside him was instantly reduced to a cool, slopping jelly. He crouched just inside the fence, his hand gripping one of the posts and listened.

Tap-tap, tap-tap, tap-tap.

What the hell was that?

It was coming from the alley and Chazz was far beyond the point where he could believe that it was anything perfectly ordinary or perfectly harmless. He waited there, his entire body trembling.

Tap-tap, tap-tap, tap-tap.

He could see a moonlit stretch of alley from where he was. A shape came hobbling into view and his heart dropped south of his stomach. It was another one of those mannequin things. Oh yes, there was no doubt of it. It moved with an uneasy, hobbling gait and that was because it only had one real leg, the other being a pegleg like a pirate in an old movie.

It kept coming.

Tap-tap, tap-tap, tap-tap.

Then it paused as if it had heard something.

It looked like a woman, an old woman with a bent back. He could see her clearly in the glow of the moon. She was dressed in ragged clothes like a bag lady, a sack slung over one shoulder. She had a wild shock of white hair that was long and stringy, but patchy on the skull itself. Her scalp seemed to shine. And her face…he couldn't see it too well, but it was grotesque and hanging like a grinning gunnysack.

Tap-tap, tap-tap, tap-tap.

She went on her way and Chazz did not relax until he heard her tapping pegleg fade into the distance. Even then, he was shaking and sweating.

He crept through the yard, moving even more carefully now, frightened of every shadow and bunched dark shape. They could have been all around him for all he knew. One of them could have been reaching out for him. No…no, he couldn't let himself think things like that. It wasn't acceptable. He was on the verge of hysteria and he knew it. He was thinking like an animal again. He wanted to run, to flee, to find a new hiding place.

What he really needed was the van or another car.

And a weapon. Not a gun or a knife but something like a good Louisville Slugger. Something he could shatter those things with if they got too close. That had to be his priority.

He sidled along a house, studying its dark windows, praying that nothing would move behind them. He was going to chance it and run across the street. It was the only way, and he had to put some distance between himself and Lady Pegleg.

A sound.

Oh God, no.

It was getting louder and coming closer and he was locked down with fear, frozen with it. He couldn't even get his body to respond. His brain was filled with white noise and he wanted to scream his head off.

Tap-tap, tap-tap, tap-tap.

She was coming again. She had paused in the alley, sensing that he was near and now she was coming back to find him. She would not stop until she did and Chazz knew this deep in the black beating drum of his heart.

He made his body move.

She was slow, he was fast. He had to keep that in mind.

He moved out toward the sidewalk, then, with a burst of manic speed, he crossed the street into the shadows of the houses across the way. He stood by a porch, panting not so much out of exertion, but of numbing fear. He waited and, *Jesus,* that tapping was coming again.

Tap-tap, tap-tap, tap-tap.

She was not in the alley over there anymore. No, no, no. She had found the yard he had hid in and she was coming up the flagstone walk that led to the front porch. He saw her hobbling shape begin to emerge from the shadows. Raw panic breaking loose inside him, he made ready to run.

Then he saw an open window.

It was there toward the back of the house like it was waiting for him and something inside him was certain that it was. But he would not acknowledge that. He *could* not acknowledge that. He needed a place to hide. Lady Pegleg wasn't fast, but she was relentless and she would keep coming and coming until she ran him to death.

Chazz wasn't going to let that happen.

He snuck over to the window and with an easy flex of muscles he slipped through into a darkened room. Murky shapes were all around him. He listened and waited, but nothing moved.

Quietly as possible, he slid the window down until it was only open an inch or two.

Then he waited.

Lady Pegleg was crossing the street.

Tap-tap, tap-tap, tap-tap.

10

Even though the van had passed by and its tail lights winked out in the distance, Ramona knew she was still in the shit. In fact, she was barely keeping her head above it. She thought for certain when she ducked into the recess between the two buildings that the van—and the horror that drove it—would find her.

But off it went.

And off she had to go.

The others had to be somewhere. Unless, of course, those doll people had gotten them. She'd already encountered two of them and she wasn't quite so naïve to believe that there were not more.

But what was this place?

What was its point?

It wasn't Stokes. She knew that much now. She didn't know where they were but it sure as hell was not Stokes because Stokes didn't exist. Stokes had burned down in the 1960s. Either they had all suffered some collective nervous breakdown and were drooling in separate padded rooms or what she had seen and what she had experienced thus far was real.

You know it's real. You damn well know it.

But that made it all worse, didn't it?

It meant reality as she knew it had split wide open and they had fallen through the cracks. They had to be somewhere. As she looked up and down the streets, she was disturbed by what she saw. It was all so…fake. So perfectly arranged. So very artificial. It was like a small town you saw in an old Warner Brothers movie. The neighborhoods of nice little houses separated by squared-off hedges and fronted by narrow streets, rows of big elms and oaks. All the houses were older two-story jobs, but very well kept. There was not a single ranch house to be seen or any other evidence of post-World War II architecture. Even the street lights—none of which were lit—weren't modern. They were more along the line of street*lamps*.

Creepy didn't begin to describe it.

And the storefronts she had passed, all the little Main Street-type businesses lined up—barbershops, cafes, drugstores, offices—looked like a Hollywood director's idea of small-town America, something envisioned by Frank Capra.

Ramona had grown up in a small town; she had lived in several, passed through dozens and dozens in her life getting from point A to point B. Some were quaint, some were ugly, some were pretty, some run-down, but they all had personality.

Stokes had none.

It was sterile and synthetic like it had been kept in a box. Small towns came together in bits and pieces through the years, but Stokes looked like it had been built according to a very specific plan and that was to emphasize its small town-*ness*, if that made any sense.

This place was an imitation.

But there had to be a point to it all.

Just as there had to be a reason why they were drawn into it in the first place.

Funny, too, how there had been a near-torrential downfall when they'd entered the valley and now not a drop of rain. Even the streets were dry as if it hadn't rained in weeks. Interesting.

She stepped out into the street and listened. Nothing. No approaching sirens. Not so much as a car passing in the distance. No cars, no people, no life. Stokes was like a fucking doll house.

She walked as calmly as possible up the sidewalk.

She would go in the direction the others had run, then check out two or three more streets looking for a sign of them, then she was fucking getting out.

If she could get out at all.

11

"I suppose we should go over there and have a look," Lex said. "I rather doubt those lights came on purely by accident."

But Creep didn't like the idea. "Fuck that. It's a trap. I know it's a trap. It's like...like...like..."

"Bait?" Soo-Lee said.

"Yeah! That's it, Lex. It's bait to draw us in. When we get there, something's going to happen and I know it. Those things'll be in there, waiting for us."

"Maybe that's exactly why we *should* go over there."

"Are you nuts?"

Lex shrugged. "Something's going on here and I got a real nasty feeling that we're not leaving until we figure out what. In fact, if we don't figure it out, we may never get out."

"I'm all for walking right out of here."

"It's not going to be that easy."

"How do you know?"

The thing was, Lex wasn't sure. He had a very bad feeling that all of this was not by accident. That it was on purpose. That this town existed for a specific reason and they were drawn into it for a purpose. "Listen," he said, "here's what we'll do. I'll go check it out. You wait here. You went to look for Chazz and Ramona, now it's my turn."

Creep shrugged. It was obvious he still didn't like it, but the idea of there being no personal danger involved, bolstered him some. "All right."

"I'm going, too," Soo-Lee said.

Creep sighed. "And I babysit the psycho."

Lex ignored that and led Soo-Lee across the street.

Creep was right, of course. Maybe it wasn't a trap exactly—or maybe it was—but there was something very weird about it like there was something very weird about this town, which, presumably, did not exist in the first place. There were no lights on anywhere and now one just happened to come on. Now wasn't that interesting?

But, honestly, he didn't think it was interesting at all.

He thought it was downright disturbing.

Soo-Lee right behind him, he moved cautiously up the sidewalk until he got to the diner. Looking through the plate glass windows he could see tables and booths, a counter with round stools.

But no people.

Somebody must have turned the lights on.

"This is creepy," Soo-Lee whispered.

Yes, it was at that.

What was also creepy was that the word DINER was lettered in each window. No name other than that, just DINER. Not the DOWNTOWN DINER or the DO-DROP-IN DINER or JIMMY'S HASH HOUSE or BOBBIE'S BURGER BARN. It was all very generic like the town itself, which made him realize that every shop and store he had seen were like that—GROCERIES and INSURANCE, BARBERSHOP and DENTIST, but none of them with any more specific titles.

It reminded him of the elaborate train set he had put together with his dad when he was in grade school. There had been depots and mountains, trees and roundhouses, and a little town where every storefront had a very generic title just like in Stokes.

This is everytown, he thought. *It's bits and pieces of every town everyone has ever seen from every old movie, every old TV show, every fucking Norman Rockwell calendar. There's a reason for that and you better figure out what it is.*

"I'm going in," he told her. "Maybe you should wait out here."

"No thanks."

He pulled open the door, and it jingled. He stepped inside.

And what was weird in the first place only got that much weirder. His first impression on coming through the door was that the place smelled old, empty, and musty...but that changed when he was three feet inside. It was like the diner suddenly came to life. He could smell hot coffee and burgers, pie and french fries. It all smelled exactly the way he thought a diner should smell, as if his own memories and expectations had been hijacked.

There was food set out everywhere.

Lex blinked and then blinked again because he was certain it was a hallucination of some sort. It had to be a hallucination. Nothing else could possibly explain it. On the counter, he saw cups of coffee that were still steaming. A cheeseburger on a plate with a bite out of it, a fry dipped in ketchup. A slice of blueberry pie with ice cream that was not even melted yet. It was the same at the booths and tables: bowls of hot soup, malteds in icy metal cups, BLTs and grilled cheese sandwiches. The soups were barely touched, malteds barely sipped, the sandwiches all with the requisite one or two bites from them as if to emphasize the fact that the diners had all just left...perhaps seconds ago.

"What the heck is all this?" Soo-Lee said.

But he didn't know.

Together, they stepped behind the counter, moving very slowly and carefully as if they expected to find a tripwire. There were no booby traps, only pots of hot coffee and a large, freshly poured Coke in a cup. A chalkboard announced the day's specials: HAMBURGER PLATE .79¢ CHICKEN NOODLE SOUP .50¢, CHICKEN FRIED STEAK $1.00.

"Can't beat the prices," Soo-Lee said.

No, you can't, Lex thought. *And when was the last time you could get food that cheap? The 1960s? The 1950s?*

Everything was fucked-up and out of whack.

They peered through the archway into the kitchen. Burgers and bacon were frying on a big, greasy range.

Lex went back out into the dining area. He picked up a fry and examined it closely.

"You're not going to eat that?" Soo-Lee said.

But that's exactly what he was going to do. He doubted the physical reality of what he was seeing so he was putting it to the test. It felt like a fry. The weight and texture were perfect...but it had no odor and he was willing to bet it had no taste.

He looked around. Incredible. This place was like the *Mary Celeste* of diners. All the patrons had been mysteriously snatched away into thin air. *Oooo-weee-oooo.* Except that it was all bullshit, a carefully constructed ruse. There had never been people here.

He dropped the fry back onto its plate. "It's fake," he said. "All this food is fake. It's like that plastic food little kids play with. And I bet that's exactly how it tastes."

The words had no more than left his lips when he felt a subtle shift in the atmosphere of the diner. It was quick and inexplicable. He no longer smelled good things to eat and drink. No, now he smelled mildew and rot.

"Lex," Soo-Lee said, grabbing his arm.

But he saw, all right. There were mice running around on the floor. A rat was on a table gnawing at a club sandwich that looked like it had been sitting there for weeks. The bread was green with mold. There were flies everywhere. A beetle crawled out of a malted cup. A burger was writhing with maggots.

Yes, it had happened everywhere.

Everywhere.

The walls were dingy, the plate glass windows dirty, the counter and tables filthy with rat droppings and food scraps gone black. The red vinyl booth cushions were torn open, stuffing hanging out. There was three inches of dust on the floors. Ceiling tiles above were water-stained, some missing entirely.

"Let's get out of here," Soo-Lee said.

Yes, that was a good idea. A very good idea because he had the most appalling feeling that the diner was decaying, and if they did not get out, they would decay with it like worms trapped in a rotting apple. Beyond the grimy counters, the chalkboard had changed now.

It no longer offered the day's specials. Now it read:

LEX FONTAINE
SOO-LEE CHANG
CHAZZ ACKELY
RAMONA LAKE
CREEP RODGERS
DANIELLE LECARR

† REST IN PEACE †

A white fear opening up inside him, Lex grabbed Soo-Lee and they raced for the door...only there was no door. It was not simply missing, it was like it had never been there in the first place. There were only the plate glass windows with their lower fringe of curtains hanging like dingy rags, but no aperture where a door might have been placed.

Soo-Lee was shaking.

So was he.

"What...what is this?" she said, maybe more to herself than to him.

But without a doubt it was an excellent question: *what exactly was this?* What sort of mind game was it and what was the fucking point of it all? Who was running it? If they wanted Lex and Soo-Lee to be unnerved and scared, well they had been successful. Lex's skin was crawling. It felt like something inside his head wanted to fly apart. He felt helpless and trapped like a fly in a web.

Christ, he felt like he was buried alive.

But he had to think. He knew that much. He couldn't lose it because whatever puppet master was running this show wanted him to. The only real weapon he'd ever had in his life was his mind and he couldn't let all this dull its edge now.

Think.

Yes, *yes.* The image of the diner had been offered to them with flawless diner perfection: the smells, the sights, even the sounds of the soft drink bubblers and coffee percolating. But he had turned his nose up at it. Being suspicious, he refused to accept the simple joy of what was offered, so it was made worse. He was being punished.

"Well," he said, very loudly, "I'm not buying this either, so you better fucking try again."

This time, the atmospheric shift was not so subtle.

He felt a wave of force pass through the room. It was actually tangible and had enough intensity to nearly knock the both of them down. It made him feel woozy and dizzy and he wondered if it had been such a good idea to challenge the puppet master of this not-so-little nightmare.

The room shifted.

The air seemed to crack open like an egg.

Lex's vision went blurry. He held on to Soo-Lee, who was having trouble staying on her feet. When they got a hold of themselves and their vision cleared—it was like the room had gone misty or out-of-focus—they looked around and saw there was more than decay and filth to contend with.

They saw bodies.

Corpses.

Soo-Lee gasped and Lex felt his stomach contents bubble up the back of his throat. For one second he thought the room was filled with mannequin people, but it wasn't that at all. It was worse. Oh yes, it was much worse. The corpses were arranged at the tables and in the booths, at the stools lining the counter. They were all pale and shrunken-looking, desiccated like scarecrows. Their faces were bloodless, their hands—skeletal white claws—were resting on tables and gripping coffee cups and holding spoons and forks.

But the worst part was that their throats were all slit.

A sharp knife, Lex found himself thinking. *It must have been done by a very sharp knife.*

The gashes were neat and bloodless, surgical. And that was enhanced by the fact that they were all sutured shut with black catgut. Their lips were likewise sewn shut with an X-pattern stitching, giving them the look of fairground shrunken heads. Their eyes were missing, too, neatly replaced by black shoebuttons. The entire effect was like someone had turned them into voodoo dolls.

But not true voodoo dolls (if there was such a thing), but the way you might imagine a voodoo doll *should* look. The sort of programmed image, it occurred to Lex, that existed in everyone's head from living in a culture saturated by cheap horror imagery.

To say it was grisly and frightening would be to minimize the absolute horror of it. There had to have been twenty of them in the diner. And not only men and women, but children, too… even an infant in a blue bunting cradled in his zombie-like mother's arms, stitched-up like a sock puppet.

Lex stood there.

He didn't know what to do or what to say. Soo-Lee was shaking, speechless, and wide-eyed. Her hand held his in a crushing embrace. He was pretty certain she was very close to going into shock.

But there was nothing he could do for her.

And nothing he could do for himself.

The other phenomena was generalized. A *Mary Celeste*-type diner emptied of people. Disturbing. Then it began to decay. Even more disturbing. But what was written on the chalkboard was beyond all that: personal and shocking.

These corpses weren't like the mannequin things. These were of a different species, but it meant something. Within the microcosm of this haunted little town, it meant something.

"All right," he said to Soo-Lee, "we walked in here, we can walk out. Physics is physics."

She nodded quickly.

"The door was right there. It must *still* be there, only someone or some*thing* won't let us see it."

That was his logic, and it was culled mostly from TV shows, paperback novels, and movies. But it gained ground in his head. What would they have called something like this on *The X-Files* or *The Outer Limits*? A mind screen? A hallucinogenic screen? Something like that. Maybe that was bullshit, but it gave him an unwavering frame of reference in his mind and, dear God, how he needed that because it felt like his world had ripped out the seat of its pants.

Clutching Soo-Lee to him, he walked to the plate glass windows.

"Right there," he said, under his breath. "It was right there."

He waved his arm to get Creep's attention across the street and the glass instantly steamed like a mirror in a bathhouse.

Got that covered, too, do you?

"That door is still there," he said.

Soo-Lee nodded quickly again. If he said it, it must be true. She had been brought down to the level of simple child-like reasoning now. The fear owned her. She belonged to it.

Lex figured the logical and rational thing to do was to walk right at the window where he knew the door had been and, hopefully, still was. Maybe his reasoning was shit, but it was time for the acid test.

Then behind him, the sound of a spoon dropping.

The sound of a stool creaking.

I don't want to see, I don't want to fucking see this.

Soo-Lee was stiff as a post. Her hand was chilled as if she had been handling an ice pack.

His mouth dry as soot, Lex turned very slowly and looked upon what the diner wanted him to see. He nearly screamed. Soo-Lee certainly would have if her voice wasn't gone and there was sufficient air in her lungs to propel it.

The voodoo doll people were alive and moving.

They weren't doing anything menacing. No horror show creeping or any of that. They were simply going through the motions of being diners, imitating what they might have done in life. They were bringing sandwiches and spoons of soup and cups of coffee to their mouths in some kind of mockery of eating and drinking, something they were incapable of with their lips being stitched shut. One of them was even reading a newspaper and two others were face-to-face in an animated, yet silent, conversation. Cups rattled and forks were set down. Coffee was poured and chicken fried steak cut into. It was like some bizarre parody of the living condition. They were mimes and nothing more. It might have been darkly comic if it weren't for how they looked and the very nature of this place.

Silently, Lex and Soo-Lee watched them.

It seemed there was very little else they could do.

"I think we can go through that door whether it's there or not," Lex said. "C'mon, let's try. It's crazy, but if we believe it's there, it just might be."

Soo-Lee was beside herself. It was obvious she didn't know what to think about anything, but it was also obvious that she had absolute faith in him. He could see that much and it gave him strength.

They turned together and reached out for the plate glass window, believing and yet not believing at all.

Behind them...things went quiet.

Shit.

They turned and the voodoo doll diners had stopped what they were doing. The playacting was over, apparently. They were all completely frozen in place. Coffee cups were held in midair, same for spoons and forks. A guy in one of the booths held an uneaten hamburger to his mouth. When it fell from his fingers, he didn't seem to notice.

Lex didn't like it.

Something was about to happen.

Something bad.

And then, as if the diner knew he was expecting it, the voodoo doll people all slowly swiveled their heads until they were all staring out at Lex and Soo-Lee with those shiny button eyes. It was very unnerving.

"Fuck this," Lex said.

He turned his back on them and went over to the plate glass windows. Reaching out with his hand, he pressed his fingertips to the window and saw them stop at the glass. Yet, even though he saw them stop, he felt the door that he could not see give an inch or two.

There was a rustling, and he saw that all the diners were on their feet now.

In a group, they were coming.

He chanced one more look behind him and, yes, they were indeed coming…except they were all on fire. Not just on fire, but melting like wax dummies as they blazed. Eyes steamed and bubbled, oozing from sockets. Noses and lips slid from faces. Faces became skulls glistening with dripping flesh wax. They all stood there as their skin superheated and dripped off in clots, revealing the bones beneath, hair flaming up like burning wigs.

The stink was unbearable.

Lex pushed and went through the door and out into the night, dragging Soo-Lee with him. He moved quickly and did not stop until they were in the street. Then he dared to turn, expecting to see a mob of button-eyed people in hot pursuit.

But there was nothing.

The diner was completely dark. There was no indication that

the lights had ever been on or that any of it had happened in the first place. He went up to the plate glass windows. Cupping his hands like binoculars to cut the glare of the moon high above, he peered in there.

It was completely empty.

"This is fucking crazy," he said.

Then the alarm began to sound again.

12

Tap-tap, tap-tap, tap-tap.

It felt like Chazz's skin was crawling with thousands of tiny insects that were skittering over his arms and up his legs, down his spine and over the nape of his neck. The sensation was so very real that he scratched at his skin until it hurt. But there were no bugs, there was only fear, and it was making his skin prickle.

He was watching Lady Pegleg.

She had paused now in the middle of the street. She was standing there, not moving, not doing anything at all. He studied her and realized that she had gone inanimate. She was just a dummy now. She had no more life than a mannequin in a store window.

What now?

He didn't find this latest development very comforting. In fact, he liked it better when she *was* moving. At least he knew what she was up to. It was like she was waiting there, plotting, thinking, playing head-games with him. Trying to jack up his unease and apprehension. If that was the case, she was doing a very good job of it.

Now was the time to get away, to do something, but he was as stiff as she was.

She waited.

He waited.

He wasn't really sure what for, other than he knew down deep that he was essentially too scared to move. All of it was too much and something in him had simply shut down. It wanted to crawl into a corner and hide and suggested he join it. Again, he wished Ramona were there.

He wished anyone were there.

He had never been very good at being alone. Even as a kid, he was not the sort that could amuse himself building model cars or reading comic books or playing video games. He was a social creature (he liked to think) and he needed others around. The truth was that he needed people to justify his own existence, people to marvel over him and his athletic grace, his good looks, and easy manner. He needed the worship. Alone, he was empty, wanting, and unsure. Alone, he had no confidence. Alone, he seemed not to exist or to be on the verge of dissipating.

And right now, he was not sure of anything other than the fact that he was certain he was losing his mind and there was no one around to tell him that he was not.

So get the fuck out of here, dumbass. Climb back out the window and go find the others. Do what you do best: run, gobble up some yardage.

And he knew that's what needed doing. He could hear Coach yelling at him, motivating him, driving him, telling him that he had the tools and he had the skills but he lacked motivation.

Oh, he was so right, so very right—

The alarm.

It started again, droning on and on. Like Ramona earlier, it reminded him of some primordial beast pulling itself up from a Mesozoic lake and shrieking out its rage and hunger. It went right up his spine and seemed to make the fillings in his molars actually ache. The windows rattled. The world echoed with grim noise. Then about the time he thought he might start screaming from the sound of it, it cut out and faded in the distance.

At that very moment, as if on cue, he felt something skitter over his shoe and he kicked out at it. He figured it was a mouse. He didn't like crawly little furry things, but most of his old fears seemed pretty minor league now. *Fucking mouse. So what?* He could live with mice.

Then it started crawling up his leg.

It was no mouse.

It was a rat.

With a cry, he reached down and felt his hand brush against a greasy pelt that seemed to palpitate with the verminous life within. Goddamn thing was no bush league sewer rat, it was a monster the size of a cat and if he doubted its intentions before, there was no mistaking them as it bit into his leg and brought a hot, needling pain to his calf.

Chazz grabbed at it, clutching a thick rope of tail that squirmed in his hand like an especially unpleasant snake. He ripped the rat away from his pants, feeling its claws tearing at the material as they tried to maintain their hold. He had no idea what he had in mind other than peeling that SOB free, but he found himself swinging it around in loose circles, seeming to enjoy the power he held over it. Once he had picked up the necessary velocity, he let it fly.

It hit a patch of moonlit wall with the sort of force that should have injured it and made it bleed. But it left no blood splotch. In fact, as it hit the wall, it simply fell apart...it broke into pieces.

Chazz let out a muffled cry.

It wasn't real. Like everything in this place, it simply wasn't real.

In the moonlight, he could see it there on the floor. Its head was hairless like that of a possum, detached from its body, the jaws still trying to bite. Two of its legs had fallen off and they were still moving, still trying to claw. But the very worst thing was that its body had broken open and he could see what looked like whirring gears inside it, spindles and springs.

There was no end to this shit.

The rat was like some windup toy.

And as this settled into Chazz's mind, mixing up in there with the rest of it and making him more confused and pushing him that much closer to complete lunacy, he heard another sound.

Creak, creak.

He looked around. It was Lady Pegleg again, it had to be Lady Pegleg again...but no, as he peered out the window, he saw that she was no longer in the street. He couldn't see her anywhere.

Creak, creak, creak.

And besides, this sound was in the room with him.

Yes, over there beyond what he thought was a couch, he could make out a dim figure. It was sitting in a rocking chair, rocking back and forth, back and forth.

Creak, creak, creak.

"Who...who's there?"

And a voice, feminine in caliber, throaty and breathless, said, "It's me, doll-face. And I've been here a long, long time."

A woman, another doll woman.

He nearly started cackling hysterically at the idea of it.

"Stay away from me! You come by me and I'll kill you!"

The voice giggled in its throat. "Oh, you don't have to worry about me, doll-face. It's the old lady who wants you. The pegleg lady. She wants your heart. You have a nice, strong heart and she doesn't have one at all. She wants yours."

"Fuck you!" Chazz shouted.

The chair stopped creaking. "You only had to ask, doll-face. You only had to ask."

The doll woman had risen from the chair now and was coming with that same clicking sound as the doll man in the street. She moved with a shambling gait, painfully and slowly as if one leg was longer than the other. He could see her reaching out with sharp fingers, long hair sweeping from side to side as she got closer.

With a scream, Chazz vaulted across the room to where he had seen a door.

He barely got through it. Her fingers dragged through his hair and then he slammed it shut behind him and he could hear her nails scraping at the other side as if they were not nails at all, but claws.

The door had a lock and he set it.

She continued to claw at the other side. "When I find you, doll-face, I'll fuck you."

Chazz threw himself backward, his skin crawling again.

He stumbled over a chair and fell into a pool of moonlight that made his fingers look ashen and almost phosphorescent like the petals of night-blooming orchids. He was shaking, drooling, chattering his teeth. Tears ran from his eyes and he could not throw together a single coherent thought.

There were a set of stairs before him, climbing to the second floor.

When he could think, he considered going up there and hiding in a room, but, no, he could not bear the idea of being in the same house as that thing in the other room. No, he had to run. He needed to escape. He needed to put some distance between himself and this place.

And this is exactly what he was going to do.

Then he saw something coming down the stairs and in his fevered mind it could be nothing but a giant, leggy spider. It had sighted him and decided he was its prey.

Clip-clop-clip-clop, went its many legs.

Chazz crawled away toward the door, thumping into it and on the other side, the voice said, "Now you have to make a choice, doll-face...me or *it*."

13

Danielle's world felt compressed.

It was tight and suffocating like a small black box. It consisted of these streets and buildings, thoroughfares and houses, all the little details that made up a town called Stokes that she knew existed only in nightmares and perhaps at the very perimeter of hell itself.

She was suffocating.

Waiting there up against the window of some nameless shop, she was suffocating. Creep was standing there, nervous, agitated, moving this way and that, unable to sit still. Lex and Soo-Lee were in the street, glancing fearfully behind them at the darkened diner. They had gone in and then came out. They must have turned off the lights after they left.

Danielle realized that she had to use her entire body to draw in a breath.

She had to actually lift herself with the motion of her diaphragm to get any air in her lungs. When she tried to tell Creep that, her voice simply would not come because there was not enough oxygen to power it.

There was something wrong here.

Something bad.

The air was gone. She had to find a place where there was air or she was going to asphyxiate. She started walking, stumbling along really, in the direction they had come from.

"Hey," Creep said. "What are you doing?"

He reached out to grab her, and she shrugged him aside and ran. Gasping for breath, seeking air she could breathe, she ran down the street and around the corner, and the faster she went, the better the air was until she was no longer gasping.

Creep was running after her, calling out her name, demanding to know what in the hell it was she thought she was doing and, oh, had there been the time she would have told him and then he would have understood.

She came around another corner and there was somebody standing there.

It was a man. A big man.

He moved with a clicking, whirring sound of gears and cogs.

Danielle skidded to a halt bare inches from him, backing up frantically. The moonlight showed her that he was not really a man, but another doll that only looked like a man. He was grinning at her and she saw that he had teeth.

"Is that you, doll-face?" he said.

And then there was a silvery flash as he swung something at her.

She had enough time to let out a small cry as something thudded against her head, the impact driving her to her knees and then to the sidewalk, where she knew no more.

14

*G*oddamn idiot.
  This is what went through Creep's mind as he chased after Danielle, who was surprisingly fast and surprisingly agile. She had the long legs of a gazelle and he figured she was some kind of jock to pour on speed like that. A runner or a soccer player. Maybe she played lacrosse and swam competitively like Ramona or raced mountain bikes like Soo-Lee. Regardless, that girl had game.

And for Creep, whose major sports consisted of marathon sessions of *Resident Evil*, she was simply out of his league.

He called out to Lex and Soo-Lee, but they were already on the way.

Man, this was just great. Like they didn't have enough problems already trying to stay alive and keep sane, now they had to babysit this psycho bimbette while she showed them how she ate the turf in the 100-yard dash.

He saw her disappear around a corner ahead and, damn, she did not break stride at all. She leaned into it and zipped around it with incredible grace. The sort of grace that would have put Creep himself right on his ass and twisted an ankle to boot.

He made the corner finally, but he had to slow way down and even so, Christ, he nearly tripped over his own feet like a geriatric monkey. But there she was. Just ahead and pouring on the speed again.

He followed her, hearing Lex and Soo-Lee gaining on him. He had a feeling they would overtake him any second.

He saw Danielle round another corner, and by that, point he was starting to think she wasn't even fucking human. Just as he was ready to give up, call it a day and hang up his cleats, something pushed him on. He was not the bravest guy in the world—outside of X-box 360, where he was nearly a legend—but he knew that if he didn't stop her, something really bad would happen to her. Something that might have already happened to Chazz and, *gulp*, Ramona.

He came around the corner at the precise moment that Danielle skidded to a halt like a sprinting wildebeest that had run smack dab into a hungry lion.

Only, in this case, a lion would have been preferable.

Creep saw the doll man standing there and he stopped, too. This guy—*thing*, whatever it was—was a huge form that towered above her like a graveyard angel. It wore a huge dark coat that looked like a moldering tarp. It hobbled closer to her with a see-sawing side to side gait, dragging one leg behind it. Its face was like a fright mask made of burlap or pale gray sackcloth, but yet it was flesh because as it spoke, the thin-lipped, crooked mouth moved as if muscles beneath were in motion.

Creep heard what it said: *"Is that you, doll-face?"*

Then it swung what it held in one narrow, long-fingered hand…a hatchet. The blade caught Danielle right at the crown of her skull, splitting her head like moist green wood. The sound it made reminded Creep of a cleaved gourd. He was hit by a wet spray of blood and brains and went right down to his knees with a broken cry.

The hulking thing began to drag itself in his direction, stepping over the still-shuddering corpse of Danielle.

Creep waited for it.

He was speechless and stunned, his mouth hanging open, fingers numbly pawing at the blood and gray matter on his face, which had the consistency of greasy gelatin from a canned ham. He was struck dumb and motionless. It felt like his own blood had drained down into his feet and he was in danger of pitching over face-first to the sidewalk.

The moonlight made the hatchet man's face look luminous.

There were tufts of white hair jutting from his malformed head, the face itself seamed and sutured, one empty eye socket set lower the other, both filled with the formless blackness of endless nighted catacombs. He had no nose and his mouth was distorted from the stitching that held it together.

Again, Creep was struck by the impression that it was a mask...but as the thing approached him, it grinned with a lopsided, mocking smile. *"Is that you, doll-face?"* it asked, raising its hatchet to strike. Gore dropped from the blade. Tissue and hair were clotted on it.

Creep waited for it, but then Lex grabbed him and pulled him away, half dragging him and half carrying him out of range of the monster.

"Run!" Soo-Lee said. *"Run!"*

She was leading them and Creep found his feet and ran at Lex's side, feeling suddenly that he could have run ten miles if that's what it took. His fear and horror became vigor, and he put it to work.

Behind them, the hatchet man followed.

15

In the brooding silence, Ramona moved up the sidewalk, doing her best to keep out of the direct moonlight and beneath the shadows thrown by the awnings positioned over the store-fronts. Each one was striped and antique. Each one out of place and time like the whole goddamn town.

She knew that in the greater scheme of things, or at least the greater scheme of the town specifically, that it meant something if she could only figure out what. Her head was too full of shit to figure it out. Too much anxiety and stress and terror and apprehension.

It was all masking her ability to think clearly, to reason.

This place was a box, a big black box, but there was a key that opened it. If only she could find it and recognize it for what it was.

The alarm had sounded again and that was trouble.

The last time it had sounded, the broken man had come to life and that other thing in the van had attacked Chazz, poor, worthless Chazz. In her way of thinking, that meant if there were other mannequin people around, the alarm probably had activated them.

She had no real proof of that, but she believed it.

For now, she had to find the others.

They had to be here somewhere. But that seemed to be part of the problem. Every street seemed to look alike. The business sections were like repetitions of one another as were the residential districts. She swore she saw the same storefronts, the same houses again and again. That was impossible, of course, because she was moving in a straight line, yet the feeling persisted.

It not only persisted, but it haunted her.

She stopped there beneath one of the awnings, one of the same striped awnings, trying to make sense of thing. Yes, reality was distorted here, but just because it was, that did not necessarily mean there wasn't a rhyme and a reason behind it all.

Oh, quit trying to fucking rationalize everything. Don't you get tired of it all?

But she didn't because that's who and what she was. She had spent her life looking for signs and portents, the systematics and mechanisms behind perfectly ordinary events. Take Chazz for example. She had known for some time he had been screwing around on her, but she didn't leave him. She didn't even broach the subject or sink to his level like many other women might have and start sleeping around. No, not her. She looked for vague clues and hints in conversations and daily activities with him that should have tipped her off that his infidelity was inevitable and wondering what she had done wrong, what she had failed to recognize, and how she must be on guard against minor infractions in their relationship that led to major problems.

And she was doing that now.

She waited there, smoking a cigarette, knowing she had to quit before swim season started…but tonight was not the night.

She was thinking about that alarm or siren or whatever it had been. She knew the general direction it came from—the east—and was very tempted to track it to its source because she felt deep inside that if she could do that, she might be able to shut it down, and if she shut it down, she might just shut this whole town down with it.

But that was foolish and dangerous.

The reasonable thing was to give up looking and backtrack to where the van had been. That was the point of entry into this madhouse and probably the escape route.

She turned around, moving faster now in the direction she had come.

The same storefronts, the same houses, the same everything.

She walked and walked and walked and it seemed she was still no closer to where she had been, wherever that was and wherever it could be in the greater scheme of this lunacy.

Bullshit, this is all bullshit, all a cheap fucking game, and this town is nothing but a cheap fucking carnival. That's all it is. That's all it can be.

She walked faster, refusing to give in and refusing to accept the grim inevitability that she was going nowhere, that she might as well have been running on a treadmill. Same storefronts, same houses, same trees, same boulevards...God, it went on and on ad nauseam.

But so did Ramona.

Because anyone that had ever known her discovered one thing sooner or later: she had a stubborn streak a mile wide and she refused, simply refused, to give up or give in. She would not be beaten by this nightmare. She would exhaust it, she would wear it down, she would make it spend itself until it was simply out of breath and the walls of perception ran thin...then she'd be out, she'd be free.

But she was the one that ran out of breath.

Scared, but mostly angry and irritated at everything, she stopped, catching her breath and making herself think. There had to be an answer here. There had to be a way out. Christ, she was starting to feel like a hamster run to death on a wheel.

Swearing, she started walking again.

Since moving in a linear fashion was getting her absolutely nowhere, she changed her tactics. She moved completely by instinct. She walked this way, turned on her heel and cut down an avenue, then down a street, up a boulevard. Her navigation was haphazard, it was random as hell. She did not think about what she was going to do, she just did it, guiding herself with pure animal sense. Her point was that this was all controlled somehow, and she was going to break down the controller one way or another, force him or her or *it* to show itself and reveal its hand.

She walked faster and faster, listening to her footsteps echoing off the faces of buildings and houses.

Then she stopped dead, knowing that she had struck a nerve with her theoretical controller.

Listen, listen to that.

Though she was no longer walking, she still heard footsteps.

She turned and there was no one there…at least, no one she could see. But the footsteps were approaching and it was not merely one set, but many sets. They made the slapping sound of bare feet, yet they had a hollow little echo to them.

She heard a low whispering.

What might have been the giggling of a child.

She felt the fine hairs at the back of her neck rise up, a chill moving upwards and over her scalp. She was being stalked by things she could not see and they were getting closer and closer.

Maybe it worked, maybe I wore it down, maybe I'm forcing its hand.

But there was no satisfaction in that because she was quite literally terrified of something—many things—she could not see. They were coming for her. The whispering grew in volume until it seemed like maybe it was a dozen children out there, hissing and piping and gibbering with a low and eerie sibilance that seemed to fill her head and echo around in her skull.

She ran.

She ran as fast as she could and every time she paused, it seemed that they were closer still. They were going to run her to the point of exhaustion. As she passed store windows, she clearly saw display mannequins turn their heads and watch her progress. Finally, she stopped and turned.

"Show yourselves already," she said, her anger rising above her fear.

One of them stepped from the shadows—a naked girl or an imitation of the same, to be more precise. She was a little thing with a matted mop of blonde hair, her face the color of frost and the texture of silken spiderwebs, her eyes like ragged holes looking into a dark and empty room. From chest to hips, she was open as if there hadn't been enough flesh to cover her. Inside…there was nothing. Merely a metal framework that was narrow and spoking like the bones of jackals.

There was no machinery.

No electronics.

Nothing that could make her work, yet she moved, she was alive. Ramona heard an insane laughter in the back of her head.

She was insane. She had to be completely insane.

"It's Ramona," the girl said in a perfectly shrill, scraping voice that was many miles from what a girl's voice should have sounded like. "Ramona, Ramona, Ramona, Ramona."

The others began to appear now, stepping out to chant her name.

Dozens of them.

Many of them were unfinished, their heads like swollen, nodding toadstools. An army of Raggedy Ann dolls from hell, faces stitched and spliced, carved and slapped together out of papier-mâché that grinned and moved like living tissue. Effigies cut from fissured deadwood and dry rot, scarecrows with pipe stem legs and spidery tree branches for hands, animate sculptures of mortuary pipes and rib cage baskets. Some lacked limbs and a few lacked heads, one of them was little more than a walking armature waiting to be fleshed out, another was a set of legs with a post-like spine and a cracked open, hairless head but nothing else.

They called her name, whispering it, seeming to like the sound of it: "Ramona, Ramona, Ramona, Ramona," they chanted, gathering volume and intensity until their voices were a whispering, shrilling cacophony: "RAMONA, RAMONA, RAMONA, RAMONA, RAMONA—"

It grew louder and louder until she couldn't take it anymore and she vented her horror in a high, whining scream. She stumbled back and away from the dolls, tripping over her own feet, silvered by pale moonlight.

They closed it on her, reaching for her.

One of them kicked its head before it on the sidewalk. It rolled over and over and over like a ball, orange locks splaying out over the cement. It righted itself, turning to look at her with empty eye sockets that could see nothing. Its mouth opened and it screamed at her, perfectly mocking her own cry again and again, cycling higher and higher with each piercing shriek.

Ramona, as close to madness as she'd ever been, dropped to her knees, her flesh crawling and her mind sucking into some black crevice of numbing child-like terror. One last shred of adult reason broke through like a beacon and she shouted: "I

DOLL FACE 65

DON'T BELIEVE IN YOU! YOU'RE NOT REAL! YOU HEAR ME? YOU'RE NOT REAL!"

But they kept coming.

She knew there was only one thing to do. Only one possible way to break the spell of madness. Her instinct warned her away from it, but her rational mind demanded it because if she did not fight them here and now, did not put this hallucination down, then it would never, ever stop until her mind was completely gone.

With a cry of rage and violence, she stormed at them, vaulting right into their midst and she felt their cold little fingers scratch her face and their mouths bite into her arms, but it did not slow her down. She fought and clawed and kicked and bowled them over and fell away from them.

The street was littered with doll parts—heads and arms, torsos and legs and hands, tangled cords and pulleys and gears…what amounted to the guts of the things. She knew she hadn't hit them that hard. Not hard enough to break them into pieces.

But they *were* in pieces.

She stumbled back, blinking her eyes, waiting for them to reassemble themselves as the mannequin woman had. But they were nothing but parts, inert and inactive, completely incapable of anything like motion. It looked like someone had dumped out the bargain bin from a puppet shop.

Do you see? Do you see? They are nothing and they never were nothing! They couldn't be anything but what they are—wood and wax, steel rods and sackclothing, plastic and papier-mâché, glue and rubber hoses and gears…don't you see? Don't you fucking see?

She shook her head because she did not see and she goddamn well knew better. Maybe *now* they were parts. Maybe they were never anything but parts machined and cut and carved. But something in this nightmare shithole of a town trembling darkly on the borderland of fucking hell had the power to *make* them move. It could make them do anything it wanted. It made them live, it made them breathe, it made them walk. Maybe it couldn't give them souls as such, but it woke something up inside them...something stalking and malignant. She had seen it hiding in the darkness of their eyes, a nameless black life force.

So maybe they were nothing but parts now, but that could change in the blink of an eye. A car was nothing but parts, too, until someone got behind the wheel and made those parts work. Then it could be made to kill.

Trying not to cry, trying not to deflate with madness, she shook until cold sweat ran down her face and then she promptly fell to her ass, panting and sobbing and making a moaning sound deep in her throat. Her face was scratched, her arms bitten, her shirt torn from sharp little fingers.

They were real and yet they were not.

They were solid, they were physical, but when she attacked them with fury, they simply fell apart.

When she had calmed somewhat, she sat there, trying to get her head working so she could get her body moving and get her ass somewhere relatively safe. Because right then her mind and body were completely out-of-sync.

And her mind was much closer to full-blown insanity than she dared contemplate.

"Just get it together," she told herself in a very soothing and motherly voice. "Get it together and get your feet under you."

Slowly, she did just that.

She got to her feet and she was not dizzy. Disturbed, yes, but no longer white inside with rabid fear. She bunched her muscles and worked out the kinks in her neck. She was ready. God yes, she was ready as she was ever going to be.

And good thing, too.

Because the doll parts began to move.

16

Clip-clop, clip-clop, clip-clop.

Chazz saw an immense hairy thing with a poison-dripping mouth, its many legs set with spinnerets swollen like balloons.

But, of course, it wasn't a spider.

There were many horrors in Stokes, but giant arachnids weren't among them. In the moonlight that splashed the stairwell he could see legs…what seemed to be dozens upon dozens of mannequin legs coming down the stairs. So many of them, in fact, that their feet were not only on the steps themselves but clopping off the walls and rapping against the stair balusters, several gliding down the stair rail itself.

This is what he saw.

This is what made white ice flow in his veins and his breath scrape in his throat. Sweat beaded his face and he had a perfectly mad desire to start giggling.

Legs, legs, legs, so goddamn many legs…they must be connected to something.

That's what he was terrified of. It scared him more than what was behind the door clawing to get out. All those legs… they kept coming and coming and he could clearly see the ball joints at the knees and something above, a body of some sort and he did not want to see that, did not want to know what that was about.

As the legs kept coming, he broke into a clumsy, stumbling run, cutting down a darkened hallway where he was certain other nightmares would be waiting for him. He saw a door. He grabbed the knob and threw it open. A breath of hot, spoiled darkness blew out at him.

It was only a clothes closet.

That's all it was.

Yet...*yet*, he saw that it was much more that that. For in the fear-induced hallucinatory narrowing of his perception, he saw that it was no closet. No, it was a coffin. It was a narrow house, an oblong box like in an old horror movie and he was holding the lid in his hand like a grave robber rooting around in old tombs for wedding rings and valuables.

He tried to let it go, but it refused.

It *refused* to be released.

Chazz knew in a steadily dimming corner of his mind that still functioned somewhat rationally that it was the closet/coffin that was making the decision here. He could not let go of it any more than he could will one of his fingers to drop off.

His hand was fused to the lid.

And whatever dark alchemy and deranged witchery were behind it, he was powerless next to it. He tried to yank his arm back with everything he had because this was not only bad in of itself, but it was trapping him here while that thing with a hundred legs hunted him down. The second time he tried it— absolutely wild by this point, his eyes like glass balls drawn into bloodred sockets, a froth of mad-dog foam on his lips—the pain was intense. It was as if he was trying to tear his hand free at the wrist.

His only reaction, other than jumping and jerking from the adrenaline coursing through him like a hot shot of pure cocaine, was to cry out in a voice that he hadn't used since he was ten years old: "*Leave me go! Leave me go! Leave me go! Oh, please, oh Jezuz Godz, leave me go!*"

But it did not let him go.

This was not only an incantation, an evocation, but an invitation as well. Inside the closet that was no closet, he could see a body in a black burial dress hanging by its neck from the coat rod. Except it was no body, no woman, but...*Danielle*. Yes, Danielle remade as a puppet or a doll or a window dummy. Her eyes were missing, her face like gleaming white rubber, her jaw hinged like that of the Tin Man in *The Wizard of Oz*. As she performed a slow, twisting turn on the rope that noosed her broken neck, the hinged jaw opened and she said, *"What's your pleasure, doll-face?"*

With a shriek, Chazz broke free.

He pulled himself back with such strength, that he threw himself four feet. Four dangerous feet into the shadow of the thing with a hundred legs.

He scooted around on his ass and saw the creature bearing down on him.

The hallway was flooded with moonlight, because it *wanted* him to see. That was a very necessary part of it. It wanted him to look upon it so he would drown in his own fear, which it would suckle and juice from him drop by drop.

It was a massive thing, a perpetual motion machine of metal pipes and wooden reeds and snapping elastic cords. A living, pulsating armature of femurs and ulnas, spoking rib bones and gleaming puppet bone slats dragged ever forward by scuttling toadstool-white doll legs that were hinged and swiveled, skeletal and fleshy, most with feet, others just wiggling stumps. All of it was welded together and threaded with knotted undulant cobwebs whose strands were thick as vines. They hung in rotting cerements and fluttering crepe and ropy sheaths. The thing spewed out sticky ribbons of them from a dozen puckering, sap-dripping orifices. It dragged dozens more behind it like a placenta.

Chazz screamed and pissed himself as it came for him.

Its legs rattled off the floor and walls and ceiling.

Clip-clop, clip-clop, clip-clop, clip-clop, went its legs, only there were so many of them it was booming and echoing in the confined space of the hallway like god-awful drums pounding and beating and hammering: *CLIPCLOPCLIPCLOPCLIPCLOPCLIPCLOPCLIPCLOP*—

As the thing pressed in ever closer, its leggy/webby form opened like a flower to reveal a cluster of blind white eyes the size of softballs and a sticky black chasm that must have been its mouth, which kept opening wider and wider like a birth canal to suck him in.

He crawled frantically away, knowing he had bare seconds.

The thing had hoped to debilitate him with fear, to put him

to his knees where he would finally scream and sob and suck his thumb, crawl into the darkest corner of the darkest closet of his dark, crowded little mind.

And he was close, so very close.

He saw another doorway, crawling faster to reach it, not daring to take the time to get to his feet. As he got through the door, the thing behind him so large that it could barely fit down the passage now, he heard its voice like a needle scratching on an old record:

"I will make my nest of scraps and bones and soiled rags. I will knit a cocoon of gray dust and old blood and virulent webs and lay the pulp of my eggs here in this womb of fractured darkness and my creeping young will feed upon you. In sorrow, shall I bring forth my children here in this deserted house. For that which brings harm also makes fertile."

Then Chazz had the door closed and locked, his sweaty fingers pressed against it. He heard the thing coming. The noise of its many scurrying legs was deafening. It made his ears ring and his teeth ache. The door actually bulged as the thing struck it, battering it again and again, pushing its mammoth girth against it.

Then it stopped.

It scraped the door with something like dozens of claws, then made a sucking sound as if it had pressed its mouth up against it. There was a slimy, wet noise like the licking of many tongues. Then the voice again, that same strident, creaking voice: *"Rinky tinky tink,"* it said of all the absurd things, repeating it again and again with a lilting child-like rhythm. *"Rinky tinky tink, there's a new one in town, I think."*

By that point, Chazz was probably mad.

He was probably struck blind with insanity. But something in him that wanted to survive would not curl up into a ball and die. It simply refused to...even when the thing began to project images of its victims into his head. He saw how it crushed them flat with its bulk until their entrails gushed from their mouths. How it slurped their juices up with its many sucking mouths and then ingested them, regurgitating what was left like husks. He saw how it tormented its enemies—blowing out their eardrums with its screeching voice and inserting hooks up their nostrils like Egyptian embalmers, drawing out their brains in spongy clots. How it nearly shook with orgasm when they tried to escape and it seized them with a thousand wriggling doll parts.

It wanted him to see it in its entirety: so it showed itself to him.

It wanted him to know its cruelty: so it showed him this as well.

And by then, Chazz could take no more. Screaming and hysterical, he ran from the door and dove straight at the window with every ounce of strength and weight he possessed. The window shattered, and he hit the ground with a rain of glass fragments.

Bleeding, bruised, his mind bouncing around in his skull like a bullet, he ran off into the night before it could get him.

But even so, he knew he had not escaped it.

17

When he got the door closed, Lex went down to his knees on the floor, trying to tell himself he had not seen any of it. He tried to make himself believe that none of it was any more real than what Soo-Lee and he had seen in the diner. But he didn't believe it. He found he *couldn't* believe it because Danielle had been murdered and that was no fantasy. He'd seen it. It was real.

Or was it?

That was one of the questions that kept dogging him. Had the idea been planted in their heads? Had it been shown to them with three-dimensional authenticity so that their overcharged imaginations and fears would do the rest?

He kneeled there, breathing, listening to Creep and Soo-Lee doing the same. Neither of them had really spoken since Danielle was murdered and he had the feeling they never would, not until he did. Not until he oiled their jaws for them and got them working again.

There was a terrible taste in his mouth, rusty and coppery but with an acidic sort of bite to it like tart fruit. He'd never tasted anything like it before and he was certain it was the taste of fear, a combination of chemicals the body secreted during times of incredible stress. An adrenaline/hormonal/pheromonal/endorphin-laced cocktail, and this was its by-product, a sickening flavor.

He was going to remark on it to the others, but he didn't dare.

He just didn't dare.

His scalp was greasy with sweat that ran from his hairline and stung his eyes. It felt cool against his hot face. He was exhausted. They were all exhausted…but the idea of anything like sleep was absurd. You didn't take a nap in the cave of a man-eating tiger and where they were was no doubt much more dangerous.

"I think we're safe for now," he finally said.

In the dimness of the house, Creep nodded his head. "Danielle's dead. She's…dead, man."

"There was nothing we could do," Soo-Lee said.

Creep laughed sarcastically. "Well, there's one thing we could have done and that was not coming here in the first place."

"And how could we have avoided that?"

"Chazz shouldn't have brought us here."

Lex sighed. "Creep…it isn't Chazz's fault."

"He took that fucking shortcut."

"Which nine times out of ten would have been just fine. It had nothing to do with him. This…all this is completely out of his control. I don't know who's behind this, but whoever they are, they have a way of rigging things, making things happen. We were brought here for a purpose."

"To be killed?"

Lex shook his head. "I don't know. There's no way any of us can know until we stop running and start thinking." He studied their faces in the shadows. "This entire place is some kind of imitation. It's not a real town. It's either a projection of one or some kind of…of physical hallucination we're all sharing."

"Feels pretty real to me," Creep said.

"It *is* real. But it's only real because someone or something is reinforcing that. When they stop, it'll stop."

"And how can you know that?"

"I can't. It's pure gut feeling and for now that'll have to be enough. Unless, of course, you have a better explanation."

Creep didn't. He sat there silently, brooding and scared. "So you think this place is a time-loop or alternate reality, something along those lines?"

"Maybe. I don't know."

"I noticed it from the first," Soo-Lee said. "Everything looked so…artificial. I remember thinking it was like a movie set, some director's idea of what a small town should look like, you know?

Everything was too perfect, too planned, too...*seamless*, if that makes any sense."

It did, Lex figured. "It's very sterile, isn't it? Like the memory of a small town seen through rose-colored glasses. Not the real town, but a synthetic, glossy, nostalgic too-good-to-be-true sort of town in a Normal Rockwell kind of way."

"Yes, like a set," Soo-Lee said.

"Exactly. I thought the same thing when we went into that diner—it was exactly what I thought a diner should be from images programmed into my mind from old movies and TV shows, Rockwell paintings and postcards. Everything was perfect just like the town itself." He thought that over and felt it was the key somehow. "I mean, hell, there's not any cars to crowd the streets. There's not even cracks in the sidewalks or weeds in yards. Nothing that would upset the perfect balance."

"And what does that mean?" Creep asked.

"It means," Soo-Lee said, "that as weird as it sounds, it's like we're trapped in somebody's dream or memory of a town. Not the real Stokes, but the way somebody wanted it to be or imagined it to be in their own self-deluded little way."

"Okay, now I'm more scared than ever," Creep said.

Lex told him how when they were in the diner, when they refused to accept the reality of it as offered, it changed. It became a darker and dirtier place, an ugly place complete with corpses and rats and flies. "It's like our disbelief pissed somebody off. Oh, you don't like this? I can make it worse."

"That's when the door disappeared," Soo-Lee said.

"Yes, exactly. This puppet master we're talking about changed the look of the diner, but it couldn't stop us from escaping. The door disappeared, but it was still there. We walked through it, even though its image was gone. So there are limits to the power of this other."

Creep was getting it now. He sat up. His eyes looked brighter in the darkness. "That means if we found where we came in, we might be able to get out. We might not see the road but it's probably there."

"Maybe."

Soo-Lee nodded. "But finding it will be the problem. This

town is a maze and I think we've all noticed that. I don't think we'll be allowed to find it. This other will confuse us and get us lost. And it'll throw more doll people at us. Anything to stop us from getting away."

"But if we could get there."

"Even if we got there, we might not know we were there," she said.

Creep slumped down again.

"Everything we've done since hitting that thing with the van to arriving here has been carefully planned, I think," Lex told them. "We're right where it wants us to be. We've been carefully herded. It threw certain things at us that would make us run and offered us shelter—this house—when it knew we couldn't run anymore. What we need to start thinking seriously about is *acting* rather than *reacting*. We have to start taking some charge of our destiny or this other will run us ragged and then destroy us with those doll things."

He wasn't really sure how much on target he or Soo-Lee were with their thinking, but it felt right. Judging by what they had experienced and seen thus far, it seemed to fit. It was like a game, like they were being manipulated by the imagination and whims of a cruel child.

"So when do we started acting?" Creep asked

"When they throw something else at us," Soo-Lee said. "We can leave this house right now. We can run in circles, but in the end we'll only be reacting again. What we need to do is wait for what is thrown at us next and overcome it. That would be the first step, I think."

Lex loved that woman. Her instincts and intuition were right on target every time.

Creep said, "When do you think it'll start again?"

"Any minute now," Soo-Lee said. "I can almost feel it beginning."

18

Creep wasn't sure what to make of them and their theories. It always seemed like Lex and Soo-Lee were on a private wavelength or something. They seemed to communicate very easily without words. But he wasn't part of that. Even in school, he had not been part of that. For all he knew, their harebrained theories would get all of them killed.

He stood up and went over to the window.

He saw nothing out there, but that didn't mean anything.

Inside, he was bunched up tight, waiting for the air raid siren or whatever in the hell it was because that's when it would start. Soo-Lee said it was about to happen and he did not doubt that at all. The thing that scared him is what form it would take.

"I wonder if Ramona and Chazz are still alive," he said.

"If anyone is still alive, it would be Ramona," Soo-Lee said. "She's always been a major dynamo. If she is, she's probably thinking what we're thinking."

"And it won't be easy killing Chazz. He won't go down quietly."

Creep didn't really care about Chazz. He didn't want him dead or anything, but his thoughts were of Ramona.

They were in the living room of a house that looked pretty much like every house on the block. An average clapboard two-story. They hadn't been upstairs yet or down into the basement and there was no point in nosing around in those places and looking for trouble.

Trouble will find us just fine without any help.

He took out his lighter and flicked it, the jumping flame lighting up the room and giving him a look at things. It was all very typical. A couch, two wingback chairs with accompanying lamps. A coffee table. A bookcase. A big old console stereo. And a TV that looked like something from a museum—a massive cabinet that sat on four legs with huge, bulbous channel and volume knobs and a bubble screen, obligatory rabbit ears up on top.

The lighter started burning his fingers and he killed it. "Notice how everything's old? There's dinosaur shit all over this stuff," he said. "No technology newer than the 1960s. No cells or computers. Not even a VHS player for chrissake. Even my gramma had one of those."

"It fits," Lex said. "This figurative other we're talking about is remembering the good old days of 1960. It can't be too much more recent than that. I bet if you go over to that bookshelf, you're going to see nothing copyrighted after 1965. Just a guess."

Creep went over there. He flicked his lighter. "A shitload of *Reader's Digest Condensed Books*. Let's see...*To Kill a Mockingbird*... *The Agony and the Ecstasy*...*Franny and Zooey*. Yeah, all old shit. The stuff they make you read in English class."

"I love *To kill a Mockingbird*," Soo-Lee said. She was an English major; of course she would say that.

Lex grunted. "I had to read *Franny and Zooey* in tenth grade. Our teacher was obsessed with Salinger."

"Aren't all lit teachers?" Soo-Lee said.

"Most, except for my eleventh-grade English teacher. Mr. Spreeg. He was big on Faulkner. Just the mention of Faulkner's name gives me narcolepsy now."

Creep ignored them. He wasn't interested in debating fucking books. The thing that was intriguing him was that old TV set. He very badly wanted to take it apart and get at the tubes. When he was a kid, his uncle Frank had collected vintage TV sets, and he had an amazing collection of old tubes. Creep loved looking at them. He wanted to open this one up and paw through its guts until he found those tubes like a diver digging through an oyster for a pearl.

The world lost something when they invented solid-state circuitry, he thought. *There's just something about old vacuum tubes.*

Which was quite an admission from a techie like him.

In the dark, he kept staring at the murky shape of the TV

and the funny thing was that he did not seem to be able to look away. He knew they were in a rough spot here, a truly horrible situation, but it was like Soo-Lee and Lex were not even in the room. His eyes were fixed on the dead TV and his mind could think of nothing else.

It was strange.

It was more than strange.

In his mind, he began to see black-and-white images of the shows that TV must have pulled in with its rabbit ears back in the good old days...grainy, fluttering images of things he had never seen and never really wanted to. The men smoked pipes and read newspapers, and the women always had aprons on and slaved away in the kitchen. The children were un-rebellious, well-mannered, and well-dressed. It was an age he did not understand. But the images captivated him and it was like he was really watching that old set.

What the hell is going on here? he asked himself, but there were no answers in his head. Nothing that made any kind of sense, anyway.

A tiny white dot appeared on the screen.

And he wasn't the only one seeing it because Soo-Lee gasped.

"What the hell?" Lex said.

The pictures were gone from Creep's head now. He, like the others, was staring at the tiny white dot in the center of the bubble screen. It was growing. It went from the size of a pin to the size of a quarter, gradually expanding. Now the screen came on and there was static, a field of snow, and wiggly horizontal lines.

Nobody said anything.

Soo-Lee said earlier that she could feel something beginning and this had to be it or, at the very least, the prelude. A picture was coming up on the screen, but it was still rolling and bleached out. It was hard to say at first what they were looking at, but Creep knew it was coming. Those old tubes took time to warm up. The image would never be HD, but it would come. In its own way and time, it would come...and maybe this was what he feared the most.

He waited there with the others, wringing his sweaty palms. The image stabilized. It was still grainy and not exactly sharp, but it was certainly clearer and they could see what was going on. It showed a family sitting around a dinner table. A 1950s family by the looks of it. A mother and father and two boys having an animated conversation. There was no sound, but a canned laugh track was a given. As the peas and chicken were passed, the boys got very excited. They apparently were launching some scheme that made the mother look comically overwhelmed and the father exasperated with a clear *oh-boy-here-we-go-again* kind of look.

"It looks familiar somehow," Soo-Lee said.

Lex swallowed. "Yes…I think it's *The Adventures of Ozzie and Harriet*. We had to watch it once in Mass Media in high school."

"When is it from?" Soo-Lee asked. "The fifties? The sixties?"

"It ran a long time, as I recall, from the fifties into the sixties. But their sons are small here and judging from the furnishings, I'm going to say this episode is from sometime before 1960."

"And why does that matter?" Creep asked.

"Because, again, our theoretical other is creating a physical image of the good old days before the social upheaval of the 1960s. This whole nightmare we're trapped in has something to do with that, with some incident that happened back then." He shrugged. "Maybe our other is trying to recreate a world before something happened."

"What?" Soo-Lee said.

"A tragedy? Something that happened to the town or them personally. I don't know."

"You're guessing," Creep said.

"Of course I am," Lex admitted.

The sitcom played on and Creep sat there, tensely, the images filling the room with flickering light. Soo-Lee's and Lex's faces were painted with a dull blue glow. What was the point of this? Was it somebody's favorite show back in the good old days or was it kind of like Lex intimated, a frame of reference for a simpler time before some horrendous tragedy? Creep didn't really care. He wanted out. It all made him panicky because he knew it was leading up to something, something bad.

The camera panned away from the joyfully arguing family and focused in on an archway behind them that presumably led into a very standard 1950s living room. They saw a shadowy gray form sitting near the wall. It was ghost-like, out-of-focus, somehow contorted as if it had been put together wrong. There was a table before it with a body on it. A woman.

Creep was certain it was Danielle.

It was too dim and shadowy to be certain, but he had the feeling it was. The certainty was like a blade of ice in his heart. The shadowy figure—it was one of those doll people, he realized—was doing things to the body. It opened the corpse up, pulling things out, plucking off limbs like the wings of flies, carefully replacing everything with items he could not be sure of other than what appeared to be prosthetic arms and legs, a bundle of gears and cogs like the guts of a clock that were stuffed into the body cavity. Then the doll person was doing something to the face, peeling and slicing, then cutting and finally sewing. Stitching up what it had made with black gut that looked like fence wire.

"Shut it off," Soo-Lee said. "Please shut it off."

Creep was more than happy to oblige. He tried turning the on/off knob, but it did no good. The TV wasn't even on and it wasn't plugged into anything.

"It won't do any good," Lex said.

Creep knew it wouldn't, but he tried anyway. He had the feeling that even if he had a hammer in his hand, he could not have broken the bubble screen. It was not part of the plan, part of the game that was being played on them.

Now the Nelsons were gone along with their sons.

The camera had pulled away from the weird anatomical plunderings in the living room and was panning over the dining table, revealing the half-eaten food on the plates, the glasses of milk half-drank, the chicken and vegetables that still steamed on their serving trays. It showed them this, then it showed them the chairs pulled away from the table. One of them was tipped over, as if someone had left in a great hurry.

The camera passed by a single window quickly, and light flickered out there beyond the curtains, the jumping light of a bonfire. But the camera didn't waste too much time with that. It pulled back now and they could see the shadowy doll figure standing in the corner, head hanging to one side as if its neck was broken. It looked like some kind of mannequin leaning there, something incapable of movement.

The body was no longer on the table.

Creep felt an icy/hot fear-sweat run down his face. What had been on the table was shambling in the direction of the camera that seemed to be fixed now as if it was sitting on a tripod. The figure came closer, moving with an uneasy limping, see-sawing locomotion. One of its arms swung back and forth with pendulum strokes, a limp and dead thing, the other was missing.

"That's Danielle," Soo-Lee said, something breaking in her voice.

The figure got closer and closer. It was still blurry and out-of-focus, but there was no mistaking that it was Danielle...or that it had *been* Danielle. Her long blonde hair was pulled over to one side of her head, gathered at one shoulder in snake-like tresses. Her face was pallid, grotesque, made of something that was not skin exactly, one eye a black fissure, the other staring out at them with a cataleptic glaze...but set back as if she was looking through the eyehole of a rubber mask. It rolled in its socket like a marble

She was trying to speak.

The clothlike material of her face moved like it was alive. Her mouth was horribly lopsided. One side of it opened to speak, but the other side remained fused as if it was sewn shut.

"TURN IT OFF!" Soo-Lee said, sitting up. "TURN THAT FUCKING THING OFF!"

Creep sat there, unable to move.

Danielle's single eye had been looking at him, now it was looking right at Soo-Lee and there was no mistaking it despite the fuzzy, wavering image. She continued to speak and Soo-Lee clasped her hands to either side of her head like she was trying to keep it from flying apart. She had taken more than she could stand and she was very close to a breakdown.

Lex jumped up and the Danielle-thing tracked him with her eye.

He ran at the TV and kicked the screen with everything he had.

Creep was sure it would never break because that's how things worked in places like this that were sculpted from the bits and pieces of nightmare. He was surprised when a crack appeared in the crystal. Danielle was slowly shaking her head from side to side as if she was disappointed. By then, Lex had kicked the TV two more times and right before the screen went black, Creep saw Danielle open her horribly synthetic mouth and scream. Though there was no sound, he could hear it echoing around inside his skull until he thought that he would be the one to have a breakdown.

Then the screen went black.

There was a tiny white dot that gradually faded. But before it did, at the very moment Lex gave it his last and most powerful kick, a sound rushed through the house that seemed to be carried on a moaning wind of burning air: *OOOOOOHHHHHHHHHHHHHHHH.* The chilling, sibilant sighing of what seemed to be hundreds of voices that cycled through the rooms and died out below them, somewhere in the vicinity of the cellar.

And that's when things started to happen.

19

Ramona stood there, watching the doll parts moving on the ground as if some sinister life-spark were circulating through them. Hands trembled, torsos thumped, and legs kicked. Heads opened and closed their mouths, whispering with needling, strident voices.

She started breathing in and out rapidly, nearly hyperventilating.

An ice-cold sweat ran down her spine

The parts continued to move as if a wind were blowing through them, making them rattle and click and tremble. As she watched, one, then two and three and four torsos rose into the air, the others following suit as if they were being worked by invisible wires from above. Dozens of them spun around in some kind of storm and then they came together with heat and motion and impact, fusing into a common whole that danced up and down before her, swaying and gyrating to some unheard melody. Then the legs stood up. Those whose feet had broken loose reattached themselves.

She let out a tiny, strangled cry.

The legs were hopping around, pale and oddly fleshy, their ball joints shining in the moonlight. She was waiting for them to walk over to her, but that didn't happen. They jumped up into the air, spinning around the common torso and then they, too, were sucked into its mass, gluing themselves to it. The mass continued to move and sway as before, but now it floated about with countless bare kicking mannequin legs that made it look like some horrible spider composed of human parts. Hands were joined with arms that clattered on the pavement and then they, too, flew up in the air, rising as if on a hot column of gas. They circled the mass of legs and torsos and were sucked into the mass, becoming part of it, arms flexing and fingers wiggling as this new and strange accumulated horror accustomed itself to its new environment.

Then the whispering heads.

They bounced up into the air, many of them fastening themselves at odd angles atop the many bunched and stacked torsos. Other heads adhered themselves to the bellies and breasts like gruesome ornaments.

Then this new and nearly indescribable mutation settled back down to the pavement, hissing and clicking and whirring. It approached Ramona with the marching of innumerable feet.

She ran.

Beyond terror, completely irrational with fear, she ran, sprinting down the street and up the sidewalk and around a corner. Pausing there, pressed up against the face of a building, adrenaline pumping through her, she made herself wait and listen. For a few seconds there was nothing and the buzz of fear inside her mellowed slightly. Listening to her own breathing, she stared at the blank faces of little shops across the street. The moonlight was bright, impossibly bright. She saw FLORIST, ICE CREAM PARLOR, and, at the very end, SUNDRIES. Yes, all very generic as before.

When was the last time there were stores called Sundries? Even if this is some weird 3-D representation of Stokes from the 1960s, things like that had to have been something of an oddity even then. A holdover from a much earlier time.

She heard the doll-thing coming again with an echoing *click-clack* of what sounded like a hundred feet marching forward in hot pursuit.

She ran.

Down the street, around another corner, cutting through an alley and across a little park that she had not seen before. When she got to the other side, she found another street and ran down it, racing around yet another corner and pausing again, her lungs gasping for breath and sweat beading her face.

Click-clack, click-clack, click-clack, click-clack, CLICK-CLACK, CLICK-CLACK—

God, it was getting closer.

It wasn't possible.

That immense gangling thing could not be getting closer, but it was. The sound of its marching feet was echoing in her head like the cacophonous ticking of some gigantic clock, getting louder and louder and louder. And it was as she realized this, that she looked across the street and saw it again: SUNDRIES. Next to it, ICE CREAM PARLOR, and next to that, FLORIST.

I couldn't have gone in a fucking circle. I couldn't have.

She hadn't. She knew she hadn't. Either this whole goddamn town was one big loop or, yet again, she was being led, pushed in a certain direction by whoever ran this place. It wanted to break her with fear. That was important somehow to the controller. She had to be broken. It wanted to run her to death like a dog.

Click-clack, click-clack, click-clack, click-clack—

It was getting closer now like it had before when it was just a collection of malevolent doll children. Closer and closer. As before, Ramona knew there was only one possible way to break the spell. She could not run from it; she had to run *at* it. It was the only way, regardless of how unbearably frightening the idea was.

CLICK-CLACK,   CLICK-CLACK,   CLICK-CLACK, CLICK-CLACK!

Jesus, it was almost on her.

She could see its shadow coming around the corner, an impossibly massive and undulant thing with marching legs, wavering arms, and nodding heads.

Sucking in a slow breath, she went to meet it before she had time to reconsider the foolishness of what she was about to do. *I won't be run to death, I refuse.* She saw it bearing down, maybe forty feet from her, its shadow already touching her and feeling cold, dreadfully cold, like the air from a freezer. She ran right at it and it chanted her name and waited for her, its many arms open wide like it wanted to hug her, crush her in its multi-limbed embrace.

No!

Ten feet from it, she turned. She couldn't do it. She couldn't let that horrible thing take hold of her. It would seize her, the arms enfolding her and crushing her against itself until her insides squirted out of her mouth like red jelly.

She turned on her heel and cut between two buildings and then she was in some huge fenced lot. A dead end. It was some kind of junkyard. She saw heaps of refuse, old barrels, uneven stacks of rotting lumber, and junked cars up on blocks. They lacked windshields and doors, the hoods raised and rusted in place, the engine compartments empty save for sprouting weeds. This was the graveyard of the town. As she stepped into its vast wasteland, she saw broken bottles glinting in the light, stacks of bald tires, and the bent frames of old bicycles. She stepped around a cracked bathtub and an overturned toilet. Things skittered amongst the refuse and she knew they had to be rats.

With each step, a little cloud of black dust puffed up.

They smelled hot, like cinders. She blinked her eyes and everything in the junkyard was smoldering. It happened that fast. Not burning, but smoldering as if the actual fire had burned out some hours ago and what was left was the choking incinerated stink, the hot ashes, and the lingering heat. She could feel it through the soles of her shoes. The junk cars were blackened, the wood charred, the tires melted into unrecognizable shapes that still let out greasy black fingers of rubber smoke.

Ma'am, please listen to me, okay? The only Stokes on Highway 8 burned to the ground back in the 1960s, I'm told.

Ramona let out a little cry because it wasn't some voice of memory echoing in her head, but an actual voice. It sounded like it was spoken from inside one of the cars. But she refused to go see. She did not want to see. Gagging on the scorched smell, she stumbled forward, sweating rivers now, her feet hot and sore, her skin feeling like it was sunburned. If she didn't get out of here and fast, she was going to become disoriented by the fumes and pass out.

It was only a matter of time.

The smoke seemed to be getting thicker. The moonlight

cast expanding shadows of it across the seared wreckage. She began to see other things in the ashes, which were ankle-deep now. Body parts. She thought they were the remains of people burned in the fire that took Stokes so many years before…but no.

They were doll parts.

Baby doll parts.

All of them oxidized by the blaze. Little hands melted, bodies folded in half, groups of them welded together, dozens of little faces looking up at her with hollow eye sockets, blistered and ruined. And all of them grinning with what seemed some macabre delight.

Despite the heat, Ramona felt chills run down the back of her arms and up her spine.

She stood there on hot feet, rocking back and forth on burning heels, trying to think and finding it nearly impossible to string two coherent thoughts together. A little voice located somewhere in the back of her skull was whispering to her, telling her that it wasn't the heat or exhaustion or trauma of this night that was mixing up her brain like a jigger of martinis well-shaken, but that which controlled this place, her hypothetical controller or *Controller,* for certainly it deserved proper-noun status.

Don't you get it, Ramona? This is the old mindfuck it's playing on you. Your resilience and obstinacy are wearing it thin. Tormenting you and breaking you down is more work than you're worth so the Controller wants this done right now. Here in this shithole dumping ground of pristine and perfect Stokes, a.k.a. Mayberry RFD, it wants you dead before you get away again and figure out more and start turning what you know against it, because you will. It knows it and so do you.

Doing the two-step on her broiling feet, images of dancing barbecued chickens parading through her head from an old TV commercial, she began to realize that there was truth in what the voice said. The fog of her brain cleared momentarily like a good clean breeze blew through her skull.

You've already figured the town out there is Stokes before the fire.

You've already figured there is a guiding hand at work here.

And you know that the siren activates these things, and it's coming from the east. That's the epicenter of this here fucking quake and you know it. The Controller might just be afraid that you'll track it to its source and put it out of commission.

What do you think of that?

Yes, what *did* she think of that?

But there wasn't exactly time for thinking because the ground was hot, the air was gagging with vapors of searing smoke, and she was most certainly cornered. Her head seemed to spin again and she started seeing things, things that were either pure hallucination or real or some bizarre combination of both.

She saw doll faces watching her from the junked cars.

High above the reaching steeples and craggy branches of the town she could see the moon like a glowering eye, and as she stared into it, it seemed to get bigger, a puffy discolored lid pulling away from the white, shining orb beneath that looked unpleasantly juicy like a pickled egg.

She saw skeletons around her. Not perfect, gleaming Halloween skeletons, but badly used things that were yellow and brown, some black as coal, but all disarticulated and shattered, jaws sprung in wide silent screams when they had jaws at all. Most of them were over near the fence in the distance, but there were others scattered about. In fact, not four feet from her there was an ancient baby buggy whose spoked wheels were threaded with cobwebs and whose bonnet was torn and flapping, a swallow's nest tucked away in the folds. And in it, oh yes, a baby that had been burned right down to the bare bones. It had worn some kind of bunting that melted to its tiny skeleton in black rags. The insane thing was that it was still burning. Its black bones were smoking, flames coming from its eye sockets and mouth.

She saw rats picking through the piled refuse. They were greasy gray bags of fur with tiny red eyes like jewels that sparkled in the moonlight. They all made a curious ticking sound as of pocket watches that were slowly running down.

She blinked her eyes and she heard a steady *thump-thump-thump* of a door swinging open and shut. It came from a small ramshackle hut set between the masts of two burned trees. Tiny ashes fell from them and made a tinkling sound on the sheet metal roof. As she watched, a man came stumbling out, holding his face in his hands. He was not on fire, but black smoke steamed from him in twisting plumes. The stink of roasted flesh and burned hair were nauseating. He stumbled maybe two or three feet and then hit the ground, breaking apart like cigar ash.

These were the things she saw or was made to see and they were all, in their own way, part of the puzzle of Stokes (or *anti-Stokes*, as she was beginning to think of it) that she needed to put together if she ever wanted to get out.

CLICK-CLACK, CLICK-CLACK, CLICK-CLACK, CLICK-CLACK.

It was coming again. Of course it was.

She nearly collapsed with despair.

She turned, coughing on the fumes, and that great ambulant collection of living mannequins was bearing down on her. It cast a long and freezing shadow before it that was like something from an old film noir. The shadow seemed equally as alive as what threw it—a black and crawling thing, expanding, throwing dozens of reaching tendrils before it. Then the thing itself entered the junkyard, a Frankensteinian patchwork of parts, a pulsating colony of heads and hands and shambling legs.

"*It's Ramona,*" the many mouths said. "*It's Ramona. Get her so she can be with us. Pull her apart and paste her parts to ours. Put her head high up on top so she can scream with us…*"

The other heads affixed to its torso did not join in the chorus. They were low, bestial things that bayed and snarled and hissed, clattering their teeth and snapping their jaws.

The thing—*Frankendoll*, was its name, she decided—moved ever forward and Ramona knew she was trapped. The only way out was the fence at the back of the yard. But getting there without being overwhelmed by the heat and the fumes would not be easy. She felt dizzy and queasy and she couldn't seem to think straight.

If you just wait here, it will all be over with soon. Very soon now.

But she couldn't allow that. She stumbled on, her mind flying around in her head like an uncaged bird, crashing into the walls of memory and reason, leaving her confused and breathless. She fought on, maneuvering around the hulks of cars, stepping over weed-sprouting transmissions, tripping over a rusting section of pipe and going down into the cinders that burned her hands. The pain was real and it was like a good, refreshing slap in the face.

The fence was about thirty feet away now, maybe closer.

You're almost there. Pour it on for godsake, pour it on!

Behind her, the Frankendoll monstrosity was still chanting her name, still pushing forward. She turned back once and looked. The sight of it nearly took the heart from her. In the moonlight, it was a cartoonish monster that could not possibly be, a gargantuan hybrid of parts that all seemed to be moving independently though they were part of the wriggling whole. Legs stomped and hands reached and heads shook from side to side. The fused torsos all seemed to be in motion like they were trying to pull themselves apart from the central mass.

The thing was in some kind of demonic rage now as it stalked her.

It kicked barrels out of its way, flipped a leaning bedspring end over end, and charged through a smoldering tower of tires, kicking up a haze of soot that filled the moonlight in dusky clouds. It would have her. And the closer it got, the more it became enraged at the idea of seizing her in its hands. It smashed through heaps of burn lumber and tossed a broken rocking chair into a collection of banged-up trash cans. Its many totemic, blistered faces were breathing out puffs of black smoke.

But Ramona did not sit still.

Even though her eyes were watering, her breath scratching in her throat, and sweat left clean trails down her ash-darkened face, she saw the fence and went toward it, dizzy and tripping and fumbling, but gaining ground foot by foot. Then the fence was very close and she poured on the speed, jumping up onto an old TV set and vaulting up at the fence. She grabbed hold of the top of it, some seven feet from the ground, and pulled herself up and over with her last reserves of strength. She fell into a grassy lot on the other side, panting and shaking, tears streaming from her eyes.

Frankendoll screamed.

With each of its many mouths, it screamed with a sound of dozens of shrieking, tortured children. Then it hit the fence, pounding and kicking and beating at it. Ramona saw the tops of its heads just over the upper planks. It went absolutely hysterical and she saw the fence begin to come apart, loose boards falling and rusted nails ejecting into the air. Planks split and fence posts fell over like saplings.

"NO! NO! NO, RAMONA! DON'T DO THAT!" the mouths cried out to her. *"IT'LL BE WORSE IF YOU DO! WE CAN HELP YOU, WE CAN MAKE IT EASY, WE CAN DELIVER YOU QUIETLY—"*

"Fuck you!" she called out at them with poison.

The doll horror went at the fence with renewed fury like Godzilla going after Tokyo. Boards were flying, planks split lengthwise, posts launched up into the air, wood splinters and blowing clouds of sawdust erupting into the sky.

"YOU STUPID STUPID STUPID MISERABLE CUNT!" the voices cried out and if it were possible for animate dolls or a hulking animate *Franken*doll to go insane, it did at that point, sounding absolutely hysterical with wrath. *"WHO ARE YOU TO UPSET THE BALANCE? WHO ARE YOU TO DARE STAND UP AGAINST WHAT WE ARE? WHO DO YOU THINK YOU FUCKING ARE?"*

But by then she was on her feet, running and running.

Where she got the energy from, even she didn't know. But it was like competing in the fifty-meter freestyle swim. Just when you thought there was nothing left, you got a burst of energy and you turned the corner.

When she finally came to a stop, she waited on a shadowy patch of sidewalk, listening for the approach of Frankendoll, but there was nothing. She was only glad that she had somehow managed to break free of the business section and was not looking at a plate glass window that said SUNDRIES.

But she knew damn well that the only reason she had gotten away was not that she had outsmarted the Controller, but that he, she, or *it* had become bored with the chase, with her very tenacity.

Regardless, she was free.

20

A phone was ringing.

It stopped Chazz dead in the middle of the street. He went down to his knees, sweat dropping from his head to the pavement like raindrops. He was being run to death and was aware of the fact, but he didn't seem to care. He only understood that he must flee. Earlier—ten minutes or twenty or thirty, who knew?—he had thought he heard a phone ringing, but he dismissed it. It was distant and fading. Maybe not there at all. The sort of sound you might hear late on a summer night when you had the windows open and thrashed in your own perspiration. A ringing from several streets away.

But if that had been fantasy, there was no denying the reality of this.

It rang and rang.

Cupping his hands over his ears, he shouted: "Answer it already! Why doesn't somebody just fucking answer it already?"

But the reason for that was fairly obvious. His brain was moving in such strange rhythms now that it took him some time to realize that nobody *could* answer it because there were no people in this town. But how could it ring if nobody called?

None of it made sense.

Unless it was Ramona or one of the others but he did not believe that.

It kept ringing and ringing.

It's for you and you know it.

No, no, he wouldn't let himself think that. Nobody would be calling him because there was no one who could call him. God, the ringing drilled right through his skull and made his brain ache. A ringing phone. An empty town. Why was it familiar?

Was it an old show he had seen or maybe some story they had to read in high school?

Don't matter, Chazz. Don't matter at all, that voice in his head told him. *The call is for you and if you don't answer it, it'll never stop ringing.*

But he wouldn't do that. He'd already made up his mind. That would be asking for trouble and he had more than enough right now. But if he wasn't going to answer it…then why was he walking in the direction of the ringing, tracking it to its source? It hadn't been a conscious decision. He was certain of that. He didn't honestly believe he had any say in the matter. His legs were walking over there and he was obeying and his lips were trembling, a whimpering in his throat.

He was on the sidewalk.

No, no fucking way. I won't do it.

He was moving toward the ringing.

I'll just turn and run.

He saw what looked like a little cab stand. The window was open, one of those sliding types like they have at ice-cream parlors. The phone was sitting inside on a ledge, a big old black phone with a rotary dial. God, it was a dinosaur, a beast from another age.

Okay, you found it, now go.

But he wasn't going. He could see the shadow of his hand reaching for it and then it was not just a shadow, but his fingers gripping the receiver. It was heavy. You could brain somebody with it like in an old movie.

He brought it to his ear.

He heard static, a windy static like a strong breeze blowing across empty fields and down lonely byways. He looked up across the street. He could see the telephone poles, the wires strung between them. The humming sound he heard had been carried to him across fields and through thickets, over county churchyards and down deserted streets and moonlit meadows. And slowly, so very slowly, all that loneliness and dark distance became a voice: "*Chazz…I don't like to be kept waiting. When I call, you better answer.*"

Jesus.

He nearly fell over, but try as he might he could not pull the phone away from his ear. The deserted streets suddenly looked that much more deserted, the shadows that much more like shadows, and the night that much darker, like some finely-woven web of black funeral silk.

"Oh, what's the matter, Chazz? Are you afraid? Are you terrified?"

And he was, God yes, he was. It was more than the phone ringing in this empty dead town, knowing he would be nearby to answer it. It was the voice itself that he had heard back at the house, the voice of the entity he referred to as the Spider Mother, the woman with a hundred legs. He had heard her speaking through the door to him and now she was calling him, baiting him with her squeaky voice.

"Do you want this to be over with, Chazz?"

His breath coming in gasps, he nodded. "Yes…I just…I just want to get out of here. But I don't know the way. I can't find the way. I just can't find it."

The Spider Mother made a hissing sound that slowly wound itself out into something like a cooing. *"You poor little thing, lost and alone, and no one to hold you. No one to make it better. No one to take away the fear and the dread. No one but me."*

"Please…just leave me alone…"

"Ohhhhhh," she said. *"That's not what you really want. You want Mama to come and hold you. You want Mama to make things better. That's what you want."*

"No, I—"

But it wasn't true. He could say it all he wanted, recognizing the horror and revulsion of the thing that spoke to him, but deep inside he was not so sure. Her voice was oddly soothing. It was peaceful, like being wrapped in dark silk and tucked away somewhere where no one could ever hurt you. But that was the danger, that was the threat, that was the seduction. The Spider Mother's voice was taking him away places, making him feel helpless like an infant. She was netting him in strands of warm, comforting spider silk, twining him in it, creating a bunting that he could sleep away eternity in, locking him down into a dark, poisonous cocoon from which there could be no escape.

"You just wait right there, Chazz, and Mama will come for you."

But he knew he couldn't allow that. He already had a repulsive, skin-crawling image in his head of her webbing him up and forcing him to suckle from the wrinkled sacs of her teats.

"No...stay away from me. I won't let you touch me."

"You're ruining it all, Chazz. You're going to make it ugly. You're going to make it hurt real, real bad."

And, yes, he knew that he was, but he wasn't about to let that thing get him. He had to fight; he couldn't give in. And with that, the phone slid from his hand and he ran out into the street, not knowing which way to go because all ways looked exactly the same. And maybe they were. Maybe it wouldn't matter which way he went because all roads led deeper into the heart of this nightmare where *she* waited for him, waited to make him suckle from her so that he was hers forever. His legs would be her legs and his arms her arms and his beating heart would bring the blood that would make her strong and deathless—

Clip-clop, clip-clop, clip-clop, clip-clop.

She was coming.

She knew where he was and she was coming now.

Clip-clop, clip-clop, clip-clop, clip-clop.

The sound of her many marching legs was echoing through the streets now, bouncing off the faces of buildings, getting louder and louder, filling his head and filling his world and if he did not run right now, he would see her coming for him any moment now, rushing out of the dark to seize him the way a funnel-web spider might seize a fly.

But she was not coming down the streets.

She was coming from above.

She was creeping over roofs.

He looked up and saw her legs coming over the cornice of a three-story building directly across the street. He dashed off, choosing a direction purely at random, not thinking, just knowing he needed to get away before she trapped him. Because, sooner or later, she would.

21

Soo-Lee became aware of two things in rapid succession: the smell and the darkness. The smell came literally out of nowhere, thickening and growing rank, filling her stomach with waves of warm nausea. *Spoiled meat,* she thought. *That's what it smells like. Like a truck full of meat that went bad.*

Which, of course, made no sense whatsoever.

Even had there been real food in the house—something she seriously doubted after her experience at the diner—it would gradually go bad as things always gradually went bad. Nothing rotted this fast, in a matter of seconds.

The second thing was the darkness.

It had been dark before, yes, but not *this* dark. Something had happened. There was not even any moonlight coming in through the windows. There was nothing. It was as if some giant cover was dropped over the house like the sort that was used for birdcages at night.

Whatever's happening, this is how it starts.

"Keep together," Lex said, reaching out and taking her hand as she reached out and took Creep's.

The stink grew worse, and Soo-Lee heard Creep make a gagging sound. The air was nearly unbreathable. The dark was more than dark, it was absolute blackness. It enveloped them like an ebon mist. It was as if the three of them were zipped inside a body bag; light no longer existed.

"C'mon," Creep breathed. "Let's get the fuck out of here."

"No," Soo-Lee told him. "That's exactly what we *can't* do. It's exactly what is expected of us. We can't run anymore. We face this and overcome it."

Lex gave her hand a squeeze while Creep's seemed to go that

much more limp. He was not with them on this. He understood the basic idea of what they wanted to do, but he had no real faith in it, no belief that it would work. But it would, Soo-Lee knew. If only he would stand with them. Their belief was important to the puppet master of this place. She was certain that he/she/ it depended upon it.

Something touched her face.

It was a light touch, like a fly had brushed against one cheek. But she knew it was no fly. Even though she could not see a thing, she could feel something substantial hovering in the air right before her face. It brushed her cheek again and though she wanted badly to cry out, she did not. She sat there, trembling slightly.

Just like in the diner, the puppet master is turning up the heat. It's kicking up things a notch. The smell and the darkness are not getting us to move, so it's trying something else. And it'll keep on trying.

Something brushed against the back of her hand.

It felt like a finger.

Someone or something was standing in the dark right in front of her. She was nearly certain of it and calmed herself. She was not going to break, not going to cry out. Its physical presence was crushing. The finger or whatever it was touched her nose, then her lips. It drew a line from her chin down her neck to her breastbone and hesitated there.

Still, she did not move.

"There's something here," Creep said, as if that needed saying at all.

Neither she nor Lex commented on what they already knew. They waited. They steeled themselves. Soo-Lee resisted the instinctive need to kick out at whatever was there. A bead of sweat ran down one temple. Her mouth was so dry she could've spit dust. Whatever was in front of her had not left. No, it had drawn in ever closer. Now its face was inches from her own. She could feel its breath hot against her face. It was not foul, not exactly. There was a distinctively musty smell to it that she acquainted with closed-up trunks moldering away in cellar damps.

You have to resist it. Your belief fuels it.

And yes, God knew it sounded great in theory, but in practice it was something else again. She was barely breathing, afraid that it would hear her, that her rising fear would charge it like a battery and she was bound and determined not to give it anything to work with.

Next to her, Creep was fidgeting, making moaning sounds in his throat.

The breathing thing was so close to her face now that its exhaled air filled her space and made it hard to suck in so much as a breath. It couldn't have been more than an inch away. Fingers brushed her neck, drew slowly down her bare arms. One of them brushed against her left breast.

I can do this, she thought frantically. *I will not break.*

Then the thing, as if sensing this, slid a hand up between her legs at the same time its cold, wooden lips were pressed to her own. All of which was bad enough, but what was even worse is that she felt its tongue slide into her mouth, only it was not a tongue, but something like a leggy, segmented worm.

It was then, and only then that she screamed.

22

Just before Soo-Lee screamed, Creep felt something in the air around him, too. Like energy that moved over the backs of his arms in prickling waves like static electricity. Whatever it was, it was building, moving toward some critical mass and that's what he feared the most: what form it might take and if he'd be able to withstand it because he was right on the edge of a full-blown panic attack and he knew it.

Something dropped into his lap and he flicked it nervously away with his free hand.

Something else fell.

It hit his head and tumbled onto the back of his hand. With a small cry, he swatted at it, feeling a bulbous body about the size of a marble smash beneath his palm with an eruption of goo that felt hot against his skin. He wiped it off on his jeans. His entire body was oily with sweat by this time. Another object dropped onto his knee and when he made to swat it, it ran over his arm on tiny, bristly legs before dropping to the floor. He immediately drew his feet up, his left hand gripping Soo-Lee's in a crushing embrace.

You know what they are, he told himself. *You know damn well what they are.*

Yes, they were spiders. The one thing he was completely terrified of and, of course, whatever ruled this graveyard of a town knew it. *Spiders.* He knew it made no earthly sense. There were no bugs in Stokes. There was no anything. Everything was meticulously sterile like a town kept preserved under a glass dome in a museum. Insects and other crawly things were not allowed. He'd noticed it earlier. It was a warm summer night and there was not so much as a mosquito to be found. Even when the lights went on at the diner, no moths were drawn to them. They should have been crawling over the glass and circling in crazy loops as they did.

But there had been nothing.

And there are no spiders either. Believe that. There are no spiders.

But belief did not come easily. His phobia eclipsed it. There were more spiders now. They were dropping on him and he squirmed and thrashed and knocked them away. He wanted to get up and get away, but Soo-Lee held tightly to his hand. It was like a séance, he thought, where people weren't supposed to break the circle, even if theirs was more of a line than a circle. But there was power to it, and he knew it. He could feel it. If he pulled his hand away, it would be like unplugging himself from them and he was afraid to do that.

No more spiders dropped on him.

But he could hear them moving around him, hanging on tiny threads and rubbing their many legs together. And something more: a high, barely audible squeaking that he knew were the sounds they made when they communicated with each other. Ordinary spiders probably didn't do such things, but these were not ordinary and the squeaking noises he heard were their voices.

They're plotting and you know it. They're discussing you and what they will do to make you let go of Soo-Lee's hand. They'll cover you. They'll bite you. They'll do whatever it takes, because they know you're afraid of them.

Next to him, Soo-Lee tensed and screamed.

It was unbearably loud and felt like a needle piercing his ear. She was going through something, too, but he doubted it was spiders. One of them dropped into his hair and he cried out. Another crept down the back of his neck and got inside his shirt. Others dropped onto his arms. He felt tiny creeping legs move over his face and a smooth, round body settle at his lips, trying to force itself into his mouth.

He screamed, too, as they began biting him, and more dropped down on him. He jumped up, scratching and swatting them, crying out with disgust as their swollen bodies went to mush under his hands and smeared him with their oozing guts. He tore and pawed at himself. Given time, he would have scratched off his own skin such was his mania.

Then something grabbed him.

He felt hands take him and throw him flat against the floor and with such force, the wind was knocked out of him. Fingers like cables pinned him. He tried to fight, to squirm away, but it was no good. He clawed at the face of what held him and felt his fingers slide into it. It was like breaking the skin of a soft brown apple. As he pushed out at it, hitting it, he realized it wasn't the face that was soft, but what was attached to it: dozens and dozens of pulpous, bulging growths that broke apart under his hands, spilling rank fluid into his eyes.

The growths were alive.

He could feel their tiny wiggling legs.

The thing that held him was parasitized with egg sacs, spider ova that were hatching. He destroyed many with his thrashing hands, but many more were born, tearing free of the sacs and dropping on him until he was covered in wriggling spiderlings. They were biting him, sucking his blood, trying to force their way into his mouth and up his nostrils, more and more crowding all the time until he could not breathe.

Until he could do nothing but scream his mind away.

23

Lex took hold of him and yanked him to his feet.

Creep fought him like an animal, hitting and kicking and clawing, and Lex finally slapped him across the face and with enough force to put him right back down. Though he could not see Creep, he could feel him cowering at his feet, moaning and sobbing, utterly broken by whatever the puppet master had thrown at him, which must have been considerable.

"We need to stay calm," Lex said, channeling some B-movie hero and knowing exactly how foolish he sounded.

Soo-Lee was at his side, practically clinging to him and Creep was shivering at his feet. They had both gone through something, but he had been aware of only the utter blackness and things moving in it. Then Soo-Lee screamed like she was being skinned alive and Creep had hit the floor, crying out and squirming, unable to even speak.

So now what? Lex asked himself. *Now what? You seem to think you're the guiding light here, so what next?*

He almost laughed at that. If he was the guiding light, then he had a very weak bulb. Soo-Lee helped him get Creep to his feet. Lex put questions to both of them and the answers were barely coherent.

"All right," he said. "We stand together and we fight together."

More B-movie wisdom, but he had no other frame of reference for something like this. They held hands in the darkness and waited for what came next and when it did, it was not what any of them expected. The lights began to come on. Not in a flash, but very slowly like mood lighting. The glow was orange like that of candles, dim and wavering, slowly brightening.

As it suffused the room, they saw that they were no longer alone and Lex had to wonder if they ever had been.

Soo-Lee gasped.

Creep made a pained sound.

And Lex sighed. *What now? What the hell now?*

He knew the room he was seeing was not the room they had originally been in. There was no bookcase or antiquated TV set or console stereo. All that was gone. They were in a workroom that looked like it was part doll factory and part Frankenstein's laboratory. Two of the walls were hung with hairless doll heads and smooth unpainted doll faces, limbs of assorted sizes, the torsos of children right up to the torsos of adults. None of them looked as lifeless as they should have. He sensed movement in the faces...subtle, secretive, impossible...but there, a slow and yet deliberate crawl of facial muscles beneath waxen skins. Even the limbs were shifting, fingers unfurling, the chests of the bodies rising and falling with measured respiration.

The flickering orange light only enhanced this and made Lex's skin feel like it was going to inch right off his bones.

He held Soo-Lee's hand tighter and that of Creep, whose own hand felt limp and rubbery.

Don't loose it, he warned himself. *This is important. Part horror show and part history lesson.*

Another wall was hung with what looked like archaic, well-yellowed anatomy prints. Lex thought he recognized several Da Vinci drawings, elaborately rendered explorations of the human body. There were dozens and dozens of them, all crowding for space, many tacked right over the top of others or overlapping one another. They were very old, most ripped and dog-eared, faded from age. There was everything from detailed explorations of the human skull to the musco-skeletal system, nervous system and lymphatics. There were also engineering prints where the organs were replaced by arcane machinery, pullies and wires and unbelievably complex clockwork gears.

There was a table, a workbench.

Seated before it was an old woman whose face was wizened, wrinkles deeply etched, mouth hideously seamed. Her hair was stringy white yarn. She didn't seem to have eyes. There was a body on the table. The body of a child or a child-like thing and she was stitching it shut, humming a melancholy tune in an off-key voice that sounded positively morbid.

Lex could not say that it was a dead child.

And he could not say it was a doll.

It seemed to be a horrid hybrid of the two. Its head was detached, a series of tiny, intricate wires hanging in bunches from the throat. They looked like the fine rootlets of a plant. Its arms and legs were likewise divorced from the body. But it was its face that captured his eye—pale and smooth, framed by luxurious yellow hair, the lips sewn shut, the eyes wide and perfectly blue, perfectly sightless.

A voice in the back of his head said, *Look away, oh Christ, look away! If she finishes putting it together, it will move. It will sit up and look at you with those dead cerulean eyes.*

The other wall was taken up by shelving that was likewise crowded with nameless glass jars and bottles that looked to be filled with liquids and powders, vessels of eyes, and overflowing boxes of swivels, sockets, gears, fine steel piping, and spooled wire.

Lex knew without a doubt that he was looking at the puppet master of this awful place.

She was the one.

Hers was the mind that held them here.

He expected her to look up at him and acknowledge the fact that he knew, but she did not. She was far too busy putting together the little boy. Nothing could interfere with her work, her obsession and devotion to her craft. Her hands were in constant motion, practiced and expert. Before she finished stitching the torso shut, she poured something from a jar into her hand that looked pink and alive and stuffed it in there. Then she began to fit the limbs in place with meticulous artistry.

It was at this point that he and the others realized that the woman was not the only one in the room. There were others sitting about in folding chairs like an audience. They were doll people, the men in suits and the women in fine dresses. Their dead white faces emoted like rubber masks, empty eyes fixed on the old woman. Several of them had empty sleeves as if there had not been enough limbs to go around.

"This is insane," Creep said under his breath. "This is all fucking insane."

His voice boomed in the silence where the only sounds were those of the old woman and her fingers moving deftly at her creation. It was like a scream in church. The effect was instantaneous: the old woman stopped what she was doing. Snips in one hand and a surgical knife in the other, she looked up with eyes that were purple-red in flayed sockets. The doll people all turned their heads and looked in Creep's direction.

One by one, they stood up.

Creep panicked and ran.

As the doll people began to move in their direction, he dashed through a doorway and down the hall. Lex and Soo-Lee had no choice but to go after him. There were several doors and he opened each one, crying out as he did so. From each doorway, another doll person emerged, reaching out to him with soft, puffy hands. He went to the doorway at the end. He threw it open and disappeared into it.

Lex and Soo-Lee went after him, avoiding the reaching hands themselves. By the time they got through the door and slammed it shut behind them, the hallway was filled with animate dolls.

We've been herded again, Lex thought as he went down the steps into the cellar after Creep. *Now they've got us right where they want us.*

24

Sometime after climbing out of the junkyard and her manic run in the streets, Ramona came to her senses and she was crawling up the sidewalk. Not sprinting or walking or even stumbling, but *crawling.* Her face blackened with soot, her clothes gray with ash, completely out of it, laid low by shock and the aftereffects of pure terror.

Finally, she stopped.

Just what in the hell are you doing?

The thing was, she didn't know. By that point, she really knew nothing. She very badly needed a good solid dose of reality but reality did not exist in this place, and without it she couldn't seem to get her feet under her. Literally. This was all a dark fantasy, a nightmare.

All right. Stop right now. Don't think. Don't try to make sense. Stand up like a fucking human being. That's a start.

It took some doing, but she did it.

She stripped off her filthy coat and breathed.

She leaned up against the brick front of a building and looked across the street. She was expecting to see the same storefronts again, but she didn't see that at all. Instead, there was a gigantic banner draped over the faces of several edifices that said: WELCOME TO HISTORIC STOKES. If it was meant to inspire fear, it had the opposite effect: she started to giggle. The giggling welled up inside her until it became full-blown laughter and she shook with it, her girlish and manic cackling echoing up and down the empty streets. Now this was funny! This was fucking comedy! This had to prove that the Controller had a very wicked sense of humor.

Historic Stokes, she thought. *Historic Stokes. Oh, that's hilarious!*

When she finally calmed down—and it took some time—she fished her cigarettes and lighter out of her pocket and lit up. Dirty and grimy and smudged with ash and smoke, she pulled off her cigarette and had to force herself not to laugh.

Then she saw the van sitting up the street and things quickly became very unfunny.

It was not idling; it was simply parked at the curb. She stood there, stiff from head to foot, waiting for it to rev up and come after her. But it did nothing. She swallowed down her fear, knowing damn well that she was not some shrinking violet, and she wasn't about to become one now. A few deep breaths. A second or two to unclench her muscles. A few drags off her cigarette. There. She was not about to fall apart again like she had in the junkyard. No goddamn way.

You were close before, real close to wearing down the Controller. Then you lost it. Well, find it again and put it to work. Do not allow yourself to be driven. Do not be predictable. Go on instinct. Act irrationally.

The van.

The van was intended to make her run screaming until she was exhausted. But no, she would not allow that. The Controller would expect her to run and hide, to find a safe place that would be, no doubt, conveniently available so she could be trapped in an enclosed space. And there the games would really begin.

Ramona took a final drag off her cigarette and tossed it.

She moved up the sidewalk at a very sneaking pace, keeping to the shadows as if she was trying to avoid being seen. This would be predictable behavior. The Controller would be expecting it. At the last moment, she made as if to run off…and then dashed across the street to the van, grabbing the handle of the driver's-side door and threw it open.

The broken man was behind the wheel.

A blade of fear went through her, but vanished quickly enough. He was slumped over in the seat, loose-limbed and limp. He seemed incapable of motion. He was a lifeless window dummy and no more.

Still…she was cautious, very cautious.

She knew how quickly they went from being inert to active.

Common sense told her to get the hell out of there, so she ignored it and did the irrational thing. The thing that was dangerous, but oh-so satisfying. She grabbed the broken man and pulled him out of the van, tossing him to the pavement. He broke into pieces. She kicked his head and it rolled into the gutter.

She waited for him to come to life, but it didn't happen.

She jumped behind the wheel and started the van up. She was amazed that it ran so smoothly. Did the Controller's power not extend to internal combustion engines? Or was she—gasp— playing into his/her/its theoretical hands again?

Fuck it.

The last time the alarm sounded it had come from the east and that's where she was going. The rational thing would be to drive out of town, so she didn't bother with that. She was going to track this bullshit to its source.

Guess what, Mr. Controller? she thought then. *I'm coming for your ass. Goddamn right I am.*

25

She was still out there.

She was still waiting for him.

Chazz could not see the Spider Mother. He could not hear her. Yet, he could feel her out there, sense her drawing closer. He was like a streetlight and she was a moth. She was circling him, drawing ever closer, creeping up just out of sight, waiting to pounce.

He was not running now.

He was simply run out. But he refused to stay still for more than a few seconds or a minute at the very outside. Every time he stopped, he threw out feelers, trying to figure out where she might be. Casting for scent like a bloodhound. And each time he did, he thought: *You can't outrun her. You can't escape. This is her town and she decides where every street leads to.*

Now and again, he could feel her eyes on him, her *many* eyes...if she even had eyes at all. It made him break out in a cold sweat. And once, several streets back, he was certain he heard the distant thumping of an immense heart. In his mind, he could see it: not the Spider Mother, but a huge, well-muscled heart in an empty lot, flabby and black-red, beating away. Not necessarily her heart but perhaps the heart of the town, the secret black beating heart of it that nourished the body. He could imagine the sewers and pipes and conduits beneath the ground being blood-swollen arteries and veins.

You're thinking crazy. You're thinking absolutely crazy, he told himself.

It was true and he knew it, but even so he was not convinced of the fact. There had been a time—long ago, it seemed—when he would have rejected such thinking out of hand as any sane person would have. But that time was gone and reality was not such a given anymore. That which once made no sense made all the sense in the world today.

"Move," he whispered under his breath.

Chazz stood up, looking around. He could not hear the *clip-clop* of the Spider Mother. Maybe she had given up, but he didn't believe that for a moment. He moved down the sidewalk, eyeing doorways, unable to decide if they promised sanctuary or danger. He moved on for another ten and then fifteen minutes and saw nothing and heard nothing. He began to stand tall again and not bent-over and skulking like some scavenging animal.

He walked with a more confidant stride.

He breathed easier.

His brain became less clouded and he began to think less instinctively, and more like a man. He had been running and running and getting absolutely nowhere. Now that there was not menace around every corner, he began to consider how he might find the others. Because, really, that was the true horror of this entire situation…being alone. The doll people and Lady Pegleg and the Spider Mother, they were all horrible, of course, but being alone against them made it so much worse.

If he had someone at his side, someone like Ramona for instance, he would fight with her (or him) happily.

Forget Ramona, dumbass. You knocked her aside when that mannequin woman grabbed hold of you. You cracked up. You showed her what you were made of. Maybe muscles and attitude on the outside, but nothing but shivering pudding on the inside.

He refused to think about that.

That's not the way it was. Yet, the idea that he was a coward haunted him and would not let him go. As much as he tried to sweep it out of his mind, it clung there like a dust ball, getting bigger, gathering all the debris inside his brain until it pretty much blotted out all else.

He started running again.

He knew he wasn't running from any real threat but running from himself. He dashed around a corner—good God, the streets were all the same, all the very same—and ran smack dab into one of the doll people. He crashed into it before he could stop himself and they both went down.

It was trapped beneath him.

In those few seconds of shock before he fought himself free, he saw it was Lady Pegleg. Her white wig was nearly detached from her scalp, hanging off to one side like a rag. Her face was loose and flaccid like latex rubber, the eye sockets filled with a formless blackness.

Chazz screamed and threw himself backward, cracking his head on the edge of a building, seeing stars. The very worst thing was that she came with him. She was stuck to him. He hit her and pushed her away, but she was glued to him. They rolled across the sidewalk together, but he could not throw her. He ended up on his back and she was on top of him, not moving or doing anything, just a dead dummy, a conjoined twin he could not separate himself from.

He screamed again, her gruesome face inches from his own.

It hung in flaps and pouches, a breathing bag of flesh that seemed to inflate and deflate with respiration. Great furrows, crevices, and deep-hewn wrinkles were cut into it. Black suturing ran from the corners of her mouth and up to her forehead where they joined more intricate stitchwork. Her face was like something sewn together out of three or four corpse faces. The suturing was so tight it pulled her lips away from juicy pink gums and peglike teeth that were all twisted and gnarled.

But the most shocking thing was that even though she wasn't moving, she was alive. She was breathing and he could feel the dull thudding of her heartbeat.

Wild and hysterical, he fought to be free of her but she clung on tenaciously.

On his feet, he smashed her into the brick face of a building again and again, trying to shatter her, to break her into pieces but she was incredibly tough and resilient. Her head bounced about on her sagging, flabby neck, her face brushing his own, her lips feeling cold and greasy like the entrails of a fish.

Somewhere during the process, she merely slid off him like a sloughed skin.

He did not run.

He went down on his ass, gibbering and mad, drool running from his mouth and tears flowing from his eyes. He did not think and he did not feel. He just waited there for her to wake up.

There seemed to be nothing else left.

26

"They've stopped," Soo-Lee said, trying to regulate her breathing in the dark clamminess of the cellar. "I don't hear them anymore."

"It's not over," Creep said.

Lex said nothing. He figured they wouldn't be down in the cellar if it hadn't been for Creep and he wasn't too happy about it. Creep had lost his nerve. Lex did not believe that they were in any real danger up there. It was weird and disturbing, but there was no true threat. Not if they kept their heads. Not if they let it play out. He knew from his experience in the diner that they could have gotten out anytime they wanted. Regardless of how the room had rearranged itself, they still could have gotten out because the "real" room was still there even if it wasn't visible.

Now he wasn't so sure.

Once again, they had been manipulated, driven to the very place the puppet master wanted them. He had a feeling they were in a momentary lull until that siren went off again.

"There's something down here," he said. "Something our host wants us to see or to find."

Creep trembled next to him. "Like what?"

"I don't know. But, trust me, nothing is by accident here."

The three of them were leaning up against a wall at the bottom of the steps. Lex had locked the door to the cellar and the doll people beat and scratched at it for some time before going quiet. He knew they were still out there, but they weren't doing anything. *A lull. That's all this is.* He was thinking the smart thing to do would be to sneak out now while they were inactive. Soon, the siren would sound again and then there would be real trouble.

But it wasn't going to happen.

He was sure there would be a dozen or so of them frozen in the hallway and he did not honestly believe that Creep had the guts to move among them, even if it meant freedom.

So they waited there, shoulder to shoulder, not able to retreat and afraid to go deeper into the cellar itself.

Lex, feeling wicked and frustrated by it all, said, "What do you think, Creep? What do you think we should do?"

"How should I know?"

"You led us down here."

"I didn't have a choice."

"You could have kept your head."

"Fuck you."

"Knock it off," Soo-Lee said. "The both of you. Since we're here, let's see what there is to see."

Uncommon bravery. Something Creep lacked completely and something Lex wasn't too sure he had himself.

"It's pitch black. Can't see a damn thing down here."

"Try using your lighter," Lex suggested.

Creep, sighing, dug it out. He handed it to Lex, not wanting to be the one to flick it as if he might be punished for the transgression. Lex took it from him and flicked it. The flame was bright and even. They were in a long, narrow corridor. There was a lot of junk piled around against the walls. Everything from stacks of water-stained cardboard boxes to old bicycle frames and a particularly nasty looking mattress that was nearly black with stains as if someone had bled to death on it long ago.

Amazingly, there was also a candelabra sitting atop an old dresser that lacked drawers. There were three red candles in it half burned down, wax melted down the stems. It was like something out of an old European horror movie

"How convenient," Soo-Lee said.

Lex stared at it. "Isn't it, though?"

But then everything was a little too convenient and a little too coincidental in Stokes. You tended to find what you needed when you needed it, particularly when it had the potential to enhance your uneasiness. On the other hand, if you needed something to get you out or make you feel safer, you'd never find it in a hundred years.

He lit the candles. "There. Now we can pretend we're a couple of dumbasses in a monster movie."

Creep giggled, but there was no mirth to it, only a low-key, slow-burning hysteria.

Lex led the way down the corridor, feeling like he was moving down the passage in a Halloween spook house waiting for the ghosties and ghoulies to leap out at him. He didn't think that was too far off the mark. There was a door at the end, but there were no cobwebs or bloody handprints on it. The knob was old, very old, tarnished and grimy from generations of hands.

He looked back at Soo-Lee in the guttering candle light.

The jumping illumination painted her face in an orange glow, casting shadows under eyes and cheekbones. It made her Asian features look somehow mystical and cruel. But she was neither. He knew that much. She was solid and practical, kindhearted.

He gripped the knob without any Hollywood drama and threw the door open. What he saw in there was pretty much what he expected to see. Not exactly, of course, because he couldn't have known, yet it was no surprise.

"Boxes," Soo-Lee said.

Creep disagreed. "Coffins. Those are coffins."

Lex and Soo-Lee looked at each other and then back at the boxes. Yes, coffins. But not the modern sort that people cried over, but cheap pine boxes that, again, were like something out of a horror movie. A Hammer movie to be more precise, Lex thought. *The Brides of Dracula* or *The Vampire Lovers.* One of those period screamers his mom always watched when he was a kid. There had to have been twelve or fifteen of them piled in an untidy heap as if they had been dropped from above.

"Shut the door," Creep said. "Just shut it already."

But Lex was not so certain it was going to be that easy. What he had in mind was stupid horror movie logic, but he saw no other way. He was certain that they needed to open a few of those boxes or they would never be allowed out of there. He told Soo-Lee the same.

"Yes, maybe," she said. "But if we do that, aren't we allowing ourselves to be manipulated again?"

"Maybe."

"No maybes about it," Creep said.

Yet, when Lex went in there, they followed. When he pried the first lid off, they pressed in closer to see. What he saw was himself. A dummy of himself. It even wore his clothes. It was what he would look like as a doll person: lips pulled in a straight line, eye sockets like deep holes drilled into a smooth and white face, fingers interlocked over the belly like those of a corpse in a casket. It wasn't alive in the ordinary sense. More like something that was *waiting* to live.

It was terrifying…yet oddly intriguing. He couldn't seem to take his eyes off it even though it made him feel like screaming.

Creep had stepped back away from the box. "Put the fucking lid back on, man. I can't stand looking at it."

Lex figured that was pretty sage advice.

He clattered the lid back in place, certain the thing would wake up at any time. Thankfully, it didn't.

"We better check the other ones," Soo-Lee suggested.

"Fuck that," Creep said. "Just stop, okay? Enough is enough. You two have to learn when to stop."

They ignored him.

They pulled off two more lids. Soo-Lee found herself looking down at a mannequin of Creep that was nearly identical to him, save the mocking grin on its face and the fact that there was no warmth, no humanity, no good or bad or anything in-between etched into the features. It had not lived and experience had not seasoned it, given it character.

Lex found Soo-Lee's doll copy.

It was even more intriguing than his own. The porcelain-white face framed by long black hair was flawless, the cheekbones high, the lips full. Unlike his own imitation, this one had eyes. Not human eyes exactly, but more like gelid orbs of pooled dark liquid that seemed to watch him. She looked very good as a doll. There was no getting around it. The copy was perfect, even more physically perfect than Soo-Lee herself. He touched its face and it was not plastic or wood or wax, but something very soft like silk. There was a tactile pleasure associated with it and he did not want to draw his hand away. He had the strongest desire to run his hand over the swell of the breasts.

"What are you doing?" Soo-Lee asked him.

"It feels almost alive," he told her.

He could not seem to pull his hand away. The touching was pleasurable, erotic even, like the very act was flooding his brain with endorphins. He needed to put both hands on her and touch her, feel every curve, run his hands up and down her.

Then Soo-Lee pulled him back.

And for one moment, he felt rage, uncontrollable rage. He wanted to hit her. It was like she had unplugged him from the greatest joy he had ever known. Then it passed and he was just confused.

"It moved," Creep said in a haunted voice. "When she pulled you away, the doll moved its hand."

It had me and it didn't want to break contact, Lex thought. *Somehow it must have been feeding on me, drawing something from me.*

Soo-Lee, practical and determined, put the lid back on and then did the same with the other box. Out of sight, out of mind.

"We need to get out of here," she said. "We don't have much time, so don't waste any of it. Let's go."

She led them away and up the stairs, unlocking the cellar door and holding the candelabra out before her. The hallway was empty. There were no doll people anywhere. Nobody stopped to consider what that might mean. Soo-Lee was in charge now and she was all business. She towed Lex along by the hand and he dragged Creep with. The workroom was gone. Now it was the living room that was a snapshot from 1960, an ad from a Sears & Roebuck catalog fifty years out of date.

Soo-Lee got them to the front door, set the candelabra aside, and stepped out into the night. Lex and Creep followed. Together they stood at the foot of the steps.

"Now what?" Creep said.

"Now we get out of here," Soo-Lee told him with an authority that could not be argued with.

They had made it to the street when the siren began to sound, wailing in the night like a warning.

27

*I*t was raining ash.

Ramona had the wipers working madly on the windshield of the van, but still she could not clear it. It was like being lost in a black snowstorm. The ash flew thick and heavy, filling the headlights and then simply covering the windshield until she was forced to bring the van to a stop where it promptly died.

There was nothing she could do but wait it out.

She sat there, pulling her shirt up over her face so she did not breathe any of it in. Even inside the van, the ash was everywhere. It drifted in a haze, covering the seats and dashboard and steering wheel, settling over the floor like deep sea silt. With ten minutes, Ramona was coated in it, too. But even so, it was still much better within the van than without where it flew like a black blizzard.

She waited.

And waited.

What if it was to go on for hours? For days? You'd be buried alive in the stuff, she thought.

True, but she knew it wouldn't last too long. It couldn't. The Controller was expending a great deal of energy to create this illusion. Oh, it was real enough—you could touch the ash, feel it, breathe it in and asphyxiate on it, but it was still an illusion. A physical illusion. It would play itself out given time. She wondered if her theoretical Controller was even doing this on purpose or it was sort of a subconscious thing, if that even made any sense.

She huddled there on her seat, breathing through her shirt, wearing her sunglasses so the stuff wouldn't get in her eyes. The temperature in the van had risen at least twenty degrees in the last fifteen minutes and already she was beginning to perspire, her clothes clinging to her like damp rags. She wiped sweat from her face and it left a greasy residue of ash and moisture that she could feel.

It was disgusting.

If this ever ended, she would need to soak in a bath for hours.

She waited there, listening to the ash brushing against the outside of the van like sand. It seemed to go on and on and she felt increasingly claustrophobic, the van feeling more and more like a coffin she was slowly being buried alive in, a crate sinking into the black depths of quicksand. Even when it ended and she was not sure that it ever would, she would be interred beneath many feet of black ash and if she got the sliding door of the van open, she would drown in a moving and shifting mountain of it.

But that was imagination and she could not afford it.

Even now, it was ceasing. She could barely hear it brushing up against the van now. She waited another ten minutes or so until it was deathly silent out there, knowing it could only mean one of two things: either the van was indeed buried or the ash storm had finally ended.

She unrolled her window an inch and ash fell in, covering her in black soot.

She unrolled it a few inches more.

She was not buried.

Good then. She opened the door and stepped out into a world painted black. The ashes came up to her calves and she moved through them, casting clouds of soot with each step as she moved away from the van into a weird, blackened world. Stokes lay gutted around her. It looked like a plastic model a boy had gotten bored with, doused in lighter fluid and set aflame. This was the aftermath.

Gone was the Mayberry RFD illusion of Stokes.

What she was seeing was the town after the fire that had destroyed it.

The sky seemed to be dark with soot, the moonlight filled with smoke and blowing ash. The neighborhoods were burned-out, houses reduced to foundations or black hulks. In some cases there was nothing but a standing sooty chimney or two, limbless trees like black stakes that witches had been roasted upon. She saw the remains of incinerated cars in the streets that looked like the dried-out, mangled carapaces of insects you might find on the windowsills of deserted houses. There were heaps of smoldering bricks and burning boards rising from the ash, telephone poles that had fallen over, and stands of bushes that had not caught fire but merely withered in the blazing heat.

It was a terrible mess.

The thing that caught her eye and held it was what appeared to be the collapsing wreck of a factory or mill on a hilltop that overlooked the town itself. From her vantage point it looked much like the aftermath of a funeral pyre or a bonfire that had burned down—a collection of blackened sticks and stumps.

Then, as quickly as it had appeared, it was gone.

Stokes was pristine and pure again, not violated and broken. The streets were clean, the windows gleaming with moonlight, the air fresh and the walks swept.

The only evidence that anything had happened at all was Ramona herself, who was black from head to foot, her hair full of ashes. She breathed in the clean air, neither shocked nor surprised at the transformation of the town.

She plodded on.

Light.

She saw flickering blue light.

It was from down the street. The TVs in the window of a shop were all operating. Again, it was like something from an old movie. She half-expected to see a crowd gathered on the walks staring through the glass. She went down there because obviously it was for her benefit and stood before the window. Six or seven archaic TVs were showing the same program—a black-and-white newscast that was grainy, the picture rolling from time to time. The news anchor with his austere suit and bowtie, hair shiny with Brylcream, was holding a sheaf of papers, a bulky chrome-plated Unidyne microphone set on the desk before him.

The picture changed. Now it was showing footage of a horrendous fire, houses and buildings engulfed in flame, black smoke churning into the sky. The anchor came back on, commenting on it. Then the picture changed again. Block letters on the screen read:

AMONG THE MISSING

This was followed by blurry black-and-white photos that she could tell were herself and Chazz, Creep and Danielle, Lex and Soo-Lee. The images kept repeating. It was designed, she knew, to fill her with terror and it was doing a pretty good job at it. The most disturbing part was that they were not photos taken in life, but in death. Each of them was laid out naked on slabs like Old West gunfighters that had been cut down. Their faces looked flaccid, their eyes sunken.

Ramona turned away.

The fear inside her ran dark until it became a poison that made her hate, made her lust for revenge. She was angry, really angry, and she knew damn well that when she got like this, she was not only irrational but relentless in her need for payback.

She heard the siren begin to shrill, which meant things were going to start heating up again. Tensed, standing out in the middle of the street, she waited for it.

She didn't honestly think, *bring it on*, but in every fiber of her being, she was daring the Controller to do just that.

28

When the alarm shrieked, Lady Pegleg woke up…at least, she once again was a living entity of some type. Chazz could see it happening. It was like some kind of 3-D hallucinatory special-effects mind-fuck, only that was fantasy and this was real. No CGI could touch this because it was so unbearably subtle, so gradual that it simply happened as you watched and was so smooth and fluid you were not sure anything had happened at all.

Is it? Is it? Is it really happening? Am I actually seeing this shit?

Granted, his brain was not actually working real well of late. It was missing on more than one cylinder, his mind filled with dust and cobwebs and narrow spaces. Hell, there were no high, sunlit places up there anymore where he could walk tall and proud, only dim, dirty crawl spaces where he had to creep on his belly to get from point A to point B.

Yes, that was certainly true.

But…*but* this was something else again.

Lady Pegleg had been lying there in an untidy heap like a discarded marionette, limbs going this way and that, head hanging off to the side, hands splayed, mouth hanging open like it was waiting for a sparrow to nest in it.

Then—

Then things started to happen. With a rattling sound like sticks and marbles shifting in a box, she stood up facing him. She was hunched over with a twisted old-lady spine, her head resting on one shoulder. She balanced there on one foot and the pegleg itself, wavering slightly like she might fall down any second. A life force took her inch by inch, making what had looked essentially like a wooden puppet moments before into something animate and possibly organic. She filled with life like a balloon filling with air.

By the time Chazz was aware of the fact that it was really happening, it was already done.

A voice in the back of his head that sounded very distant, said, *this would be the point where you run if you have any sense left.*

But he wasn't running.

In fact, he wasn't doing anything. He was just watching her, feeling helpless and hopeless, a dreamlike sense of self-preservation trying to take form in his head but never really coming together. Lady Pegleg had made no threatening moves and he could not take his eyes off her. She was watching him— even though she had no eyes—and he was watching her. He felt like prey. Once, when he was in tenth grade Bio 2, he had watched Mr. Berry drop a mouse into the cage of a pet rat snake named Herman. The mouse had been very excited at first to be out of the cramped little cardboard box it had made the trip from the pet store in. It jumped and frolicked with the pure joy of freedom…then it saw Herman. It squeezed itself into a corner of the cage, shivering with pure terror as Herman slowly, relentlessly moved in its direction.

Chazz felt just like the mouse.

Maybe Lady Pegleg had no eyes as such, but there was something alive in the holes of her face and it was directed at him. She was watching him like Herman watched the mouse, preparing to strike.

Chazz knew he should do something, anything.

Get up off his ass at the very least and face this threat with the only tools he had, his strength and speed. But he wasn't doing that or anything else because he was simply wrung out. He felt like one of those dingy rags his stepmom would hang out on the line after she gave the kitchen floor a serious scrubbing. He was limp and sodden and incapable of action.

Lady Pegleg waited there, filled with menace but making no moves. She was dressed in some kind of moldering smock or shift, a raggedy black thing that reminded him of crow feathers, shiny and well-plucked. It draped from her in tattered scarves and bolts.

Good boys will be rewarded, she said, her voice echoing only in his mind. *Bad boys will be punished.*

She took a few steps in his direction, then a few more, and he watched her come. *Tap-tap, tap-tap, tap-tap,* went her peg. She stepped fully into the moonlight and he got a real look at the bag of her face, at the deep crevices and gnarled pockets of tissue, the ruts and suturing, the discolored gums and overlapping yellow teeth, the lips like dried onion peelings. It wasn't tissue, he knew, it was some kind of material like burlap, finally woven yet alive. It was flaking, coming apart, threads and ribbons of it hanging down like locks of hair. A trail of dried blood had seeped from one of the sutures.

Do you want to see your friends? Lady Pegleg asked in his head, knowing it was what he wanted the most of all. *Yes? Well, there is only one way to find them and that is through me. I can take you to them. I can join you to them. I can make you all whole again. All you have to do is take my hand and I'll take you away from the fear and into the light. I'll introduce you to she who makes and unmakes and she who rewards those who don't run like scared little boys. Just take my hand…*

His own voice in his head told him with finality that this was it, he either came to his senses and came to them very quickly or he took her hand and sank deeper into the mire of this nightmare until his lungs filled with black silt and his heart filled with black terror and he sank like a brick. This was it. This was the defining moment.

Lady Pegleg held out her hand to him, palm upwards. He could see metal rods or bones straining beneath the flesh.

He knew what he was going to do and stood up.

He'd bowl this window dummy straight over, cut right through the line and into the endzone and there wasn't a damn thing she could do to stop him. That was his intention. So nobody was more surprised than he when he reached out and took her spongy hand in his and felt her wriggling fingers engulf his hand like tentacles that would never let go.

He screamed with one last act of desperation.

But it was too late by then.

Far too late.

29

The doll people were coming.

Not one or two, but groups of them from every direction, moving like metal filings following lines of force to a central magnet. And that magnet was the house. Soo-Lee, Creep, and Lex watched them coming, hobbling and weaving and dragging themselves forward, but never veering from their set path.

We'll drown in them, Creep thought. *There's so goddamn many that we'll be buried alive in them.*

"We better get back inside," Lex said. "This looks like a siege."

But Creep didn't like the idea. "Fuck that! Let's run for it!"

"We can't run for it. There's nowhere to run *to,*" Soo-Lee reminded him.

She was right. He knew she was right. They were trapped and, once again, their decisions were being made for them and they were reacting rather than acting just as she and Lex had said earlier.

"C'mon," Soo-Lee said. "Back into the house. It's all we can do."

Lex started backing up with her, but Creep didn't follow because he saw a way out. At last, a way out.

"Creep," she said. "Let's go."

But he shook his head vehemently. Obviously, they weren't seeing it or they'd be thinking what he was thinking. "Look!" he said. "Over there!"

They still weren't seeing it.

Their faces were blank, practically bovine in the bright moonlight. They didn't see it and they weren't getting it. Christ, it was right there! Just up the street! A fucking car! How could they not be seeing it? The beauty of it was that it was an old sedan from the days before steering wheel locks. It would be no big deal to hotwire an old car like that. He had a pocket-knife with him and that's all he would need.

"The car!" he cried. "Right over there! *Look!*"

But they'd already seen it and it was obvious they didn't like the idea of it. He knew what they were thinking: it was a setup. The puppet master (as Lex liked to call him or her or *it*) had put the car there so they would foolishly jump into it. Creep knew there was a certain amount of sense to that…particularly in this place where there were no cars, but fuck it, he was scared and he couldn't think straight anymore. He needed to get out. The way he was figuring things, even if he had to fight a couple doll people for it, then it was still worth it.

Beat the hell out of holing up in that damn house and trying to survive through some *Night of the Living Dead* scenario.

He took off, running to it.

Lex and Soo-Lee called out to him, but by then the doll people were closing from every quarter and they didn't chance coming after him. Which was good, because he wasn't going to hide in that fucking house, waiting for those things to get him.

Behind him, Lex and Soo-Lee were still calling out.

They were going to feel real stupid when he rolled up out front with the car and got them the hell out of there. As he approached it, he saw one of the doll people rise up from behind it like a gas-filled balloon. It was a man whose face ran like white greasepaint as if he were under a hot lamp. He had no eyes, but that didn't stop him from looking right at Creep and it sure as hell didn't stop Creep from letting out a little cry.

He looked over his shoulder.

Lex and Soo-Lee had gone back into the house and the streets were filling with doll people. There was no going back now; they were everywhere. He was alone, and he either did what he came to do or—

The doll man came shambling around the car, his mouth opening and closing with a rigid, mechanical movement as if it was wired like the jaws of a puppet. And maybe it was. Creep tried the driver's-side door. Locked. That brought a jolt of panic.

He ran around to the other side, the doll man scarce feet behind
him. The passenger-side door was locked, too.

But the rear door was open.

He threw himself in there, slamming the door and throwing
the lock. He quickly pushed down the other rear lock and
breathed a sigh of relief. The doll man was ineffectively slapping
at the windows.

*Hit them all you want, dipshit. Car windows only break easily in
movies.*

Now, he would hotwire this sonofabitch and get the ball
rolling. It was going to work out and he knew it. He could see it
playing out in his mind. That was the only thing that gave him
pause, because things never worked out this easily in real life
and especially not for him.

What the hell?

He hadn't really noticed at first, but now he was seeing it:
there was no color in the car. It was completely washed out. It
wasn't real easy to tell with nothing but moonlight, but he was
seeing it all right—the inside of the car was black-and-white like
in an old movie. His hands were a cream color, the car itself
varying degrees of gray.

He pulled himself up to hop over the seats, deciding he
wasn't going to be thinking about what that might mean. It was
a trick of the moonlight and he sure as hell didn't have time to
be freaking out about shit like that. There were things to do and
he was the only one who could do them.

The keys were in the ignition.

The keys were in the fucking ignition!

Now that was a real break, and it made him more paranoid
that this entire thing was going to blow up in his face. He started
climbing over the seats. There were several doll people out there
now, converging on the car. *Yeah, well fuck you,* he thought.

Then something hit him.

There was no one or nothing in the car with him, yet he
felt something like a hand strike him square in the chest and
knock him into the backseat. Maybe it wasn't a hand exactly.
Maybe it was something more along the lines of a wave of force.
Regardless, it had physical impact.

Creep pulled himself up.

This was how things went bad and he knew it.

Stupid dumbfuck! You knew it was too good to be true, but you went for it anyway!

Seized by panic, expecting that invisible force to hit him again, he reached for the door handle...except there was no door handle. It was like the back of a police car, no handles. He tried pulling up the lock but it was fused. He tried the other door. It had no handle either. He peered over the seats. He knew there wouldn't be any handles up there either because that's not how it worked. This was a trap. This was a fucking Roach Hotel— *Roaches check in, but they don't check out.* It was at this point that he lost it, pounding against the windows, beating on them until his fists ached, knowing he was not going to get out, but like an animal in a cage he was unable to accept it.

The doll people were gathered around the car now.

Dozens and dozens of eyeless white faces were pressed up to the windows, crowding in, more and more of them until he could see nothing but those grim visages, faces of splintered wood and cracked plastic and melting wax and burlap that hung in threads.

They were all grinning.

They were all laughing.

It was then, as tears rolled down his face and his mind seemed to fly apart inside his head, that he heard the keys hanging in the ignition jingle as if they had been grasped. He clearly saw them move. The car started up. The doll people retreated as the sedan pulled away from the curb.

It drove off down the street, Creep beating against the rear window as it disappeared into the night.

30

Standing in the middle of the street, Ramona heard something that made her jump. It wasn't much of a sound. Merely a clattering as if something had been dropped, but in the silence it was big and unexpected and she knew it was but the first stirring of what was going to happen next and the very idea chilled her.

You were raging a minute ago. You were ready to take on the world. Where's that anger now? Where's that determination?

She didn't know. It was just...gone. It dried up inside her, evaporated, leaving her standing there shriveling in her own skin, trapped in this hell zone of a town, this twisted and very fucked-up dream and she honestly did not know what to do about it.

Yes, you do. The east, the east. That's where this is all coming from. Track it to its source. You know what you have to do.

And, yes, she did.

It was a very simple strategy, of course, but executing it would not be so simple at all and she knew it. She heard another clattering sound and this time it came from above as if something had dropped on a roof up there. She could hear it rolling down and falling. Then something hit the pavement not three feet from her. It landed with a meaty thud and exploded like a pumpkin, spraying her with goo and what appeared to be a stringy tissue.

It was a head.

Not a human head, of course, but a doll head...yet, one that was grotesquely well-fleshed. She screamed and brushed the tissue from her. God, it was warm. This wasn't something from a doll shop; it was flesh and blood even if the very idea of that was impossible.

Clatter, clatter.

Something else now. A hand. A mannequin hand. It landed three feet away and began to crawl in her direction. Another hand fell and then another. A leg came down and clattered on the sidewalk. Then an arm, another head—this one was empty, rolling like a ball in her direction.

It was raining doll parts.

Still another head came down. A woman's head with dirty blonde hair. It barely missed her. It rolled over and over, blood exploding from its mouth with a gurgling sound.

But that's not possible, a voice in Ramona's head told her. *It's nothing but a mannequin head and mannequins don't bleed, they're not real and they can't bleed because they're not alive, not alive, not alive—*

But it *was* alive.

The blood-spattered face was moving, the mouth trying to say her name.

The doll parts were falling everywhere now. Some were breaking apart upon impact, but most were quite lively. Ramona stood there, hearing them dropping around her, unsure what to do. She had to get out of there, but in what direction should she escape? The longer she hesitated—the entire rain of parts had only been going on less than a minute by that point—the more limbs and heads there were. She was standing on the one spot where nothing was falling, but before long she would be trapped on her little island in an ocean of animate parts.

The heads were screaming her name. Legs hopping in her direction, arms crawling and hands pressing forward like albino spiders.

A woman's head dropped a few feet away, rolling in her direction. It had bulging white eyes and whipping red locks, its jaws opening and closing. *"RAMONA,"* it shrieked. *"RAMONA! RAMONA! RAMONA! RAMONA!"*

Ramona screamed, unable to keep her cool now as the doll parts converged on her and more heads rolled forth crying out her name. Something hit her shoulder and clutched there. A doll hand that was hot and flabby. Its fingers dug into her flesh as it crept toward her throat. She pulled it loose and tossed it. Other things fell on her. Smaller things that writhed in her hair like worms. Screaming again, she pulled them free along with locks of her hair—fingers. They were crawling over her scalp, one of them sliding down her neck and creeping down her spine.

She squirmed, tearing the fingers from her hair and slapping away one that tried to worm its way into her mouth. She fought, screeching and hysterical, as another worked its way into the valley between her breasts and the one tracing down her spine forced its way down the back of her skinny jeans. Down on her knees, oblivious to everything else now, she unzipped her pants and pulled them down, seizing the finger as it attempted to slide up her rectum.

The body parts moved in.

A hand clutched her wrist and another slid up her thigh. More fingers dropped into her hair. One of them pushed itself between her lips and she bit down on it and it went to a mucid pulp between her teeth. Gagging, sickened, she spit the remains out as waves of nausea rolled through her.

But there was no time for that.

All the parts were pressing in and there was no time for anything but flight. Juiced with absolute terror, she broke free with manic acceleration, knocking everything out of her way and batting aside a head that came spinning end over end out of the shadows. She tore more fingers from her and threw herself into the first doorway she found, that of a clock shop. The door was open as she knew it would be because nobody locked their doors in Stokes, not in the good old days of 1960.

As she got through the door of the shop, the bell jingling above, a hand grabbed her by the throat and she fought frantically with it as its fingers squeezed her windpipe shut. She stumbled to her knees, tearing at the fingers, finally yanking them free, the nails cutting trenches in her neck. The hand was slimy with some hot secretion like sweat.

But it can't sweat, you know it fucking can't sweat, there's no way it can sweat—

When it continued to move in the moonlight, she stomped it until it came apart, her eyes starting from her head and teeth clenched, her blood boiling with panic.

It stopped moving.

She clung to a glass counter filled with watches, trying to catch her breath, trying to keep her mind from spraying into a fine mist in her skull.

Thump, thump, thump.

Mute with horror, she looked behind her and felt her knees go weak. She stumbled back against the wall. Doll faces. That's what she was seeing. Dozens and dozens of shining white doll faces hitting the plate glass windows... not dropping away, but hanging on, suckering themselves to the glass with their mouths, like snails clinging to the sides of an aquarium.

They crowded the windows, all with the same sucking lamprey mouths and feral eyes as red as wet cherries, but luminous and bright like tensor lamps. Staring, searching, sweeping the confines of the store with a lewd, diabolic glare, they watched her. The eyes looked to her like the running lights of ghost ships coming at you out of the fog. Noxious and poisoned eyes that fixed her to the wall like a pinned beetle, knotted her insides, making her want to crawl into the darkness within herself and cry.

There were so many faces by that point that they covered the windows, the mouths sucking at the glass with the repulsive, slobbering sounds of babies at teats. All of them were oblong and distorted, made of some white undulant tissue that would not hold its shape. They inflated and deflated, forever shifting and mutating like images in fun-house mirrors. They waited there, watching her, pulsating like jellied ova.

Ramona suppressed a mad desire to start giggling and stumbled back into the shop, through a door and into some kind of workroom. Dizzy, nearly in shock, she hit the floor and lay there, shaking. Hot sweat rolled down her face and her teeth were chattering. This was it. It was just too much now. She was going insane, and she welcomed it. There was no point in fighting; better to accept things and go quietly mad.

Still blackened with soot, sticky with sweat and ashes, her pants unzipped and her coat gone, her shirt torn open and her scalp aching from the hair she'd torn from it, she closed her eyes.

No, Ramona, don't go to sleep. You can't go to sleep now.

But it was too late. The exhaustion and trauma had emptied

her and she felt her mind dropping into darkness. Bare seconds after she warned herself against it, she was sleeping.

31

As soon as they stepped into the house, Soo-Lee screamed. She felt weak and dizzy, completely overwhelmed by an irrational terror without form. It filled her like black ink, and she was utterly powerless to fight against it. She slumped against the wall, white and shivering from head to foot. It took her a moment to realize it wasn't a wall at all, but the things leaning against it—doll people. They were crowded there and her hand actually sank into one, a cool fluid squirting over her fingers.

She cried out for Lex, but he was not there.

She knew damn well that the archway leading into the living room should have been right in front of her, but it wasn't. It just wasn't there. And, worse, neither was Lex. There was a wall where he had been standing like she was in some kind of carnival haunted house complete with sliding doors and hidden passages.

"LEX!" she shouted. "LEX!"

But there was no reply, only her voice coming back to her from what seemed a dozen different locations, forever bouncing and echoing but not losing its volume. Such a thing was not physically possible, but it kept up until she had to cover her ears with her hands.

When it ended and she could think again, she tried to be reasonable, logical. This was just like the diner. What she was seeing was a physical illusion, but that didn't mean it was necessarily real. Lex was probably close by. She had to *let* herself see him. Drawing in a deep breath, Soo-Lee reached out again to where she knew he would be in the dark and she touched more doll things. Something like a wet, furry mouth nipped at her finger.

The puppet master is turning up the heat. You are terrified, and that is energizing all this. Just try to calm down.

She did try, but to no avail. She could not overcome the vein of hot white terror that moved through her in waves. To beat it would mean she would have to convince herself that the walls were not lined with waiting doll people and that would mean touching them, thinking *through* them, and reaching out for what was really there.

Impossible.

Entirely impossible.

She tried again and nearly gagged on her own fear. It filled her throat like warm vomit. No, there was no thinking around something this big, this omnipotent, this starkly real. Meeting it face-to-face was beyond comprehension. She needed to move. Trembling, she began to shuffle forward, following the passage and letting it take her away, hoping that movement and distance would somehow wear this dark fantasy down until reality reinserted itself. The passage seemed to veer from the left and to the right, back and forth, slowly moving ever downward until she was gripped by a crushing claustrophobia.

Ahead, there was light...dim, guttering yellow light but light all the same.

She went to it, moving faster now and when she reached it, she had to put a fist to her mouth so that she did not scream again. The light was coming from the doll people that crowded the walls in some medieval vision of hell. It came from their hollow-socketed eyes—a flickering yellow glow. As she stood there, up and down the passage each set of eyes lit up like Christmas bulbs and the reason for that, she knew, was because it was important she see just how many of them there were so she would realize how weak and insignificant she was by comparison.

Their mouths were all yawning open as if they were screaming...screaming out the pure terror of what they were and maybe what they had once been. The screams were silent. Her ears did not hear them, but in her mind they were high-pitched and hysterical, scraping her nerves raw.

She stumbled along, gasping for breath, her head filled with the shrieks of the dead, damned, and deranged, her eyes rolling in their sockets as they took in all the swarming figures around her bunched together, the screaming faces and surreal, frightening architecture of their bodies: the dangling limbs and skeletal bodies, torsos laid open to reveal the intricate clockwork guts of gears and cogs and wires and pulley systems, the elaborate bone-like armatures. The faces of doll babies were paper skulls, leering and ape-like, bodies like shattered vessels and ossuary baskets.

Something inside Soo-Lee was caught between a laugh and a scream at what she was seeing, at all the leering, jeering, ogling, staring doll faces that pressed in from every quarter. So many, so very many. Looking upon them evaporated her will and made her heart feel like a swamp that had been drained, leaving nothing but black mud and rotting organic detritus behind. In her mind, she could see her soul leaving her body like a thousand glimmering fireflies exiting her mouth.

It was all subjective, but she was forced deeper into the barren underworld of herself.

You can't fall part now. You can't! Lex is trying to reach you so try to reach him!

Yes, she knew that was important, but knowing it did nothing to lessen her claustrophobia. It increased by the moment. The passage now seemed to be entirely made of doll people. They grew from the walls like piebald mushrooms—lumped, mounded, bulbous, and crowding, synthetic faces pushing out like expanding soap bubbles until there were no walls, only more and more faces of grinning sackcloth, sloughing burlap, carved wood, and vacuum-formed plastic. They seemed to be multiplying around her through some perverse binary fission, faces splitting into more faces that divided yet again into still more. She watched with unblinking, fearful eyes as the face of a smiling mannequin woman cracked open with a rubbery, shearing sound like a soft-shelled egg and four, then five puckering baby doll faces emerged like hungry chicks, oval mouths opening and closing, suctioning like blowholes.

It happened again and again as faces and bodies ripped open to disgorge clusters of puppet babies still glistening with the foul slime of afterbirth.

Soo-Lee fought down the urge again to scream and laugh simultaneously, to vent the gibbering madness inside her. This is what it was like to go insane. It felt like her mind had gone to a warm, melting glop that would drain from her skull or run out of her ears.

The multitude of heads around her seemed to inflate like balloons, alive but inert, animate yet lifeless, their shrill mewling cries reverberating through the passage and pushing her far beyond the boundaries of sanity.

Their glowing eyes seemed to watch her, peering deep inside her.

Even the angled ceiling above now was formed of hanging mannequin things. Faces like demonic baboons sneered and grinned overhead, dangling limbs swaying back and forth in some unheard charnel rhythm, sharp fingers like darning needles brushing the top of her head and tracing the back of her neck with splintered nails.

No matter which way she turned, their awful cadaverous visages pressed in closer and closer, their luminous eyes making bodies move and limbs reach as shadows crawled and crept. She could hear them whispering and giggling with scratching, mocking voices. She could feel an unnatural heat coming from them and smell the dark fetor of their breath.

The wise thing would have been a full retreat, but there was no going back now. Behind her, the walls had pushed in and sealed the passage with doll parts and the walls around her were pressing in ever closer. She stumbled along faster and faster, falling, getting up, falling again, faces moving in closer and fingers like tree roots tangling in her long hair. Hinged mouths called her name and begged her to join them.

As she fell yet again, she looked up to see the swollen belly of a doll woman. It was cut-away like that of an anatomical model to reveal a doll fetus within suspended upside down in the amniotic sac. It was a plastic stillborn thing…yet it was sucking its thumb with slurping sounds for a lack of anything better to suckle. When it turned its shriveled, eyeless face on Soo-Lee, she crawled away on all fours, making a pained moaning sound in her throat.

It's a lie, she told herself.

It's an illusion that has been created to unhinge your mind, to amplify your fear and thereby enhance the power of the puppet master. You know that. You've known it all along, yet you keep cooperating. You keep reacting instead of acting. It was a stupid dumbfuck bonehead play to come down this passage and you knew it, yet you did.

Yet, you did.

This stopped her. Jesus, she was crawling around on her hands and knees like an animal, like some mole scrabbling about underground. She stood up, standing tall. She had to think herself out of this mess before it got any worse…if it could conceivably do so. The way behind her was sealed up. Or at least, it seemed to be. What of it wasn't at all? What then?

Soo-Lee turned on her heel and moved back the way she had come.

The doll things that were the walls of her tight little world got agitated right away. They shook and trembled. Fingers grasped, limbs kicked, mouths made a low sighing sound.

Still she pushed forward.

Either she broke the black magic spell of this place or was broken.

There could be no other way.

She kept moving, walking faster now, and as she did so, really pouring on the steam, the passage opened. She blinked her eyes several times to be sure of it, but, yes, it was opening.

It can't possibly be this easy.

But maybe it was. She almost believed this until she saw the black hulking shape stepping from the shadows at the far end. That it was one of the doll people she did not doubt any more than she doubted that it was coming for her. She was breaking the rules of the puppet master's little game and she was going to be punished now, broken upon the wheel of Stokes, as it were.

She began stepping backward, her resolve dispersing inside her.

No, no, no! she warned herself. *Don't back down! Don't give in to the fear! The illusion was dissolving, the house of cards was ready to fall so this…this…thing was sent to reinforce the nightmare and you're yielding to it! Do not yield! It's only as powerful as you make it!*

As if the form could easily read her thoughts, it growled with a low throaty sound.

Soo-Lee trembled.

It wanted her to tremble, it *needed* her to tremble, because the more she trembled the more deadly it became. Her fear was the hot air that inflated it. Without that, it was nothing but a shriveling rubber sack...but even knowing this did not help because she was completely terrified. She could only see a hulking dark shadow moving steadily in her direction, but the terror it inspired was very real as the growling continued. As it came on, the glowing eyes of the doll faces winked out one by one. It was bringing darkness with it, a shifting wall of blackness.

She could not bear it.

She literally could not bear it.

As the lights were extinguished, the doll people lining the walls stopped moving. It was as if this thing was drawing the life from them as it came on. She could not see its face, only the dying lights winking off teeth that looked long and gnarled.

32

The clocks were going off.

Ramona came awake in a panic there in the darkness of the clock shop. She jumped and shook. Every damn clock in the place was ringing off—grandfather clocks and cuckoo clocks, anniversary clocks and alarm clocks. *BING, BING, BING! BONG! BONG! BONG!* The shop was echoing with a constant ringing and gonging and shrilling. The effect was not just startling, but shocking.

It meant something, she knew that much.

In fact, clasping her hands over her ears, and calming somewhat, she knew it could only possibly mean one thing: the Controller wanted her awake. It—for she had trouble thinking of this significant other as a human being—did not want her resting. It did not want her getting sleep. It wanted her worn out and on edge because the games would work so much better that way if she was physically and mentally exhausted.

But there was more to it than that.

She was bound and determined to track this nightmare to its source, which was somewhere to the east and that could not be allowed. The Controller had tossed Frankendoll at her and then rained mannequin parts down on her. It would stop at nothing to scare her, confuse her, hurt her, and possibly even kill her.

And these were things Ramona very much needed to keep in mind.

The intelligence behind all this was not only twisted but sly and cunning and extremely dangerous.

But those clocks, those goddamn clocks...

Ramona sat there, knowing she had to do something as the

clanging noise seemed to fill her skull and hurt her ears and even make her molars ache, if such a thing were realistically possible. It would drive her right out of her head and no doubt that was the point.

Without really thinking or planning, she got to her feet quickly, more agitated and pissed off than anything. "IT WON'T WORK!" she shouted above the racket. "DO YOU HEAR ME, YOU DIRTY SONOFABITCH? *IT WON'T FUCKING WORK! I'M COMING FOR YOU AND YOU CAN'T FUCKING STOP ME!*"

She was expecting her defiance to bring hell down on her perhaps in the form of a rampaging doll army...but that didn't happen. What did happen was so subtle she nearly missed it. There was a change around her in the very air of the clock shop as if the atmospheric pressure either increased radically or decreased. The hairs stood up on the back of her neck and her ears popped as if she were on a plane gaining altitude.

Then...the clocks stopped.

Each and every one of them ceased their ringing and gonging. The silence that replaced the cacophony was practically *loud*.

Ramona stood there, waiting, breathing, feeling arrogant now and daring the Controller to try something else because she was learning things and she was ready to fight.

But there was nothing.

Not right away.

Don't sit here and wait for it, she told herself. *Don't give it time to manufacture fresh horrors. These things must take energy so don't give it the opportunity it badly needs, do not play into its hands.*

Wishing she had a flashlight because the store was so unbearably dark, she moved around the counter, stepping carefully into the back room, which was as black as a buried coffin. There had to be a door here. A back way. She stood there, trying to be unpredictable. That was very important, and she knew it. She had to keep the Controller guessing, so she turned on her heel and went back out into the shop to the front door.

She peered out into the dark streets.

They were empty, completely untenanted, and in their emptiness was their threat. She didn't see any of those doll faces out here. There were still sticky smears on the glass from their sucking mouths and Ramona could not pretend that the very idea of that didn't disturb her greatly.

She pushed open the door.

Still holding on to it, she took two steps out and let her instinct make the decision for her. It told her to go out the back way. She turned on her heel again and went back inside. She dug out her cigarettes and lit one up. The flame of her Bic turned the shadows into living, sentient entities around her that slid along the walls and crouched in the corners and crept over the faces of clocks, so damn many clocks.

She stood there by the display case and smoked.

She could feel the Controller reaching out for her, trying to figure out just what the hell she was doing. But being that she didn't know herself, second-guessing her would not be easy. Not easy at all. Her instinct and woman's intuition were supercharged and she knew it. They practically made her skin tingle and her blood feel like it had become hot steam.

She was trying to feel for the Controller herself.

There would be something in the air when it decided to strike, when it sent a new horror to torment her with. It, again, would be subtle, but it would be there and she had to be ready to sense it. That was the key.

But there was nothing.

She took a few last drags from her cigarette and tossed it. It struck the face of a clock in a shower of sparks, the glowing remains of it smoldering on the hardwood floor. *Let this goddamn place burn down*, she thought. She stepped into the back room again and flicked her Bic. It was pretty much as she expected the back room of a clock shop would be and that was no surprise. *Everything* in Stokes was as you thought it would be. In the flickering light of her Bic, she saw grandfather clocks with their guts hanging out, dissected cuckoo clocks, and workbenches strewn with the anatomy of timepieces: pendulums and cam wheels and main springs, gears and cogs and pulleys.

Lot of the same stuff the doll people seemed to be made of, she thought, not missing the significance.

There was another door beyond the benches and shelves of parts.

The lighter burned her fingers so she had to let the flame go out. Carefully again, she moved amongst the clocks and workbenches, banging her hip on a table. She reached out in the darkness for the door...and it wasn't there.

Shit.

She could feel something in the air again. It had shifted. Something was about to happen and she felt a shiver spread across the back of her arms. It felt like her guts had pulled up into her chest as if they were seeking the protection of her rib cage. Her mouth went dry. Her eyes wide. She fumbled and nearly dropped the lighter. She flicked it.

Jesus.

There were several doll people standing around her in a loose circle. They appeared to be women. They were entirely naked, like undressed mannequins, made of some smooth white material, their breasts mere buds lacking nipples. There were bald, tiny hairline cracks running over their gleaming craniums, their eyes black holes. Their mouths were moving, opening and closing as if they needed to say something.

One of them made a sort of cooing sound and reached its white fingers out for her. Ramona slapped the hand away, and it broke free from the wrist and clattered to the floor. All of their mouths instantly went wide, expanding into black chasms, and they screamed with a high strident wailing.

"NO!" Ramona shrieked at them as they all came at her, reaching for her.

There was no quarter. As their cold hands seized her, she went wild like a fighting cat, clawing and kicking as they scratched at her, pulling out locks of her hair, pressing in, screaming in her face. She battered down two of them, punched the head off a third and when another grabbed her from behind, she let out a rebel yell of sorts and pivoted, snatching the doll woman's arms and flinging her with everything she had. The doll woman shattered against the wall. She was in the dark with them, trying to get free, bumping into workbenches and shelves, and fighting the women with everything she had.

Then the wailing stopped.

She dug the Bic from her pocket and flicked it. The shadows

jumped away, the orange flame reflected on the walls. The doll women were gone. Ramona turned this way and that, seeking them out, her mind teetering on the edge of madness. It felt like an open bleeding wound.

Then behind her: breathing.

And a giggling.

Then something hit her and she was driven to her knees, bright purple dots blazing in her head. She felt herself hit the floor. She felt herself going out cold and there was nothing she could do to stop it.

No more than a few minutes had passed when she opened her eyes.

In her mind, a voice was saying, *What? What? What?*

Confusion. Anxiety. Shock. She tried to concentrate, to bring herself out of the fog...but it was slow and she'd taken a good hit to the back of the head. She knew that much. And she knew she was in terrible danger...but the blow to her head combined with exhaustion made her loopy, her body thick and numb. She opened her eyes and they shut almost immediately. There had been a dream, it seemed, a dream she was still dreaming... something on her chest, a weight, a movement, a suction.

It was no dream.

There was something on her chest and she could feel a cold little mouth suckling her left breast greedily.

With a cry she sat up, knocking whatever it was clear with a sweep of her hand. She heard something clatter to the floor. Whatever it was, it was crawling toward her now. It made a slobbering, gurgling noise that made waves of nausea roll through her belly.

The Bic.

It was still clenched in her left hand. She flicked it and the room grew bright. She saw the thing scuttling over the floor to her. It looked like some swollen infant, hairless, its flesh bleached white. It had no eyes, not so much as a nose, just a grinning black aperture for a mouth that was wet and shining. It moved with spasmodic jerking motions like some jack-in-the-box from hell as it got closer and closer. Its breathing—because, yes, it was certainly *breathing*—was clogged and phlegmatic.

Ramona was on her feet by then, the lighter trembling in her hand.

She backed away and hit the wall. No, not the wall, the door. She could feel the knob digging into her back. As that twitching, hungry little horror was nearly on her, she fumbled the door open and the moonlight flooded.

That's when the thing leaped.

Like a jumping spider, it came right off floor in a rolling white blur and she kicked out at it with everything she had, catching it dead-on. It broke apart into pieces that continued to squirm and rattle.

But by then she was out the door, running and trying to button her shirt back up, not sure if she was even sane anymore.

33

There in the darkness of the sedan that moved slowly to an unknown destination, Creep retreated further and further into the void of his own mind. How long he crouched there on the backseat, shaking and delirious, he did not know. Only that suddenly, as if a light had gone on in his brain, awareness returned and he heard a voice in his mind say, *Just what the fuck do you think you're doing? You waiting for Mommy to come and chase away the boogeyman?*

He sat up straight.

Not being the bravest or calmest of people in the best of times, his nerves jangling like wind chimes, he was afraid to act. He was afraid *not* to act. Regardless, the unpleasant reality of his situation remained: he was in a big black car that was driving itself down dark streets, moving leisurely like it was part of a funeral procession.

He figured that probably wasn't too far off the mark.

Everything was still in black-and-white inside the car. It was madness, but there was no getting around it. He could see color outside the car—a red STOP sign, a yellow curb, a purple flowering lilac bush fronting the street—but inside it was all grays and whites and blacks.

You going to sit here and do nothing, you pussy?

God only knew how far away from the others he was now. He had to bring this to a halt one way or another. He had to get out of this fucking car right now. Which was a great idea, but how was he supposed to do that? He was terrified and afraid to move, afraid to try anything in case whoever was controlling this decided to make it worse for him.

But you have to do something.

God yes, he knew that...but what?

He was staring at the steering wheel, watching how it rotated itself smoothly to the left or the right when the car needed to take a corner. The turn signal lever was even pulled down and then pushed back up. It was insane. *He* was insane. None of this could be happening, yet it was, and he was seeing it.

Waiting there helplessly for a few more moments, he became aware of a hot, spoiled smell in the car and waited for some dead thing to materialize on the seat next to him. He waited for it to dissipate as if maybe the car had driven past some rotting animal in the road, but it did not dissipate—it grew stronger, hot and sickening.

A drop of liquid fell on his face.

With a start, he brushed it away...his fingers were wet with something black. Blood? Dear God, was it blood? But he knew it was. In old black-and-white movies, blood always looked black and he remembered finding that very disturbing as a child. *Black stuff leaking from people. Not red, but...black.* As this crossed his cluttered, seesawing mind, another drop landed on the tip of his nose and another struck his scalp. It felt hot, very hot.

More black blood fell. It was seeping from the ceiling as if the car were horribly injured. It dropped onto his head and ran down his face like hot oil. He crawled away, pushing himself up against the opposite door. The seats were oozing blood now. As he pressed a hand against them, dark blood pooled. Then a strip of upholstery hung down from the ceiling a few inches from his face...only it was not upholstery, it was not cloth or leather or some nappy knit fabric that had torn loose.

It was flesh.

It was living tissue.

No, not *living* tissue but dead tissue. He could smell the odor of putrescence wafting from it. He had all he could do to keep his stomach down. The car was not metal and wood and rubber and plastic...no, it was a living thing, an organism that was dead or dying. It was decaying around him and he was trapped in it like a mouse in a rotting pumpkin.

Creep sat there, stunned and nearly breathless by the idea.

It could not be. He was hallucinating…tripping. He wasn't here at all. He was in a padded room somewhere, heavily sedated and screaming his mind out.

Panic broke inside him, sharp and cutting as a voice in the back of his head said, *first it'll rot with organic decay, then the worms will come crawling out of the seats and the flies will cluster and the vermin will swarm as it goes to mush. And you'll be here. You'll be here to witness it all—*

He couldn't take any more of it.

He just couldn't.

Shrieking and wild, he bashed at the windows as the ceiling dripped and great fleshy strips were torn from the moist, putrid seats as he thrashed. The stench of gassy decomposition was getting thick in the air. It was like a seeping green mist, hot and gagging and utterly repulsive. He could taste it on his tongue, feel its foul juices like dew against his face. He tried to pull himself over the seat into the front and his fingers sank into the spongy tissue they were made of, black juice gushing over the backs of his hands.

Everything was rot and ruin and there was no escape.

Manically, he tore at the upholstery, ripping it with his fingers, gouging his nails into its pulpous tissues and somewhere during the process, he screamed as his mind emptied itself.

34

As Soo-Lee was lost deeper in the tangles of the doll passage, Lex did everything he could not to lose his cool. He told himself it was all illusion, whether physical or psychological, it was still an illusion. He had to ignore his base animal instincts of fear and the need to flee blindly. He had to maintain here or he was lost, completely lost.

But finally, as reality was completely torn asunder and reinvented around him, he lost complete control. "YOU'LL HAVE TO DO BETTER THAN THIS!" he cried. "THIS IS NOTHING BUT A CHEAPJACK PARLOR TRICK! IT'S FUCKING SECOND-RATE AND SO ARE YOU!"

Raging made him feel better, it made him feel stronger. Oh, he was still terrified, but he was doing the only thing he *could* do and channeling that terror into hate and anger until his hands were balled into fists and his body was shaking and his teeth were clenched. He was in a long, narrow corridor backlit by itself whose walls were pleated with some pink shiny material that expanded and deflated as it breathed. Because it *was* breathing and he could hear the low, hissing respiration. He tried to block it out and pretend it was not there at all because it seemed like if he acknowledged the sound of it and the horror it inspired, the louder and louder it got.

Like a child working a nerve. Knowing just how to annoy and disturb his or her mother and keeping at it, working it until she wanted to scream.

"It won't be that easy," Lex said softly and resolutely. "I know your secret. You're alone and you're afraid and you're trying to put that fear on us. Misery loving company. But it won't work. Because you're weak."

His defiance was worth something, it seemed.

No sooner had he spoken those words than the breathing sounds quieted until he could barely hear them. The walls were not breathing now. They were trembling minutely and they still looked like they were made of soft pink skin, but they were no longer breathing.

He thought for a moment there he heard a terrible and distant sound of anguished sighing.

Then the walls started to breathe again. Breathe? No, they were gasping for breath painfully like the lungs of a dying man, as if the more oxygen they took in the more their physical reality would be assured.

"You're not real," Lex said, kicking a section of wall.

The amazing and nearly comical thing about it was that a blue-purple contusion appeared instantly. If the entire affair hadn't been so fucking demented, he might have laughed.

The walls were still breathing deeply, but they seemed calmer now as if they refused to be rattled by him. They swell with each breath, inflating and becoming puffy like air filled sacs. They pressed in closer. He wasn't afraid of walls made of skin that breathed? Well, time to check him out on the claustrophobia scale. The walls pressed in ever closer. They would crush him, asphyxiate him with their own fleshy mass.

Lex kicked out again and again, but though they bruised they would not retreat.

It was then that the most extraordinary and unpleasant thing happened.

Oval nodes appeared on the walls, hundreds and hundreds of them to either side. They expanded until they looked like the glossy chambers of bubble wrap, only an aqueous pink. As they continued to expand, each distending until he thought they would explode from internal pressure, they split open one after the other. They were not blisters of a sort, but eyes—green and blue and brown and hazel and violet, some horror-movie red and others a glimmering turquoise. He was in a chamber of flesh now being watched by thousands of eyes that were juicy and running with snotlike fluid that dripped in gouts.

The walls continued to push in closer and with them came the eyes, countless living unblinking marbles fixed on him, staring at him, looking inside him until his skin literally crawled, and he hugged his shaking body out of sheer horror.

No, no, no, a simple child-like voice said in his brain. *Not this, not fucking this of all things.*

He knew he couldn't let it break him. He had a few minor-league phobias—fear of extreme heights, flying—but nothing incapacitating. But the puppet master was bound and determined to break him. It was trying claustrophobia and ommetaphobia—the fear of eyes—and scopophobia—the fear of being stared at—and the scary thing was, it was working. Lex felt like he was shivering inside his own skin.

This was how it would break him.

This was how it would own him.

The eyes were even closer now, perhaps sensing an edge. They were large, swollen and glistening, crying tears of slime. They were no longer evenly spaced, but crowding now like bubbles until the walls and the ceiling above were nothing but eyes. They expanded and popped open, clustered like fish roe, forever watching. Within moments, he knew, they would touch him.

"*No,*" he said under his breath. He could not allow it. The others needed him and he knew it. More so, Soo-Lee needed him and he could not let her down. But the fear had disabled him, made him feel loose and liquid inside and there was nothing left to fight with.

Don't let it, he told himself. *Don't let it win. Fight! Use your mind! Think! Think!*

And whether or not it was a conscious thing, he did the first thing that seemed reasonable: he jabbed his index finger into one of the eyes. The effect was not unpleasant, at least not for him. At least not initially. He buried his finger all the way in it and felt it flinch with the invasion and possibly pain. It was hot and soft inside, not much different than sliding his finger into a sexually excited woman. Soo-Lee felt much like that, it occurred to him.

But it didn't last.

The delicious—and obscene—tactile sensation was replaced by a grim suction from inside the orb. It felt burning hot in there. The flesh of his finger was stinging as if he'd jabbed a jellyfish. As he yanked his finger back out, the eye closed like a pink puckering mouth around his knuckle and he had to yank with everything he had to get free of it. A gelatinous goo like egg albumin spurted over his hand. It made his flesh burn with a stinging sensation. But worse…he felt a sharp jabbing in his left eye as if he'd poked his own eyeball.

Despite the pain, he jabbed another and another, feeling them burst with a spray of slime, *and* feeling the jabbing in his own eyes. But despite the pain, he would not relent. He took out six more eyes that way until the agony made him go to his knees.

When he opened his eyes again, trying to rub the hurt from them, the walls of eyes had retreated a few inches, which told him they did not care to be wounded. That was it then. Despite the pain, he would blind them all. Looking out through swollen, burning eyes, he prepared to do so…but something happened. As he watched, each individual eye sprouted tiny, wiry sets of legs that looked bristled like those of a spider. Each eye had four legs. And with the capacity to be mobile, they detached themselves from their sockets in the wall and flooded over him.

Lex let out a cry, slapping at them and smashing them beneath his fists. He kicked and punched the walls, crushing the eye spiders under him and rolling through their numbers until he was wet with eye goo and fragmented little legs—still kicking—were stuck to him.

They crawled over his face and nested in his hair, surged down the back of his shirt and scuttled up his pant legs and the only thing he could do in his mania was to get out of there before he drowned in them. His head filled with a shrilling white noise, he dug right into the walls, tearing out cobs and masses of pink tissue as he tried to tunnel free.

35

Soo-Lee crawled on her hands and knees through the passage of dolls until she realized there were no dolls and that she was actually moving up a set of stairs. The transition had been quick, and she had no idea if that had been real and this was an illusion, or if it was the other way around. She paused there, trying to acclimate herself to what was happening.

She was halfway up the stairs, and could see the polished balustrade gleaming in what seemed soft candlelight, the sort generally reserved for romantic dinners. The spindle balusters were dark oak, shining with wax. The stair runner was a soft floral carpet. It was quite elegant.

Where the hell did this staircase come from?

She didn't know and she honestly didn't care. Being out of that awful place of dolls was enough. The carpet felt nice under her hands. She was exhausted. She lowered her head to one step, luxuriating in the feel of the nap beneath her cheek.

Yes, this was nice.

She needed to call out to Lex, but she didn't seem to have the strength or the air in her lungs. Her entire body was aching, the muscles sore and tense. Her eyelids closed and she drifted off, when there was a loud banging somewhere behind her.

She lifted her head.

Thump, thump, thump, the noise came again.

Below her was a foyer with dark paneled walls and a shiny parquet floor. There was an antique coat tree, several large floor vases, and a cabinet with many drawers that looked like something from the 18th century. Beyond was a massive six-paneled door. Wavering shadows slid over its face.

Thump, thump, thump.

Somebody was knocking at the door. Knocking? Hell, they were beating on it with their fists. They wanted in badly.

Soo-Lee knew who it was.

Or, better, *what* it was.

It could be nothing but the hulking figure she had seen in the doll passage, that shadowy stalking figure. It was still after her and it meant to have her.

She pressed her lips together because she did not dare make a sound, a scream rattling in her throat. The fist pounded on the door again and it felt like the entire house shook with it.

Move!

Sobbing but refusing to give in, she pulled herself to her feet with the aid of the stair railing. She stood there uneasily, her knees feeling weak. Already she could smell the thing that was coming for her—it stank of aged tapestries moldering in dark cabinets and heavy mildewed drapes, worm-eaten and threaded by spiders. A sickening, nitrous stench of antiquity that she acquainted with dusty Egyptian tombs.

She scrambled up the stairs and was faced by a corridor that moved in either direction. It was set with antique gas jets that threw a guttering, uneven light. As the pounding came again, she tensed, knowing she had to go and get behind one of the many doors she saw. Any of them would do. She needed to shut one and lock it tight and wait in the darkness…and pray.

Thump! Thump! Thump!

It was louder now, more insistent. She could hear the doorknob down there being rattled frantically. Each time the fist hit the door it was like a nail being driven into her. She could nearly feel the pain. It made her stomach tighten like a fist.

She ran to the left, trying door after door and finding them locked one after the other. They could not be forced. She did not really believe there was anything behind them. She threw aside a heavy tapestry at the end and found herself looking at a dusty window. Maybe this was the way out. She rubbed a clean spot in the pane and peered out through the glass. She saw the moon riding high above jagged rooftops, skeletal spires, and reaching chimneys. Far below were narrow, crooked streets cutting between leaning buildings. It seemed that the window she looked out of was a hundred feet above them as if the house itself was suspended in the sky.

There was a rending crash, and she knew the door below had come off its hinges and the thing that sought her was now in the house, pushing writhing shadows before it as it came out of the dead of night, bringing a smell of dry rot and subterranean vaults.

Soo-Lee ran back down the corridor.

At the top of the stairs she paused, but only momentarily. She could not see the thing down there, but she could hear its clomping painful gait, the sound of one leg dragged behind it. It stench blighted the house. She saw jagged shadows begin to creep up the steps.

She ran in the other direction, trying doors until she found one that was open. It was a trap and she knew it had to be a trap, but fear pushed her through it. She closed the door as quietly as possible, locking it and stepping away from it into a room that was immense with a king-size Gothic canopy bed set near the far wall, red velour curtains tossed aside from massive carven teak posts.

The bed was baronial and exquisite, a chamber of dreams. It was like something from an Elizabethan novel. Red and black velvet pillows were piled in abundance, the comforter and blankets a deep scarlet. Oh, to sleep in such a bed. To lie in it, to—

Thump, thump, thump.

He was at the door now and Soo-Lee knew there wasn't a damn thing she could do about it. She was the fly that had entered the spider's web out of its own free will. In those last few moments before the door crashed in, she was not sure if any of this had been her idea or not. She had been carefully worked and carefully herded, not acting, but *re*acting, and free will did not seem to be part of it.

But there had been no other place to go, a weak and wounded voice in her mind said. *There had been no choice, no real choice.*

Maybe that was true and maybe she just lacked the strength, regardless, as the lock snapped and fell to the floor and the door swung in noiselessly, she knew that such things as choice were concepts she no longer had and would never have again.

The smell of the thing filled the room.

Its crooked shadow snaked over the floor in her direction.

Oh, please…dear God, no…no…

She saw a distorted scarecrow-like figure moving in her direction, a twisted carnal grin on its lips. And as she screamed, hands like pale tarantulas reached out for her.

36

"*S*ssshhhh," a voice that was soft and warm cooed in his ear. "*There's no need of that now.*"

What was left of Creep's mind heard the voice but rejected it. There was no one. He was alone in the car and a manic fear in his brain assured him that he would always be alone, forever and ever. Yet, he could feel someone next to him, a form, a presence, a physical disruption of the ether around him. He was alone but not alone.

The car was still dripping, still rotting around him. Now it had rolled to a stop right in the middle of the street as if it no longer had the strength or ability to move any farther.

"Who...who's there?" he heard his own voice speak before he could squelch it.

"*It's only me,*" the voice said. "*Only me and I'm your friend.*"

The voice sounded oddly like Ramona's, but Ramona couldn't be in the car with him, there was just no way. Though he was woven in a tight little cocoon of terror, Creep knew that he had to prove whether or not there was actually someone there. His eyes told him there was not, but his other senses disagreed. He reached out and gasped as he touched something, something he could not see. It hadn't been awful, just startling, so he reached out again and touched hair, long tresses of hair that slid easily between his fingers. It wasn't bad. He liked the feel of it. He kept running his fingers through it, noting that while the scalp was not soft, it wasn't quite firm either. It had a rubbery give to it that he did not like, yet his fingers could not stop stroking the luxurious locks.

"*You see? I'm nice to touch. I'm nice to feel,*" said the velvety voice that made something in him relax and release tension.

He ran both hands through the hair now. Oh yes, it was silky and fine, long hair that was glossy to the touch. He felt something skitter over the back of his hand. He brushed it aside, but there were others, many others. The scalp seemed infested by them. He should have been horrified, but he was not. He began picking the skittering, leggy things free, grooming the head of hair like an ape plucking nits from the pelt of another ape.

"That feels nice," the voice told him. *"You have no idea how long they've been nipping at me and burrowing. Pull them all free."*

Yes, that was exactly what he wanted to do. He could conceive of nothing else remotely as satisfying. He plucked the wriggling insects free and flicked them away into the front seat. Sometimes they bit him, but mostly they just wanted to get away. One of them, a very swollen individual, sprouted wings and flew away, momentarily brushing against his nose.

"I'm like you," the voice said. *"I'm broken…I am not whole. But together we can be complete."*

Yes, there was a logic in that he could appreciate.

He plucked more of the vermin free, searching through clumps of hair for their hiding places. He could sense them before he found them. With deft, practiced fingers, he seized them as they emerged from the scalp and made short work of them. He was not tossing them away now; he was crushing them like squirming little berries, feeling a rising excitement as he squeezed them into pulp, into clots of cold jelly that dripped from his fingers. They did not like to be killed, but he had to kill them because they infested the scalp.

Though he still could not see the mysterious other on the seat next to him, he could hear her cooing her delight. Sometimes her limbs made rustling sounds like tree branches scraping against roofs and sometimes she made low slithering sounds that were disturbing but strangely enticing.

"You're making me feel so much better," the voice said to him, nearly breathless with pleasure. *"When you're done, I'll make you feel better. I'll do things for you that you only dreamed of. You'll never*

want another after me. I know things. Secret things. And I want to show them to you. Do you want to learn?"

"Yes," he muttered. "Oh yes."

After all the bullshit he'd been through tonight, much of it bad enough to break any man, he was finally catching a break. He had finally found a friend that he could trust. She was beautiful. That much he knew. He could only judge by the feel of her hair—ecstasy—and her voice, which was pure desire. He still did not know her name, but that didn't seem to matter. Such things were trivial. He continued cleaning the vermin from her hair until it seemed there were no more and she made a high, whining sound in her throat like the song of cicada.

"Feel the seats," she said. *"Do you see?"*

Creep hadn't really noticed, but sometime during his grooming of her the car had stopped rotting and stopped spilling blood. Like him, it was whole again. It was solid and safe. The odor was gone, too.

"You helped me and I'm helping you," she said, her voice now deliciously throaty and seductive. *"Now you need to relax."*

She pushed him back on the seat and he was only too willing to lie back and let her do things for him now. She grasped his hand with fingers that were very cold and pressed it to her chest. Her skin was unnaturally smooth. His hand was between her breasts and he could feel the excited throbbing of her heart.

"I'm alive like you are," she said as if there had ever been any doubt. *"Do you want to see me?"*

"Yes, yes."

Straddling him, she took shape there in the backseat and it seemed that long before he actually saw her he was seeing her in his mind. Her hair was long and dark. The moonlight made it gleam. Her face narrow, the cheekbones high, her eye sockets huge and empty. Her lips were full and as she smiled he could see that her teeth were long and sharp like those of a viper and he knew she wanted to impale him with them. No, that wasn't right, that wasn't what he had expected at all.

"Get off me," he said. *"Get the fuck off me!"*

Her legs were scissored around his hips and she was not

letting go. Her hair was graying now, bunching up on her head like a withered bush, her face set with fissures and cracks, the skin flaking away like old wallpaper, revealing a shriveled visage below that was like a soft, rotten plum. His dream lover looked like an old lady three months in the tomb. Her hair was crawling with termites that burrowed into her scalp like the bark of a dead tree. They crawled over her face and winged from her eyes.

"I told you I was broken," she said. *"Now you'll be broken, too..."*

Creep let out a cry and fought against the thing holding him down, not knowing if it was real or if any of it was real, only knowing she would do horrendous, unspeakable things to him if he did not stop her now. As insects flew in his face and her breath went to black rot, he tried to throw her and pull her arms from him. One of them had flesh on it that crumbled under his fingertips and the other was little more than a mechanical armature. And her fingers, as they gripped his throat, were not fingers but the talons of a wild beast.

Pressing herself hard against his groin, her cracked doll face came in close to his own. And though it was a dead thing, an animate mask and little more, the pink tongue that wriggled between the doll lips and sought his own was very much alive.

37

When Chazz broke free of Lady Pegleg's grip, he knew he would pay for it. He knew he would not be allowed to simply escape. That wasn't part of the game and he knew it. He ran away from her, putting on great speed, and then something hit him in the back. It punched into him with the force of a battering ram, throwing him six feet before he went facedown on the ground.

Then he could hear her coming for him.

She moved up the sidewalk with the casual stride of an old woman who is in no hurry and knows she will get where she is going in the end. *Tap-tap, tap-tap, tap-tap,* went her peg as she closed in on him. He lay there, numb and senseless, his limbs tingling.

What did I tell you about bad boys? she said inside his head. *What did I tell you?*

She tapped her peg on the sidewalk to emphasize this. Though his brain was half in dream, he remembered very well what she had said. *Good boys will be rewarded. Bad boys will be punished.* Yes, that was exactly what she had said and now she was going to punish him.

Chazz knew he had to move, he had to *motivate* (as Coach had once said) or the game was lost. Rescue would not be coming. There was no one to save his ass but himself. But he had to want it and if he wanted it bad enough, he could achieve it. Dozens of inspirational speeches echoed through his head and he forced himself up onto his hands and knees. That was the first step. Then he would get to his feet and then...and then—

Owwwww...Jesus.

Lady Pegleg kicked him. She kicked him with her peg right between the legs, giving the old jewels a good hammering. Chazz clenched his teeth and went down again. *The bitch! The filthy fucking bitch!* The pain cleared his head as it always did and anger eclipsed fear and indecision. He rolled away before she could kick him again.

BAD BOY! she shrieked in his skull. *BAD BAD BOY! YOU WILL BE PUNISHED! YOU WILL BE EMASCULATED! I'LL TEAR OFF YOUR LITTLE BALLS WITH MY TEETH AND SPIT THEM IN YOUR FACE! DO YOU HEAR ME?*

And Chazz heard her all right.

He bounded to his feet and when she reached out to grasp him with a hand like a scaly and withered bird's claw, he punched her right in the face, giving her the kind of piledriver that he had decked Joey McCawber with in 10th grade. But Lady Pegleg did not go down. Her head snapped back and for one insane moment he thought it might pop up like in Rock 'em Sock 'em Robots, but it didn't. She stood there, trembling, a strange whirring sound coming from inside her. Her head snapped back to the extent that she was staring straight up at the moon overhead, then there was a creaking noise and a crackling like dry twigs and it righted itself. Her black eye sockets looked out at him, her sagging face hanging in pockets and loose folds. He had popped some of the intricate suturing of her face and blood that was black like crude oil seeped down her cheeks.

You do not hit Teacher! she screamed in his head. *You never, ever strike Teacher! You will be brought to the Principal, the Maker and Un-maker! There you shall be laid at Her feet!*

Chazz stepped back so she could not seize him, because he knew if she did, she would never let him go again. She stood there, staring at him. Her gray lips had split open and shriveled back away from fissured pink gums and gnarled yellow teeth. She licked them with a mottled tongue.

Now your hand, boy! Give Teacher your hand!

Chazz, delirious with it all, made to swing on her again. As he did so, something—it felt like a hot wave of force—hit him in the face and with such power, he heard the cartilage in his nose split like a walnut and he was pitched to the ground, blood seeping from his mangled nostrils.

That's how punishment starts, Lady Pegleg informed him. *Soon you'll see how it finishes with a bad little boy with broken balls, a bad little boy de-nutted and de-boned and castrated, laid prostrate before She who Makes and Unmakes!*

Before he could do much but moan at the pain of his nose, she gripped his hair with one scaly claw and dragged him down the sidewalk by it as her peg went *tap-tap, tap-tap, tap-tap,* and she pulled him off toward the east where he would be sorted out.

It didn't matter how much he fought, her hand would not release him and her strength was irresistible. All his defiance got him was a guttural growling from her and a tightening of her fist, which nearly pulled his hair out by the roots. He tried to pull her hand away but it was soft, slimy with some secretion that felt like petroleum jelly.

"Please," he panted. "Please...just let me go."

But she continued dragging him off. *Yes, bad little boys always beg in the end. But your begging has only just begun! Better to save your voice for when the real pain begins, you miserable little shit!*

Limp and sobbing, Chazz was drawn to his ultimate destiny.

38

Even though it was coming for her, Soo-Lee did not scream because she had no voice. The scream was inside her, echoing through her skull, but she could not give it vent. Her throat was constricted, her lips pressed tight, her jaws locked. She would die silently now and in great agony and there was very little she could do about it. All that had come before was merely to soften her up for this terrible moment. As the grinning horror shambled in her direction, she realized she had been meat being tenderized and now she would feel the teeth.

As she backed away from the thing with the flayed face, she was certain she had seen it before somewhere. Wasn't it the haunter of her childhood nightmares? A grim shape that stalked the ebon byways of her subconscious mind? Maybe, maybe not. All she could be sure of was that it was not alive in the generally accepted sense of the term—it was a zombie armature, an animate articulated puppet sewn with something that was not exactly flesh and not exactly cloth.

There were too many thoughts and emotions in her mind, all of them sharpened and made deadly by a fear that was so huge inside her that it was nearly incapacitating. The thing seemed to know this, suckling it, growing fat on her terror. She could practically hear the hollow thumping of its heart. It stopped about four feet from her, fixing her with eyes that were not eyes but deep black sockets. *"Is that you, doll-face?"* it said and that brought the scream cycling out of her, practically ejecting from deep in her guts.

It was a walking carcass, overstuffed, lumpy and disfigured, rawboned limbs standing out at right angles from the body, fingers stiff and splayed. The face was at once some sloughing bladder of putty and a deflated masklike balloon, a grotesque jigsaw puzzle that was stretched and pulled by crude suturing not of gut or thread but of some heavy string like packing twine that had been stitched in and out of the flesh in grisly intersecting lines that created bulging pockets of flyblown tissue.

Knowing that it offended her, it grinned with a hacked mouth that made her knees feel weak. There were no lips, just a ragged hole as if it had chewed away its own mouth in a feeding frenzy. Its slatlike gray teeth looked capable of just about anything.

Soo-Lee did not move away fast enough, though God knew the will to do so was most definitely there. It reached out for her and grasped one of her arms in a hand that was like a loose glove, the fingers digging in painfully. The creature whispered something to her, but in her state of abject terror she could make no sense of the garbled words or the scraping puppet voice that spoke them.

It spoke again and this time she heard what it said all-too clearly: *You will be my beautiful bride, doll-face. And upon our marriage bed, I will know you.*

No, not an *it*, not exactly, but a *he* and his intentions were obvious.

Soo-Lee screamed and fell back, tripping over her legs and hitting the floor on her ass. She scrambled away, finding her feet, as the scarecrow man got closer and closer still.

He was grinning...if that lopsided, cadaverous grimace could indeed be called such a thing. Loose ends of stitching twine dangled like yarn from his face, which, up close, was yellow and white and gray, corrugated and cracked open like dry clay. It was in constant motion as if there was something beneath it that badly wanted out.

The scarecrow man seized her again with a speed that seemed impossible.

She reacted immediately this time, peeling its fingers away from her arm. They were strong, their grip like iron...yet they were hideously spongy. She managed to peel them free, one of them squishing with a hot spray of slime like a swollen, juicy caterpillar. With a cry of disgust, she turned away and felt the scarecrow man groping for her. Guided by sheer instinct, she clawed out at him with her nails, catching him in the face. Her pinkie snared a loop of twine and she heard it pull free with a sound like thread yanked through a buttonhole. He let out a cry that was half-anguish and half-rage.

Before she could make good on her escape, one of his hands grabbed her by her swinging ponytail and dragged her back. With what seemed little effort, he swung her around and launched her directly at the bed. Her head cracked against one of the posts. She recovered, but not very easily. She climbed to her feet, dazed and sluggish, clawing out at him again but missing entirely.

For godsake, run! If he catches you, he'll rape you!

Somewhere in the depths of her brain, a voice that was not hers tittered at the very idea. A mannequin raping a woman? A dummy exhibiting physical love? A horny puppet? Yes, the mind certainly boggled and it made no sense whatsoever, yet there was no doubt in her mind that he was going to force himself on her and if he was successful, she would go mad. There would be no alternative. She would go stark raving mad.

As she tried to escape, he seized her again. He battered her head against the bedpost until she went limp. She felt fingers like hooks rake across her back, tearing her shirt open and scraping against her spine. The pain was bright and energizing, but when she tried to fight, he slammed her face into the bedpost again.

When she came to, she was on the bed and he was on top of her, pressing himself down. His face was badly unraveled, the entire left side sagging like a wet paper sack. She could feel the dark sweet stink of his breath blowing in her face as he panted excitedly, the black sockets of his eyes like ragged holes. His entire face was inflating and deflating as he breathed, a sloughing expanse of stitches and seams and loose flaps.

She screamed and threw him, sliding off the bed and hitting the floor on her knees. Her head hurt and there was blood all over her face. But the truly frightening thing was that she was naked. He had meticulously stripped her and she was crawling across the floor, nearly out of her mind.

The lights went out.

The darkness was absolute and unbroken.

Soo-Lee got to her feet and stumbled about, bumping into things and upsetting other things which, thumped to the floor or shattered at her feet. She could hear him breathing. Was it to the left? The right? Just behind her? She had to find the door. Her outstretched fingers brushed against a leathery mask and she screamed again. She whirled, moving this way and that, trying to find the door and trying to keep away from him as he stalked her silently.

Something touched the nape of her neck.

She clawed out at it.

Something clutched one of her breasts and she knocked it aside.

She circled, started, stopped, searching, feeling her way around and knowing that she would never find the door because that wasn't part of the game. Sobbing and terrified, nearly in shock, she tried once more and he grabbed her by the throat. *"Is that you, doll-face?"* he asked as his other hand roughly kneaded her left breast. She fought and clawed and kicked, but it was no good. His breath was hot and searing now like the air from a blast furnace. His excitement was making him burn from the inside out.

"Please," she heard her voice whimper. "Oh...please..."

"No need to beg, doll-face," he breathed. *"No need at all..."*

She clawed out at him in defiance one last time, fingers tearing into him, and he came apart in motheaten rags and mildewed shifts, dusty wrappings like those of an Egyptian mummy. But none of the damage she did cooled the fire that burned in him.

The next thing she knew she was on the bed and something rough and knobbed like a rawhide bone was pressing into her and she screamed one last time, venting her horror and madness and violation...at least until his mouth closed over her own in a flaccid and rubbery pouch.

39

By that point, Lex had no idea where he was or what the hell was even going on. He remembered the eyes, the many eyes, how they crawled like insects and then digging into the walls that held him that felt like living tissue. And then, and then—

Then he couldn't be sure because everything was twisted up and turned inside out. He tried to make sense of it, to apply logic, but even his fine and reasoning brain could not explain any of this. He recalled the car that had taken Creep away, then getting separated from Soo-Lee and what followed.

Jesus, had that just happened?

His sense of time was distorted, stretched like taffy until minutes seemed hours and days seemed seconds. He had to get a grip. He had to put this in some kind of perspective. He had to find Soo-Lee. The amazing thing was that he was outside. He was sitting on his ass in the cool grass outside the house. He had no memory after he began trying to dig his way out. Somehow…the house had ejected him.

Ejected?

No, he had a sense that it had been more along the lines of *vomiting*. Like a dog that couldn't keep something down, it had regurgitated him. And why was that? Because he was refusing to accept any of it and refusing to buy into it? Was that it? Maybe. Yet, he felt there was more to it than that. Hell, something in him was certain there was more to it than that.

Why does a dog vomit something out? Why must it get something out of its belly?

But the answer was simple: a dog—or any other living creature with a stomach—vomited things out that were destructive to it, that would make it ill. Lex proceeded along that line of thought. Okay. Why was he destructive? Partly because of his stubbornness. That made sense. But there was another reason that he was a diseased cell in the body of Stokes.

And the answer to that was obvious.

So obvious it was ridiculous.

Oh, come on. It can't be that simple.

But maybe it was. He had dug through the walls. He had injured the house and in doing so injured Stokes. It was absolutely insane, yet he felt that there was something to it. He didn't honestly believe the walls of the house were *really* living tissue. That was a hallucination, an image placed in his mind to scare him or offend him, to revolt him to the point where he wouldn't think of trying to tear through them. And, perhaps, for the house *and* for Stokes that was a weak spot. Maybe wherever the illusions were heaviest were the weakest points, places he and the others had to be warned away from.

He couldn't be sure.

It was all so mixed up. He believed everything in Stokes, including the town itself, was a hallucination, but not necessarily a psychological or mental hallucination but a *physical* one, if that made any sense. Some things were nothing but illusions, but others were very real. But telling them apart was not easy. They were mixed together, woven into a common skein, perfectly joined.

And all of it was the result of the fucked-up mind or morbid intelligence that brought it together and made it real. Whether that was on purpose or accidental remained to be seen.

Lex got to his feet.

He was going back in the house. Soo-Lee was in there somewhere. Probably crouched in a corner, scared out of her wits. And that was the danger: if she believed what Stokes showed her, it could most certainly harm her or even kill her.

His head feeling screwed on tight again, that dizzy sense of unreality fading fast, Lex walked up the flagstone path to the porch. He didn't think there was anything that could really stop him, he didn't believe that—

Whump! Whump! *Whump!*

A series of explosions blew the windows out of the high,

leaning house, a wave of heat hitting him and throwing him five feet as blazing wreckage rained down all around him. The house was on fire. It went up with a series of explosions as if a propane tank or something in the cellar had ignited.

Covering his head with his hands, Lex ran for the street as another wave of heat slammed into him and pitched him to the pavement. *Soo-Lee…oh dear God, Soo-Lee,* was the only thing that ran through his mind. Brilliant red flames jumped from the windows and licked up the siding. Two attic turrets on the roof blazed up like match heads. Burning shingles, boards, and debris erupted into the air as the roof exploded, vaporizing into a rolling orange cloud that leaped skyward. It all came falling down like a storm of fiery meteorites—lathing and timbers and planks and what appeared to be a smoldering staircase that crashed not ten feet from him in an explosion of flames and sparks.

He hobbled away from the inferno, coughing on clouds of black smoke that filled the streets.

And from all around him, maybe from the other houses and the very town itself, he heard what seemed like hundreds of voices screaming: *YAAAAAAAAAAAAAAHHHHHHHHH!* It was much like when he had kicked the TV screen in the house. All those voices, only this time it was the sound of agony.

The entire world around him flickered yellow and orange like a candle guttering in a carved pumpkin. As he looked back, even the trees in the yard were on fire. It was a real three-alarm conflagration and the house looked like some great burning barrel flaming in the night. As he stood there, his arms singed from debris, a section of hair burned from his head, and his face dark with soot, he muttered Soo-Lee's name and sank to his knees.

How long he knelt there, sobbing, he did not know.

He only stood up when there was a violent roaring and the house fell into itself in a blazing pyre of glowing orange timbers and a cloud of red sparks rose into the night. The house was gone. It didn't look like there was anything standing but the blackened fingers of chimneys.

And Soo-Lee was gone with it.

She could not have survived it.

The puppet master did not want you going in there. It did not want you undoing all it had done. It had to keep you from finding out something or hurting the house further in your quest so it…it cut off a thumb to save the hand.

And it used fire. It was always fire at the root of things. Back at the diner, when all else had failed the corpse dummies had burst in flames. When he and the others saw that old sitcom from hell on the TV, there had been flames flickering outside the windows. Yes, at the root of all this there was fire.

Numb, caught between waking and nightmare, Lex stumbled up the street, moving blindly with no set destination in mind. Earlier, before the fire, he had thought he could simply walk in the house, grab Soo-Lee, and walk out again, leave Stokes by hurting it enough that he would be expelled.

But now he was not interested in leaving.

He wanted to stay.

He wanted to find the puppet master and destroy him/her/it.

And it was at that very moment as if he had channeled some psychic feed, that he looked east and saw an orange glow on the horizon that slowly died out. He did not think it was a trick. He needed to go there for that was the fountainhead of this nightmare.

Without further ado, going on nothing but intuition, he moved to the east to meet whoever or *what*ever was running this show.

40

A flashlight.

Ramona decided she needed one of those more than anything. When she came upon a store whose windows read HARDWARE, she let herself in. The door was open. Of course, it was open. Everything was open. In Stokes, you could trust your neighbors and you didn't have to worry about things like thieves or *city people*. She was certain she had not thought that. That it was placed in her head or she picked up on some psychic vibe that was floating around. *City people*. No, that wasn't a term she would have used. It was a phrase from someone who'd spent their life in small towns because they liked it that way and they were terrified to leave.

City people. Those rat-infested places are rotten with 'em. And most of 'em are dirty, slinking foreigners. Immigrants. Trash from every corner of the world.

She gasped. There it was again. She was beginning to believe it was the voice of the Controller. A narrow, paranoid, xenophobic mind.

Is that was this is all about?

There was no way to know and maybe she was better off not knowing.

Finding the flashlight was easy enough.

In her mind, she had been thinking about some little Tekna LED flashlight, but such things had not yet been invented in Stokes so she had to be satisfied with a heavy stainless-steel Ray-O-Vac outfit that needed three D-cell batteries, which were easy to find as well. There was a certain satisfaction to having the flashlight in her hand. It was heavy and solid. Unlike modern ones that would probably shatter if you smacked someone in the head with them, this baby would crack a skull.

Okay then.

Time to move.

She walked randomly, edging steadily east, *knowing* she was edging east even if the Stokes she saw was repeated endlessly. That was part of the ruse. To confuse you and frustrate you and turn you around, make you doubt yourself. It was a maze, yes, but like any maze there was a path through it if you just used your head.

And then...breakthrough.

I'll be damned.

Stretching before her was a large park, your average small-town park with benches and trees, the shadowy hulk of what she assumed was a war memorial in the distance. She saw a fountain nearby that was silent until she looked at it and then it came to life—sparkling water jetting orange and blue and green, lit by from lights below.

"Very nice," she muttered.

Guiding herself with the flashlight, she walked over a little footbridge that spanned a bubbling creek. Frogs chortled among the lily pads. The handrail was carved with the names of lovers. Interesting. She studied them all in the light, checking out the dates carved in there. Not a one more recent than 1960. Just as she'd suspected. The great fire had burned this damn place flat and what she was seeing was nothing more than an idealized memory.

Ramona crossed the bridge and was back on the grass again. She kept moving the flashlight beam around in arcs to spot any doll people before they spotted her, if that was possible. But there were none. They had slipped into dormancy again as if the Controller needed to rest now and then. Whoever was doing this must have been spending a lot of energy to maintain the illusion.

She came to an open area with a bandshell and rows of wooden seats bolted to a concrete slab. Ah, just the place to listen to a concert on a summer evening from the city band. She told herself to keep moving, but she was rooted to the spot. There was something here. Something important and she needed to trust her instincts on that.

What? What is it?

She knew she had to shut her mind down and let it happen. This place was speaking to her and she had to hear what it had to say, something she couldn't do if she cluttered her brain with thoughts. It was like yoga: empty your mind and connect. She wasn't sure if it was working, but she had the sudden inexplicable urge to walk up to the bandshell, so she followed her instincts and went up there. Between two lush rows of hedges, she sidled up to the stage and placed her hands flat on it.

There was something here.

She could feel it.

Yes, it was gathering around her, nothing exactly negative or even positive, just a flow of energy, of memory, and she went with it like a leaf floating down a creek. In days long past there had been band concerts here every Thursday night. Turning, she could see them in the dark, all the good folks of Stokes sitting there tapping their feet and snapping their fingers as the band behind her played on, brassy and off-key like all small-town bands, but nobody seemed to notice. Out on the green beyond, vendors sold hot dogs and balloons and peanuts and root beer. She noticed that the men wore suits and the ladies wore summer dresses and large floppy hats with flowers on them. Even the children were dressed up.

Was that real?

Is that how it truly was or how the puppet master wanted to remember it?

No thinking. Just feel.

Let it happen.

It was like a weird electricity was running through her, galvanizing her bones and feeding through her arteries and all of it running right up into her head and making her feel dizzy and woozy. Now all the people were gone. It was high summer and the grass was yellow. It was uncut, wild. Weeds had sprouted. The root beer stand was still there—shaped like a root beer barrel, of course—only it was faded from the sun, the service window boarded over. Birds were nesting on its roof.

A few warped planks had popped loose and creaked in the breeze. The entire park was overgrown and abandoned. Even the little footbridge in the distance...the railing was splintered, cattails clogging the creek. She shouldn't have been able to see that from this distance, but she saw it just fine. Just as she saw that on the railing somebody had carved:

FUCK STOKES

The image of that was like a cold shard of glass sliding into her belly. Yes, for the Controller—and these memories belonged to him/her/it—that was pain. It was an insult. It was a slap in the face.

Ramona could very much feel the Controller's anguish... anguish that verged on rage. She could smell a stink of burning rubber. Yes, over near the creek there was a pile of tires somebody had lit on fire. Teenagers. They were drinking and swearing, openly pissing in the grass. Something had happened here. Something had made picture perfect, placid, pure-as-the-driven-snow Stokes go belly up.

But what? What the hell was it?

Now Ramona could see an old woman sitting on the edge of the stage, a hunched-over, skeletal thing like a bag of sticks. Despite the summer heat, she was wrapped in some dark shawl that looked old and well-used like herself. Ramona could see her face. It was ancient and puckered like a peach pit, the skin pale and set with fans of wrinkles. She was muttering something. Her teeth were gray, narrow, rotting black at the gums. One eye was dark and glistening, the other blemished white, blanched almost silver.

"I'm here alone," her voice said. "Do you hear me? Alone."

Ramona was only a few feet from her. Her own throat was so dry she could barely speak, but she managed one word: "Why?"

"Gone," said the old woman. Her good eye swept over the park and its ruination and there was something cold and predatory about it, a depthless blackness in it that seemed to reach deep within her and perhaps beyond into some chasm of darkness. The warm summer breeze ruffled her white hair. Her lips were pulled back from gums going brown with age, teeth clenched in uneven rows, black grit packed between them.

"Yes, all gone now," she said in a voice that was cynical and betrayed. She attempted something like a smile, but it didn't work—her lips were twisted, brown, and ugly like dead earthworms fused together on a sidewalk.

Ramona was not certain the old lady was aware of her presence, then she craned her neck and looked at her, not so much with the good eye but with the silvery blanched one. At first Ramona thought there was some pale growth covering it like a pterygium, but now it looked as if the eye had been bleached white. The old woman speared Ramona with it and Ramona gasped.

There's power in that eye. Maybe not in it, but in the deranged mind behind it. Something is there. Maybe something hereditary, something unbelievable.

"They think they can all leave, but I have other plans," she said, this time directly to Ramona. "I've named each and every one, haven't I? Their names went in the book, *my* book, and once written there is no deliverance but through me and I am a hard mistress. They'll know soon the hold it has upon them. Reckon, they will." There was a triumphant glee to her voice, the manic delight of a disturbed mind whose vengeance was nearing.

Ramona stood there, shaking, sick inside.

I don't want this shit anymore, she thought. *I didn't know what I was doing. I just want to go now.*

But, no, it was not that easy. Not so easy for the residents of Stokes and certainly not easy for her. She had plugged herself into this and until the energy stopped flowing, she was part of the circuit and there was no backing out.

She stood there, still trembling, wanting to run but afraid to move. The old woman's dead eye impaled her and held her there as easily as a bug on a pin. She was no longer speaking, but Ramona could hear her. It was her thoughts now, all the terrible and unspeakable things echoing up from the snake pit of her subconscious mind.

(Disloyal and unfaithful, that's what they are. Treacherous, treacherous.)

*(They would leave this town, which is my town, the town my
family built and cried and bled over, but I won't let them. This is my
town and it belongs to me and they belong to me. Its guts are my guts
and its blood flows in my veins and I suffer as it suffers and who do
they think they are to turn their back on it? I will take them under my
hand and teach them the error of their ways and my hand is a firm
hand, an unforgiving hand and as I have made I WILL DESTROY
AND AS I DESTROY I WILL REMAKE IN THE IMAGE MY
HANDS KNOW BEST!)*

Ramona almost fell over. She felt like she had been dipped
in freezing water. An icy sweat broke out on her brow and
ran down her face. It made her scalp feel greasy. It ran down
her spine and dripped between her breasts and beaded her
thighs and it was only through the auspices of years of physical
training that she was able to stay on her feet.

*(NOW IT COMES AND ONCE COMING CANNOT BE PUT
DOWN! IT TAKES HOLD OF THEM! IT OWNS THEM! THEY
ARE WHAT THEY ARE NOT! THEY ARE REMADE INTO
WHAT THEY CANNOT BE!!!)*

Ramona clutched her head in her hands because she did not
want to hear the words anymore. She did not want them in her
skull, she did not want to feel them burning through her brain
and distorting her mind, tearing it open and filling it with a
black crawling darkness. Because the images were too strong
now; they were devastating. The looming terrible faces and
reaching white hands and huge empty eyes like blank windows
looking into some black dimension of suffering.

The next thing she knew, she was on her knees in the
grass, the world tilting around her. She was gasping for air and
shaking, her head hurting and her eyes refusing to open out of
fear of what they might see.

"C'mon…" she heard her voice say. "Pull yourself together…"

In the darkness she sat there with the flashlight next to her.
It had gone out, and she didn't bother clicking it because she did
not want light. She wanted the security of night, of nonentity.
She was content to hide in the shadows.

But afterimages still burned in her brain.

She was tortured by them.

The stalking black shapes that were not men and women and yet were not exactly dolls or mannequins but some morbid, awful hybrid. Men, women, and children who were no longer men, women, and children but soulless artificial things that did the bidding of the deranged mind that brought them into existence—

"Enough," she said under her breath.

Grabbing the flashlight, she stood up and leaned against the stage of the bandshell, trying to catch her breath and bring her world into focus. Slowly, slowly, she pushed the nightmare images from her head, feeling that she knew many things and yet knew nothing at all. Stokes had dried up, it had died and gone to decay, abandoned, deserted, a ghost town of sorts. That had been the beginning of it. Then other things had happened, and she did not think the fire was the worst of them.

Ramona stepped away from the stage and walked out near the seats that stood like a silent jury in the moonlight.

That old woman. Her family must have built the town and the town went to shit, as small towns sometimes do, only she was not going to allow that. She had a hold on the townspeople. They were hers. She owned them and she would not let them go. She was like a little girl playing dolls...except her dolls were people.

Sighing, Ramona looked to the east, or what her internal navigator told her was the east. As she did, she was nearly overwhelmed by a sense of fear and excitement. It seemed to fill her throat and she nearly choked on it. She was close now and getting closer all the time. The bits and pieces she knew would soon be married to something more that would explain the madness and expose its dark, agonized roots.

Mumbling beneath her breath, she began moving through the park now to the east and knowing that nothing could stop her. Whether it was where she wanted to go or where she was being compelled to go, it didn't matter. She stumbled along, her mind getting sharper with each passing moment.

When she reached the outer edge of the shadowy park, she paused. "I know things now. I know things."

And then, behind her, a voice said, "You don't know anything."

41

It was a factory.

There was no doubt of that. Though at first sight it had looked like some surreal interpretation of Dracula's castle as might be seen in an old horror comic, it was indeed a factory. It even had the old multipane windows on the second-floor common to such industrial sites. Yes, Creep knew, something had been made here. Something secret. Something lost and now found again. Something that should not be but was.

He was inside now and it didn't seem that he had entered so much as was sucked inside. The car had deposited him at the door and driven away, leaving him to stare up at the factory with horror and fascination. It was like some immense dark egg brooding in a nest, waiting to hatch. That was his first impression. His second was that it looked like a fortress of gray stone block—three-story, flat-roofed, the first-floor windows tall and dark and set with iron bars, giving it the look of a prison or a madhouse.

A voice in his head, tittering madly, had said, *You punch in, but you don't punch out.*

He moved through the darkness, bumping into things and threading through shadows that did not seem to be shadows at all. Though he had never been in this place before, he seemed to know that there were three levels of machinery. That it was laid out like a wheel, all sections connected by long corridors that led to a central hub. If there was an epicenter to the place, it was the hub, which was like a hollow cylinder that led from the ground floor to the skylights three stories above.

He didn't question how he could know these things.

Like the voice in the back of his head that kept asking him

just what the hell it was he thought he was doing, he ignored it.

He was here because this is where the car brought him and this is where he had to be.

He was in a narrow chamber, he knew that much. At the far end was an archway that connected to the corridor that would bring him to the hub. But he was not ready to go there yet. Part of him—a part he desperately tried to bury—was afraid to go there. He would stay here and see what this room had to offer.

You are now in the beast, a voice in his head informed him. *The beast that the puppet master made.*

Creep considered that...and then things started to happen.

The first was that the siren began to whine, cutting through the night with a shrieking, painful sound. But where before it was distant, now he was practically at ground zero and it cut right through him.

The siren rang and the beast woke up. It stretched and yawned and growled. Except it was not a growling as such, but the noise of the factory as it came alive in the darkness—roaring and clashing and jangling, machinery trembling and gears grinding and wheels meshing. Vats poured out steam and pipes shook and great presses hissed and molds cracked with great heat as belts rumbled and chains clanked. It was a cacophony of noise, of whirring and rumbling, tanks bubbling and levers shrieking with metal fatigue.

It was a ghost factory, and he had to cover his ears from the constant hammering noise, though nothing seemed to be moving. All of it was auditory and within seconds it stopped, the factory seizing up again.

Bump.

Creep walked into a table. He stood there, rubbing his hip, thinking and trying not to think, trying not to remember the series of events that had brought him to this place at this time. He could see things on the table before him, which was like some immense industrial workbench. The room was filled with such benches. It was here that things were put together. He knew this even if he really knew nothing else.

In his mind there was a single thought: *touch.*

He needed to touch what was on the tables. He needed to

explore what was offered with his fingertips even though he knew instinctively it was a very bad idea.

Touch.

You must touch.

You must feel.

By then, he already was. His fingers roamed over disparate objects. Coils, bundles of wire, gears, metal rods…then, then something soft. He did not know what it was but he could not stop touching it. It was flabby and warm and he felt like he was a kid again at a Halloween school carnival, exploring the contents of bowls in the darkness. Weird, squishy things that were supposed to be a dead man's brain and eyeballs and guts but were actually a sponge soaked in gelatin and grapes in watery brine and great cold globs of spaghetti.

But this…whatever it was he was touching…it was not fake. It was alive and it pulsated beneath his fingers like a living human heart.

He explored further.

Yes, fingers, he found fingers. Fingers that were cold and inert until he touched them, then they came alive, brushing against his own. He found glassy orbs that must have been eyes and a jar of tongues that greedily lapped at his fingertips. Whatever he touched came alive.

He moved to the next bench.

His hand reached out, knowing it must touch what was there. He felt something silky like soft, soft skin. In fact, it felt very much like skin but doughy with no tensile strength. He ran his fingers up and down the cool, waxy material until he realized that what he was touching was a woman. There was the button of her navel set in the flat belly and, higher, the expanse of her ribs and two rounded breasts that lacked nipples. He kneaded them, disturbed by the fact that unlike real flesh, the indentations of his fingers stayed. They were like tiny craters. No, no, no! That wouldn't do. Feverish now, a shrill laughter rattling in his throat, he smoothed out the indentations, forming the breasts into perfect cones.

Yes, that was better.

His fingers continued to investigate. He found the slight mound of a hairless pubis between the thighs and he rubbed his fingertips over it gently so as not to mar its perfection. His index finger explored its cleft that was cool to the touch but gradually seemed to be warming and moistening as he toyed with it.

No, this isn't right. This isn't a woman. It's a doll.

As if to prove this to himself, his hands discovered that she had no legs and when he explored the sockets of her shoulders, he found she had no arms. There was no head. From the stump of the neck there was a knob with a glassy, smooth ball at the end. There were other things…cords, slender steel rods.

Yes, it was a doll, the beginning of a doll…yet, the very idea of the torso and how it responded to his touch was enormously exciting. He ached with a carnal thrill, growing hard even though he knew it was wrong and completely perverse. Perverse? Hell, it was *aberrant*.

But he couldn't stop himself.

He had both hands on the torso now and sweat thick as olive oil ran down his face as he shook with desire, trying to fight the perfectly obscene urge to climb up on the table and mount what lay there. Even now it was warming to his touch. The skin felt more like skin and he was certain he could feel tiny goosebumps. And, yes, the breasts had nipples now and they were hard under his fingers. One of them exuded a tiny squirt of milk that was burning hot against his hand. He could hear moaning, impassioned female moaning…but the torso could not moan, it had no head.

But he could see now, not only the torso but other things on the table and one of them was a face. Not a head, but more like *half* a head, the front half with a face attached to it as if it had been cleaved from a skull. The face had no eyes, but its mouth was grinning, the lips formed into a perfect circle, moaning with pleasure. There was a clicking sound and he saw a severed hand, its knuckles clicking as its fingers drummed the table in anticipation. Another hand reached out and grasped his wrist, sliding its thumb back and forth against his palm.

Creep realized he was crazy.

He was crazy with terror and crazy with lust and he couldn't seem to break the spell the woman had over him…or her parts had.

Do it! Stop this! Pull away or she'll put herself together and then she'll be the thing in the car!

One of her detached legs—which was finely muscled and sleek and very feminine—began to move. It rose up, its foot brushing against the side of his face and he found himself licking the toes as the other leg wrapped around him, clutching him tightly. One of the hands was unzipping him, freeing him, stroking his cock with firm, frenzied motions. The torso moved in closer until the head of his penis was pressed against its synthetic vulva.

Obscenity! Vile, disgusting, perverse obscenity! he heard a voice cry out in his head.

The torso pressed against him and he met it, pushing until he felt the head of his penis slide into the torso which, visibly trembled with shuddering waves of pleasure. He probed deeper into the silken, hot chasm as together they rode the rising spike of pleasure and were made one by the act. Creep was moaning. The face was gasping, its teeth locked together, its breath coming in short, sharp bursts. The legs held him in a vise-like grip now that was practically crushing, and the hands gripped the edges of the table while the torso arched its back, as it could feel release coming, getting nearer, building into a white-hot climax and—

Creep screamed and pulled out, peeling the legs from him.

He barely had the strength to do it, but he managed it, his flesh rippling and his cock pulsating, but some deep-set, inborn revulsion of what he was doing and *who* he was doing it with finally greased his skids enough that he not only slid out, but stumbled back five or six feet with absolute skin-crawling self-loathing.

The face screamed with cheated hatred.

The torso thumped against the table.

The hands balled into fists and drummed alongside it.

And in Creep's head, it sounded like a thousand rusty hinges screeched at the same time, filling his mind with noise, which was the hysterical, insane cry of the torso and its attendant parts at being denied not just their oncoming orgasm but the seed he would have given them that they not only wanted but needed. They needed his life to pump up their own.

The screeching continued, rising higher, a shrilling that sent his nervous system haywire and filled him with cold-hot bolts of electricity as if he had just pissed on a downed power line. It jolted through him and he stumbled away, losing his balance, vomiting and chattering his teeth as he went to his knees, quaking and pissing himself. His eyes rolled in their sockets. His nose ran. Vomit and bile oozed down his chin. He was gone, completely out of it.

Pull out of it! Pull out of it! You don't have much time!

He got to his feet as the noise in his skull died out and he heard, with a rising note of terror, the sound of the thing on the bench trying to hastily assemble itself into a being of wrath. He could no longer see anything. The darkness was thick and enclosing and that made it all only that much worse.

He had to find a door, he had to find a way out.

If he went back, it meant running into the thing that was even now refitting itself...but if he went forward, that would lead him to the hub that was the black, diseased heart of this industrial madhouse. He moved blindly forward, bumping into things and tripping, barking his knee and smacking his head. But he didn't slow down. He would bull his way through here.

He charged faster and ran right into another bench, his hands going down to stop him from pan-caking face-first onto its surface and what it held. He sank right up to his elbows into something that was surely a dead man, probably several of them. They were soft with decay, worms threading through them and maggots crawling over the back of his hands when he pulled them free. And the stink...dear God, foul beyond measure.

Creep did not know what the bodies were there for. In his fevered mind, he could not even imagine. He moved away, trying to suppress the giggling in his throat, and ran smack into a wall. He felt along it until he found the archway that led into the corridor. The air seeping out from it was cooler as if it led to a tomb.

Behind him, he heard something step off one of the benches and a voice like a knife blade scraped over a rusty barrel: *"Is that you, doll-face?"*

42

Chazz was not entirely sure what was dream and what was reality, he only knew he had found a safe, dark place and he was never going to leave it. He could remember being dragged away by Lady Pegleg to a dark and spooky place and then getting free somehow, retreating into this hidey hole where he knew he was perfectly safe. As long as he did not move and made no sounds, he would be safe here. It was like when he was a child and had done something bad. His stepmother would lock him in the closet because she thought it terrified him, but it did not terrify him. It only made him feel warm, enclosed, and secure.

His hidey hole was like that.

It was a tunnel. Very dark, very safe. It was warm and soft in there and no one could get him. It was the place he often visited in his dreams, a prenatal memory of comfort and sanctuary.

Lady Pegleg was near.

He knew that much. She was seeking him out but she would never find him. She droned on and on and if he concentrated, he could shut out her awful voice, which was a thousand forks dragged over a thousand blackboards.

Don't listen to her! Don't let that voice in your head or she'll find you and punish you and you don't want that!

No, he didn't want that. When his stepmother punished him—her burning cigarette was the worst—he had always known if he just took it, it would be over eventually. She would get bored with her own sadism and turn her twisted mind to new endeavors. But Lady Pegleg wasn't like that because she wasn't really human and things that were not human had an amazing capacity for patience. They could wait like bricks in a wall or cracks in a sidewalk. Ten minutes or ten years meant nothing to them.

"Go ahead, little boy, hide up inside your mama's rotten fuck-hole, fester between her legs and worm your way deep into her dirty cock wallet!" said the voice. *"Explore that well-worn, well-plumbed, well-bagged slunk tunnel! Squat in there, you little wart, in the depths where filthy men blew their cream and chowder! A fine place for you!"*

The voice echoed in his hidey hole and he told himself he must not listen because if he listened, she would *know* that he was listening and she would track him down, follow him to his source in his mother's ultra-secret wellspring. He must shut it out, because if he shut it out, then it would not exist and he could not let it exist because if it existed, then he soon would not. And although he tried desperately to be quiet, so very quiet as he had done in the closet when he was a boy with black eyes and purple belt marks on his ass and cigarette burns on his legs, he could not stop the low, frightened whimpering that came from his mouth.

"A-ha! A-HA!" said Lady Pegleg with unwholesome, slavering delight. *"I hear you, bad little boy! Don't think you can hide from Teacher because Teacher will find you as Teacher ALWAYS finds bad little boys! I'll pull you out, my darling little cockswallow, and then I'll lunch on your balls! Tender and sweet, are they? Soft to the tooth? Why, like fuzzy delicate little apricots that I'll bite until the juice runs down my chin!"*

Chazz stuffed his hand into his mouth so he would not scream as he had screamed when he was a little boy and his stepmother touched a lit cigarette to the tip of his little boy penis. He stuffed his hand in as far as it would go because he must make no more sounds or that witch would have him and make a fine meaty stew of his balls in her boiling black cauldron whose sides were greased with the remains of manhood boiled like prunes. He tried to do anything but listen to the voice and slowly, slowly, it all started coming back to him about the concert and the drinking and the van and Stokes and Ramona, dear hot little Ramona with her greedy hole and busy mouth, who would do anything to keep a man happy because her own manic OCD maintained that she was always at fault regardless of what happened and that meant she must work harder and give more to make things right. And Chazz had never really realized that's what it was always about with her, but he knew it now and it sickened him because he knew something in him had recognized that immediately and exploited it to its fullest. Poor, dear Ramona. He had used her and preyed upon the one chink in her armor, utilizing her inadequacies the very way his stepmother had once utilized his own. *If you don't do what I say, then your father will be angry and he'll send you to a foster home and we'll go away to sunny Florida and we'll never think about you again, you miserable little shit.* And as Chazz realized this, he realized how fucked-up he was and how fucked-up he had always been since his mother's death and his stepmother's abuse. The latter much more than the former had sculpted him into the selfish piece of shit he was and the idea of that brought great pain. Dear God, he would make it up to the people he wronged. He would make it up to Ramona because she was the only good and decent thing he had ever known in his twenty-two years of struggle, disappointment, and abject misery—

But...it was getting lighter in the tunnel only it was not the tunnel that was doing it but him. Yes, he was sliding down it into the cold, cruel, and wicked world once again and he did not want to enter its heartless environs now any more than he had wanted to twenty-two years before. He was sliding down, down, and there was nothing to slow him or break his fall as the malevolent world of Stokes waited for him, smiling monstrously and grinding its yellow ball-shearing teeth together.

The tunnel was rejecting him.

More so, it was expelling him like something harmful that did not belong and perhaps had never belonged. The placental membrane had broken, and the water had run and his safe hidey hole was forever gone and never again would he knew its safety as things got brighter and a twisted yellow claw reached up and grabbed him by the ankles.

"Breached little bastard, are we?" said Lady Pegleg as she pulled him out and held him up by the ankles like an infant that needed life slapped into it by a firm and ready hand. *"Ready to*

enter the world on your feet? Not you, young master! On your hands and knees with offerings to the lady who waits!"

Screaming and twisting in her grip, Chazz could see the room he was in taking shape around him with infinite slowness. Going from a dim gray blur to a sharp clarity so that he could see the walls that were hung with doll parts—faceless heads and arms, legs and torsos and hands. He saw jars of glass eyes, hinged jaws, numerous blank faces hanging from hooks. Among them were tacked yellowed anatomy prints and racks of gleaming instruments: knives, saws, probes. He had been brought here, he knew, not just to be de-balled, but to be taken apart carefully and meticulously.

And the worst part of it, the very worst part was that he had an audience.

There were several dozen doll people in grim attendance, gathered in seats like medical students preparing to watch the dissection of a cadaver. They were all chatting away in some unintelligible tongue, many of them calling out and holding up white hands as if they were at an auction.

"They're bartering for you," Lady Pegleg said, leering at him with the patchwork mask of her face. *"You have so many fine, fine parts. Your heart and balls are already mine. There will be no discussion of that, young master. But…oh, your legs, your arms, your eyes and face…oh so many wonderful goodies! Eh, what's that? The fine lady over there would like your manhood and she shall have it!"*

Chazz could see the lady in question.

She was a dreadful thing slumped in a chair, a swollen collection of animate parts like some fat, overfed infant that jiggled with rolls and bulges and deep-hewn crevices. Her flesh was pulsating. She was naked and lacked arms. Her body was horridly bulbous and rounded like a collection of smooth pink medicine balls married into a common whole, the offered gash between her legs like an axe cut that ran from her pubis to her belly. Her breasts were immense breathing spheres with juicy cherries in place of her nipples. Red juice had bled from them and stained her plump, uniform pinkness. He could barely see her face behind those bloated mammaries, but he saw enough of it to turn his guts to sauce. Her head was topped by wavy wheat-yellow hair set with bright blue bows, her plump lips a garish red and her eyes—set in pink blubbery sockets—were faded white marbles like the eyes of a waterlogged corpse.

Lady Pegleg giggled and stomped her peg upon the floor. *"She's most anxious for what you have!"*

By this point, Chazz was insane and he didn't bother screaming or crying out. It was simpler to just titter with the others and grin maliciously when Lady Pegleg reached down between his legs and grasped what was there in her hand, fondling and squeezing it roughly.

The bulbous woman shuddered with delight, shivering and rolling, the gash between her legs widening into a black cleft that could have swallowed him whole.

43

Soo-Lee crouched in the corner on a bed of straw as the blood ran down the inside of thighs in red streams. She was naked and cold and disoriented and could not seem to remember how it was she had come to this place. Maybe she had been here forever, sitting like this, her back up against cold cinder block walls, her arms stretched out, her fingers splayed against the blocks. Maybe this is who she had always been and maybe everything she thought she knew before was just a dream she had while she waited and waited, listening to the sobbing of a broken voice.

Sobbing?

Yes, she could hear it. The pathetic sobbing of a woman that she recognized as the sound of violation when all you knew and all you trusted in had been torn out by the roots, dirtied and dragged through filth, then tucked back inside you by greasy fingers. Yes, she knew that sound because once upon a time she had sobbed like that. But that was long ago and maybe it had not happened yet or it had happened before and she could not be sure. The sobbing, pained and pitiful, went on and she realized it was her voice but that seemed to mean nothing to her. She could only feel the pain in her belly, the deep gnawing pain, which was bright and cutting.

The blood continued to squelch from between her legs, creating a widening dark pool that glued her in place.

My blood.

My life.

She put her hands on her belly.

It was huge and round, the skin taut like it might tear from internal pressure. It was like a ball filling with air, inflated by gas. Even her navel stuck out now like the tip of a thumb. Inside, there was something. Something that shifted and rolled like an uneasy sleeper, nipping and gnawing at her.

You were raped, a voice told her.

No.

You were raped by a doll.

No!

You were raped by a puppet.

NO!

You were raped by a mannequin and it planted its seed and—

NO! NO! NO! NOOOOOOO!!!

She slapped her hands against her belly again and again like she was drumming on a bongo, hearing the sounds and feeling the deep-set agony it brought. If there was something in there, something alive but not alive, human but puppet, flesh but wax and wood...she would kill it. She would tear it out and pull it apart with her hands. Her fingers arching into claws, she made to do that very thing.

But something began to happen.

Something that dropped her mind into a white blankness of nonentity. It started with her toes. A coldness that numbed her and sucked the warmth from her veins and replaced it with an icy sludge. It threw out frigid roots that grew up through her legs and netted her thighs and infested her belly, climbing inch by inch up into her chest. Her well-abused sex felt like a flap of rubber, her bones like frosty sticks, her breasts like pert bags of ice, and it continued on and on, pushing the heat from her and replacing it with a chill blackness that swallowed her internals and stiffened her limbs and fingers, finally engulfing her brain, locking it in a black static that hummed incessantly but did not feel or emote any longer.

Soo-Lee could hear a voice telling her how it was going to be and how it *had* to be and there was no will in her to refuse it. Defiance was no longer amongst her natural rhythms. Acceptance and obedience were all that she knew. In her head, the humming went on and on until she knew nothing else *but* the humming that was a beautiful red silence that encompassed all and everything. Her lungs were sacs that breathed, her eyes were black glass that did not see, and when the thing began to chew, digging its way free, clawing and biting and finally bursting from her belly with slopping and slithering sounds, her face cracked open in a smile and she looked down at the wizened horror that was slicked red with her own blood and said, *"Is that you, doll-face?"*

44

Though Ramona knew it was probably a mistake, she went with the woman to her house that fronted the park. Inside, there were lights from guttering candles and she brewed them tea. The woman said her name was Mrs. McGuiness and she had been in Stokes a long, long time and knew how things worked. That was the sugar she used to get Ramona to go with her. That was the bait that drew the fly into the spider's web.

Mrs. McGuiness was a large, but sickly woman. She was round and fleshy, but her skin was yellow and dry. But beyond that, her blue eyes were friendly in their puffy sockets and she said she knew things and Ramona desperately wanted to know what those things were.

As she sipped her tea, Mrs. McGuiness said, "Now, I can imagine you were pulled in here as oftentimes people are...but where is it you thought you were going?"

"I'm going east," Ramona told her. "I'm tracking this to its source."

"That's a foolish proposition."

Ramona shrugged. "God loves fools. Better to take the fight to the source than be on the defensive."

"You certainly have a tongue on you."

Ramona ignored that. She was beyond the point where such things mattered. She looked at the tea in her cup and decided it was probably black with poison. She would not drink it. "You told me I don't know anything."

"You don't....you're only guessing."

"Then tell me what I don't know."

"It's quite a yarn."

"I've got the time."

Mrs. McGuiness shrugged. "So you say. I've been here a long time, as I said. No one but the Mother herself has been here longer. I was one of the ones that did not try to run and did not conspire against her, so here I stay. I am provided for. I am left alone and I am not a synthetic thing that obeys its master because it has no soul."

"Who is the Mother?"

Mrs. McGuiness rattled her cup against its saucer. "*Who?* Well, maybe *what* might be a better question, but no matter, no matter. She is Mother Crow. She is the last of the family. The last one and the most practiced of all."

"Practiced in what?"

"Well, in the arts of the doll makers, the puppet masters. The Crows were not simple toy makers, dear. Oh no, oh no no no. Their figures—because that's what they called them, *figures*—were more often than not mechanized. You see, the Crows weren't always doll makers. Back in old Europe, they were clockmakers, artisans of fine precision instruments and delicate clockworks. They applied those skills, secrets, and techniques to their dolls. Not the window dummies, of course. Nobody likes their window dummies walking around, now do they?"

"This is…this is all so insane."

The old woman smiled at that, as if she understood the feeling all too well. "You said you were going east…do you know where it was you were *really* going?"

"The siren," Ramona said. "I was seeking the siren."

Mrs. McGuiness nodded. "Smart girl or maybe not so smart at all. The siren sounds and those things out there wake up, don't they? Like wooden puppets deciding they are no longer wooden, eh? Well, listen. The siren is the shift whistle that puts them to work and it is Mother Crow who sounds that whistle as she's always sounded it as generations of Crows sounded it before her."

"Shift whistle for what?"

"The factory, child, the factory. The place where the dolls are made…at least, where they *were* made. Now other things go on there that would chill your blood to know of them." She dismissed that with a wave of her hand. "Now listen. Before the fire of 1960—and I can see by your face that the fire is known to you—the Crow factory on the hill was the lifeblood of Stokes. Nearly the entire town worked there, and it was a good town, with good people who lived a good life and were respectful of one another. Not like the vermin in the big city. These were *good* folks and this was their town and the Crow family provided so that all might flourish. You're far too young to know about this town or the factory, but once upon a time when the factory went nonstop and was the blood of this town, dolls were made up there. Dolls for children. Puppets, marionettes, even dime-store dummies of particular artistry. Crow figures were world-famous and the orders just rolled in and people were fat and happy and the town thrived. And watching, always watching, over the town *and* the factory, was Mother Crow, good Mother Crow like the old woman who lived in the shoe, loving each of her children more than she loved herself."

Ramona lifted an eyebrow at that. She did not seem to remember the Old Woman in the Shoe being a loving mother, but that was neither here nor there. "So let me guess. The factory went belly-up, closed, people moved away to where the grass was greener, and Mother Crow took it personally."

"That tongue," Mrs. McGuiness said, shaking her head. "That awful tongue."

"I got something wrong?"

"Yes, dear, you did. When they needed her, she was there for them. But when she needed them, they abandoned her. They took the good name of Crow in vain and paid no homage to who she was and what her fine family had done for them."

Ramona nodded. "People need to eat, ma'am. I'm sure they hated leaving, but they had to go where there were jobs so they could feed their kids. I hardly think that's a crime. What the hell did she want from them? Their firstborn?"

A darkness passed over the old lady's face and Ramona figured she had gone too far. There was a time and place to speak your mind and mouth off and maybe this was not it. But she couldn't help herself. She had been through too much, seen and experienced things that left her nerves not only on edge but humming like telephone lines. Proper conduct and etiquette seemed to have no place now. Her back was up and she was ready for a fight and she didn't have the patience for trifling bullshit.

The darkness shadowing the old lady's face remained a moment too long and Ramona wondered what horrors were hiding beneath, sharpening their teeth.

"Maybe she did want that," Mrs. McGuiness said, her breath coming fast now. "Maybe she *deserved* that. She and her family had given blood and they wanted some in return, and maybe all she really wanted was the simplest of things: loyalty."

Ramona nodded. Yes, the Old Woman in the Shoe who whipped her children soundly and put them top bed. "Maybe. But maybe she asked for too much. Loyalty is great but it won't put food on the table. Was Mother Crow willing to support everyone out of her own pockets?"

"Her pockets were as empty as theirs!"

"So they had no choice. They left."

Mrs. McGuiness nodded. "Not all of them, not right away. But family by family they hightailed it out and left a graveyard in their passing. That's what Stokes was, a big old graveyard and when the wind blew on dark nights, you could hear the emptiness of it and feel the sorrow and sense the desertion. Those are things you can feel in your soul, missy, and the soul of the town was blighted like a summer field, diseased black to its roots, and that's when it bled. I don't expect you to believe it, but those that were still around—I was one of their number—we all saw it. Blood began to seep from the earth, bubbling up like crude oil but it was no oil—it was blood. You could smell it and taste it in the air. It came up through cracks in the street and filled yards and ran in the gutters. It terrified some and others were in rapture over the mysticism of the whole thing. These were the ones that would bow down before it and offer prayers to God above and lower things that crawled below."

Ramona sighed. "And Mother Crow? What did she say about the blood?"

"Nobody knew. She was hidden away up in that silent old factory like a spider in a crevice and she wasn't coming out for no one."

Spider was right, Ramona figured, because that crazy old woman in her own way had webbed up the town and she wasn't too happy about the townsfolk—*her* people—slipping out of her grasp like flies sneaking out of a spider's web. But the blood? How did you explain that? Either Mrs. McGuiness was confused and deluded by the years or exaggerating to make a point or something very weird had happened and with all Ramona had seen, she would not have doubted that things could happen in Stokes that could not happen elsewhere.

"How do *you* explain the blood?"

Mrs. McGuiness rattled her cup again. "The seed of that is belief, missy. That's what lies at the core of it. This town was dying fast. It was gasping its last breath. And like anything that lies wounded and worn on its deathbed, it was bleeding out. A malignance had seeped into this town and as its flesh went to rot so did its bones and blood as the body decayed. And we saw it. Yes, we all saw it. Houses were falling apart, trees standing and leafless. The water in the creek went bad and the sky boiled black, and there was a graveyard stench to the wind. Impossible, you say? You think I'm talking symbolically, don't you? I am *not*. I am talking literally. This town was diseased. We didn't know it then but there was a good reason for it. You see, up in the factory, Mother Crow was dying, too. The collapse of her family business, which created the collapse of Stokes, was like a knife stuck into her. The malignance that blighted the town started in her and spread down from the factory into the town. I told you the blood of this town was the Crows' blood and so it was. As she sickened and died, so did the town. By then, there weren't too many left. Maybe twenty families, no more. But they witnessed it."

She went on to say that Mother Crow might have physically died, but something in her refused to lie quiet. Whatever it was—stubborn pride, anger, or dark witchery—it lived. It grew stronger up there and it seized hold of the town and decided to make those that were planning on getting out pay an awful price.

"It wanted sacrifice?" Ramona said.

"Yes, of a sort. You look at me like I'm insane, my dear, and maybe I am, but I saw things. Awful things visited upon those who were not loyal to the family that had given them life and breath and allowed their children to grow strong and vital. I saw these things. However it could be, it was. That dark machinery up at the factory was still turning out *figures* of a sort and one by one, those in the town below became those figures or were replaced by them until there were no people left…just walking dolls."

"Then there was the fire."

Mrs. McGuiness looked pained by that. "Yes, they said it started in the town and burned its way right up to the factory and when it was done, Stokes was a gutted ruin of black trees and standing chimneys, cinders and wreckage blown by ash. But what was up in that factory, what had been Mother Crow, was still up there, something that fused itself with the machinery, something so powerful it remade the town in its own ideal image and now and again, it needed people. People like you. Because that's the key to it, my dear. You and your friends, you don't have to die or let them horrors run you ragged and suck the spirit out of you. Stop fighting. Settle in as I have. Accept things and be part of the Mother and her town and she will provide all that you will ever need or want."

Ramona sat there.

She had no voice to speak with. It was all bullshit. Not that she didn't believe it was true, but the very idea behind it was mad bullshit. Did old Mother Crow really think she could suck people into this netherworld and they would be content to live in the graveyard of Stokes and accept what she offered and make homage to her, their bright and shining fairy queen who guaranteed a happy ending each and every time? Fucking madness. That's what it was. Ramona was more intent than ever to get up to that factory and sort this out.

"I'm not about to accept this," she said, "and neither would anyone else in their right mind. Mother Crow or whatever she now is has to be stopped. This insanity has gone far enough. Who the hell did she think she was? Who gave her the right to own those people?"

That darkness passed over Mrs. McGuiness's face, but this

time it stayed like shadows creeping in at twilight. It darkened the wrinkles and ruts of her face, casting gray pools under her eyes, which were no longer that striking perfect blue, but yellow and runny like the yolks of poached eggs.

The monster was nearly out.

"She did *everything* for them! While they slept, she toiled! While they prospered, she bled! They were her wheat and she treated them lovingly and with great care, scything the weeds that grew up around them! There was no sacrifice too great for Mother Crow! And she only asked for loyalty and...and *obedience!* And these were hers by birthright! By who she was and what she was and the name she carried and the family she was born into!"

Mrs. McGuiness was standing now and her sallow lips had pulled away from long graying teeth in a sour grin.

"They worked their shifts! Eight to four and four to midnight and midnight to eight, oh yes! But she worked them *all* until there was no separation from her and the factory and the town itself! All in one and she wanted them to understand that nothing is free! That everyone must sacrifice and everyone must suffer for the good of all and in the end, we are all owned! Do you hear me, you silly little twat? In the end, *we are all owned!*"

Ramona was on her feet now, too.

She let Mrs. McGuiness rant because there was no talking a zealot out of their beliefs. Mother Crow, while she lived, sounded like the dark lord of all micro-managers and control freaks. She probably drove people away with her obsession and misguided attention to small, meaningless details. They called it boss*itis*, Ramona knew. That was when a boss felt he or she had to work more hours than their employees to prove that they were sacrificing so much more and working so much harder. But as their employees soon learned, the more said boss worked, the less he or she got done and it was all just an excuse to hide their rampant OCD, which demanded that they oversee every meaningless detail that could have easily been taken care of by their employees. She had worked for a man like that once. Like most bosses of that stripe, he was suspicious and paranoid by nature, believing that his employees were trying to fuck him but there was really no need since he was fucking himself so damn hard.

"I'm leaving now," Ramona told her.

"YOOOUUU ARE NOT GOING ANYWHERE!"

As Ramona stood there, Mrs. McGuiness got louder and louder, her voice scraping and screeching like a reed instrument being played with a sawtoothed file: "A WHORE like YOU cannot understand the responsibility of Mother Crow and what she did and what she must do to maintain this town! YOU do not know the suffering and torment and anguish of birthing this town whole again! YOU cannot see nor feel that the blood of Stokes is her blood! That it is her child that she brooded and nurtured and will never EVER let go of! YOU are nothing but a synthetic little whore like your entire generation! *VIPERS! WHORES! COCK-WHORE! WITCH-WHORE! SLUT-WHORE! USER AND TAKER AND ABUSER! YOU DO NOT SEE THE PURITY OF MOTHER CROW'S VISION, AND YOU CANNOT SHARE IN THE BEAUTY OF WHAT SHE HAS MADE! LIKE ALL THE REST! VERMIN! YOU ARE—"*

"Shut up!" Ramona shouted at her. "YOU...JUST...SHUT THE FUCK...UP!"

As she tried to pass, Mrs. McGuiness, who didn't exist now and probably never had, gripped her by the arm and in that instant, it felt like something exploded inside of Ramona. Her head was filled with glaring light and fireworks and hot steam. This was not Mrs. McGuinness (just as she had suspected all along), it was Mother Crow, a projection of Mother Crow, who still brooded up in the ruined factory like a tick on a blood-filled artery, like a rat in a bone pile. This was *her.* And Mother Crow knew that she knew and the understanding that flashed between them was not mutually advantageous, but mutually destructive because they both saw the power and wrath of one another and shrank in fear and rose up in anger. Ramona felt like an expanding bag of hot blood that might burst at any moment. The realization that she was being touched by the parasitic horror that engineered this nightmare was almost enough to make her scream.

In fact, it did make her scream.

And as she screamed, she yanked her arm free, very aware of the fact that where Mother Crow/Mrs. McGuiness had gripped her was now cold and numb and that pretty much said all that needed saying about the leech herself.

As Mother Crow's anger spiked, the house began to tremble and the wind, which had been nonexistent, began to whip outside, moaning at the windows as if it was in pain. For a moment or two, it seemed like the house was *wavering* slightly in and out of reality, shifting between solid and something far less substantial than a gas. The spell of Mother Crow was either weakening or she was tiring of putting forth the massive mental/psychic energy of making Stokes real.

"YOU'LL GO NOWHERE!" she shrieked at Ramona. "NO ONE LEAVES UNTIL THE MOTHER ALLOWS! NOT NOW AND NOT BEFORE, YOU CUNTING LITTLE WHORE! YOU FILTHY DIRTY LEG-SPREADING COCK-EATING LITTLE TRAMP! YOU HAVE NO SAY HERE! YOU HAVE NO—"

And it was at that moment, as Mother Crow made another grab for her, her eyes wild and her sneering mouth flecked with white saliva, that Ramona swung the flashlight at her face with pure rage. The Ray-O-Vac's stainless steel shell, heavy in of itself but with the added dead weight of D-cell batteries, split Mother Crow's Mrs. McGuiness mask like dry pine. Ramona felt it sheer through the mask and then imbed itself into something soft and pliable just beneath.

"EEEEEYAAAWWWW!" cried Mother Crow, her mask cracked open to reveal something gray and grinning beneath that looked like the fissured face of a mummy. "DIRTY DIRTY DIRTY BITCH! TREACHEROUS LIKE ALL THE OTHERS! JUST LIKE YOUR LITTLE FRIEND UPSTAIRS! THE ONE WHOSE WOMB BLEEDS FOR THE DARK SINS SHE HAS WROUGHT AND MADE COVENANT WITH! THE GOOK! THE CHINK! THE SLOPE! RICE-PICKING ZIPPERHEAD DOG-EATING RICE NIGGER CHINATWAT!"

The phobic racial slurs blew out of her mouth like vomit, empowered by a black cesspool of a mind that was probably rank and rotting when she was still truly alive. She was nothing but a sack of poison, intolerance, hatred, and fear. *Fear* because that's really what this was all about: that's what had kept her mind, her spirit, her essence on this side of the grave. Fear of change. Fear of anything that was different. Fear that she had lost her omnipotent sway over the good folks of Stokes and that she could no longer squeeze them in her arthritic fists until the blood ran from them. Fear of the loss of control. And, ultimately, the fear of being alone, of having to look the demented, vindictive hag she indeed was right in the face.

Ramona, shouting herself now, battered Mother Crow until the hag's head split open, half of it sliding down a few inches and giving her the look of some fairground monster reflected in a shattered mirror. Things broke inside her face as Ramona kept hitting her, but she did not go down despite the snapping and cracking of her anatomy or the black viscous-looking blood that ran from beneath the remains of the Mrs. McGuiness mask.

"GO THEN!" she said in a mocking voice. "GO SEE YOUR LITTLE TWO-DOLLAR GOOK WHORE FRIEND WHOSE LEGS ARE HINGED TO SPREAD AND SEE WHAT SHE HAS PUT FORTH!"

Then the mask fell completely away and Ramona saw the sardonic face of Mother Crow revealed. It looked like grinning wicker, the eyes juicy red meat, the teeth long and sharp…and then she was gone. There was nothing to mark her passing but a wisp of smoke and shards of the Mrs. McGuiness mask on the floor. And overhead, Ramona heard something bump along the floor.

The flashlight in her hand, terror opening her up like knives, she went to the stairs and started up.

To what waited there in the darkness.

It was then she heard the siren ring.

45

Lex heard it, too, as Creep did inside the factory. It registered with all ears in Stokes. Some woke and others trembled. Lex did neither. He was on the twisting road that led up to the factory on the hill and nothing could stop him now. He knew where he had to go even if he had no idea what it was he was supposed to do.

I'm coming for you, he thought. *That's all you have to know. Whether you summoned me or it's my own idea, it doesn't matter. I'm coming for you.*

As he climbed the tree-lined road and the hulking shape of the factory grew larger, he told himself that whatever he did it would be for Soo-Lee, who was kind and special and good and much better than he had ever deserved. Whatever came now, whatever he had to sacrifice and how much of his own blood that he had to spill, he was doing it for her because he owed her that much.

Up ahead, at the turn of the road, he saw a figure standing there.

His first impulse was to call out to it, but a tremor of anxiety in him canceled that out. He knew it wasn't a person. There was nothing really alive in Stokes.

He began walking faster.

The shape beckoned to him, then moved off into the shadows. He decided he was going to catch it and tear it apart with his own hands. Nothing less would satisfy him. He was walking even faster now, catching momentary glimpses of the figure as it moved in and out of patches of moonlight with that peculiar seesawing motion indicative of the doll people.

He came up to the next turn of the road and saw a pool of

something wet on the road. He knew it was not accidental. Like the song said, it never rained in Southern California and it sure as hell never rained in Stokes...unless whoever or *what*ever that waited in the factory for him wished it to.

He kneeled down by the pool.

He knew it was blood before he touched it. He dipped his index finger into it and it was very warm, almost hot. More like fluid that leaked from a transmission than something that leaked from a living body.

Standing up, he resumed the chase.

The figure was at the next bend waving to him.

So you're bleeding, he thought. *I suppose that means something but I don't have time for puzzles right now.*

He kept coming upon more and more puddles of blood. If the thing he was following was human, it would have dropped by now. There would have been no blood left in it. Apparently, this thing could bleed endlessly; the reservoir never ran dry. Another splotch of blood followed by another, then a spreading pool that was slowly draining into the ditch at the side of the road.

Lex was now a big-game hunter following a blood spoor.

The puddles were getting bigger and bigger and now he saw that in-between them were footprints. Small, delicate-looking footprints that he thought were female.

Soo-Lee, he thought. *That's what the puppet master wants you to think, but you know it's bullshit. It's all part of the game.*

Now the factory was before him, across a field of shorn grasses. It was a big, industrial-looking place, flat-roofed, squared off, perfectly geometrical like a series of blocks piled atop one another. Though the moon shone down from above, it did not touch the structure. It remained perfectly dark as if it had been snipped from black construction paper. The figure waited for him, beckoning—and bleeding, no doubt—in the freezing penumbra thrown by the place.

Lex stopped.

In fact, it didn't seem so much that he had stopped but *was* stopped. It felt like he had run smack into an invisible wall of force. That was purely subjective, of course, but he stopped dead, his feet feeling like they had grown deep roots into the soil. He stared at the shape of the factory as Hansel and Gretel must have stared at the candy cane cottage of the big bad witch. Then he actually *did* feel waves of force coming out at him, pushing him back, making his knees tremble with his own weight. The force was sheer hate, and he thought for a moment he could see bright red eyes looking out at him from one of the upper windows.

Yes, this was it.

If he had doubted it before, well, there was no doubting now. The epicenter of the Stokes nightmare was right here and he could feel its lines of force radiating out like the silken threads from a spider's lair. There was real power here, black and ugly killing power. It was like standing before a transformer. The air was energetic.

Lex knew he could weaken and walk away or he could fight. Only the latter would weaken the puppet master. The former would make it that much stronger.

He took a step forward, then another.

The electric hate of the place made his head ache and droplets of sweat the size of corn kernels ran down his face. He wiped them away, more determined with each step that brought him closer to the diseased heart of Stokes. It was then he felt a blast of heat like demon's breath. The air was filled with churning smoke and he could hear screams, the screams of souls burning in the surrounding inferno.

He pushed forward and the smoke cleared and there was the doll person, only it was no doll person but a doll woman and that woman was Soo-Lee reaching out to him with pale white hands, a wolfish hunger seeming to emanate from her.

He could hear her voice: *It hurt me. It tore me open. It ripped out everything inside. Why did you let it? Why did you let it hurt me like that?*

Lex did not know exactly what she was talking about.

He could hear her words in his head so she wasn't exactly speaking, but he heard her just fine. And beneath each word there was imagery of what had happened to her in the house after they were separated. Seeing it, it felt like he was kicked in the stomach. He shouted, he cried out. Tears ran from his eyes. He shook and nearly went over. He felt physically ill.

And then a voice from deep inside him said, *"ENOUGH! ENOUGH FUCKING GAMES!"*

And that changed everything.

It changed it very fast.

The flawless smooth perfection of the Soo-Lee doll began to change. Flames licked up through her clothes and her long, beautiful hair ignited with a sickening stench. Her face bubbled and ran. She was like a wax image tossed into a fire and she burned. She screamed as her flesh melted and her limbs began to curl. Her features ran down her face in flowing runnels.

This isn't Soo-Lee, Lex told himself as resolutely as possible.

This is a projection, a physical hallucination that wears her face. It's a mask and beneath it, there's something else. Let it show itself.

The thing continued to melt until its face split open like immense jaws and revealed the monster hiding beneath that easily stepped from the burning, melting wreckage of Soo-Lee and was only connected to her by a few strands of flesh. What he saw was a hunched-over, wizened creature that reminded him a little too much of Norman Bates's mother in the rocking chair. An old woman in a black dress with a white ruffle at the neckline, sexless puritanical garb buttoned right up to the throat. Her face was a skull covered in corrugated gray flesh, her white hair pulled into a strict little bun atop her head. But unlike the corpse in *Psycho*, this thing was very much alive as it came at him in a deadly dark shape, puffing out smoke like exhaust fumes. Its teeth were long and sharp, its reaching hands like chitinous claws.

But Lex did not run.

And when it reached out for him to peel his face free, he reacted like a cornered animal and attacked it. He hit it in the face with three good shots that made the head bounce about on the withered twig of neck before something snapped and the head slumped to the left shoulder. That didn't spare him the nails that opened grooves in his face or the awful feel of the thing as he took hold of it and threw it to the ground, jumping up and down on it and hearing it snap and crackle beneath him like dry sticks.

When he finally calmed down, there was nothing on the ground.

But the door to the factory was wide open.

If he wanted an invitation, then here it was.

46

In the darkness of the corridor that led to the hub of the factory, the *nest*, as it were, Creep could hear things moving around him. Not doll people, but what he thought were rats, hundreds of rats that skittered over the floor and climbed the walls and dangled by their claws not three feet above, dropping foul pellets on his head. He could see their gleaming eyes, but they did not frighten him because he had the oddest feeling that they were actual living creatures who were frightened of him and in a mad exodus to reach shelter.

Behind him, something was following him.

He could hear the slapping of its feet as it came for him to finish what he had started.

About twenty feet into the corridor, he realized that he had stepped off into some nighted cavern that stretched on to infinity, an endless back chasm from which he would never return.

He had seen such a place only in his dreams and knew it would run on and on for miles and never, ever would he be any closer to its end than he was right now. But he couldn't turn back. If he did, *she* would get him, so he had to keep moving and moving until he could move no more. To stop was something worse than death. To go on, madness. There was no in-between. He would go marching along until the flesh dropped from his bones because there simply was no alternative.

He realized he should have been terrified, but he wasn't.

Not yet.

Not just yet because he knew that there would be an end because the director of this little play would get bored and he would cut the scene. That's when Creep would be afraid. That's where the real fear lay.

Then, as if on cue, he was looking into the mouth of hell.

He had reached the hub because it was necessary that he reach the hub. Only it wasn't exactly as he had imagined it. It was a kiln, a blazing blast furnace that ejected glowing tongues of flame. The smoke made his eyes water, and the heat singed his eyebrows.

There was the choice.

Go back to the thing that followed him or step into the flames.

That was his choice. So without further ado, he did what he had to do.

47

Her heart seeming to throb in her throat, Ramona mounted the stairs to search for Soo-Lee. She clicked on her trusty Ray-O-Vac and used it to peel back the shadows like layers of blankets on a bed. She studied each one, watching, listening, and feeling for threat. It was close and she knew it, but it wasn't ready to show itself yet. When the time came, she knew, it would spring out of the darkness at her and sink its claws into her throat.

You've pissed off Mother Crow now and she'll have something special waiting for you up here.

As she climbed, she noticed a certain mildewed smell in the air, which was out of place in Stokes. Odors like that were for other towns and the teeming animals that called them home, but not Stokes. Stokes always had a summer scent to it—lilacs and hydrangeas, hibiscus and marigolds. At least in the deluded mind of the spook that could not forget and could never let go.

That's why Ramona noticed it and it gave her pause there on the stairs.

This was the smell of a deserted house, an unused and unoccupied dwelling where the dust formed thick on the windows and desiccated flies piled up on the sills, where the carpets went green with damp rot and black patterns of mold grew over the walls. Such a thing could not be in Stokes, at least Mother Crow's fanciful image of it.

But it was here, and it was growing stronger as if the house were some great gourd that was rotting around her. And maybe it was at that.

The flashlight revealed water-stained wallpaper that was discolored with yellow rings of seepage. It showed her loose ceiling tiles and a dusty floor. She could smell the pungent odors of mice and rat droppings, hear busy creatures gnawing inside the walls. She had to step over the mummified corpse of a little bird with one outstretched wing. Spiders hung boldly in massive webs in the corners.

Interesting.

In Ramona's mind, she could hear Mother Crow's abrasive voice: *I showed you beauty and perfection, but a city whore like you couldn't understand that. So I give you this instead. I give you the filth and abandonment that you know best. I leave you to writhe in your own dirt. This is your element, pig.*

The air was growing cold as Ramona reached the top of the steps. She could see her breath now.

"Soo-Lee?" she called out. "If you're up here, call out! If you don't, I'm leaving!"

She felt a little thrill at that because she knew she was fucking with Mother Crow's carefully laid plans. This whole thing was setup for her benefit. She *had* to go up here. She *had* to see what was waiting for her. Mother Crow would accept nothing less.

She thought she heard a thumping from down the hallway. There was a door there. She approached it, staring at its cobwebbed surface, which was grimy from generations of dirty hands. She knew she was not going to like what the room would show her, but if she turned back now, she would not have been surprised if the stairs were simply gone.

"All right," she said, fear shivering beneath her words. "I'll play your game. Then later, you can play mine."

The door was locked when she gripped the knob. She expected some electrical charge to sweep through her at touching it, but there was nothing. Just an old doorknob on an old door in an old house. Was Mother Crow trying to second-guess *her* now? She had the urge to step back and think this through because this was mind against mind now and she could not afford to make any mistakes.

Bullshit. That's exactly what she expects you to do.

Ramona took a few obligatory steps back, trying to appear unsure and filled with anxiety, which wasn't too hard because that's exactly how she felt. Then she stepped forward and the door was not locked. She threw it open and smelled a warm, meaty reek that reminded her of thawing pork. She panned around with the flashlight, taking in a large bedroom that lacked everything save a metal bed frame tucked in the corner.

"Soo-Lee?" she said.

Something cracked open in the air at that moment and she heard it, though probably only in her mind. She saw an image of an egg cracking open and some furry thing pulling itself out. It was symbolism of some sort and she recognized it as such.

The light picked out a slumped form against the far wall.

"Shit," she muttered, her breath catching in her throat.

At first, she could not say that it was Soo-Lee up against the dirty brick wall. She saw a naked female form, long-legged, a sweep of lustrous black hair hanging over her face. The hair, if nothing else, triggered recognition because she had known very few women outside of fashion magazines that had such beautiful hair. Soo-Lee was dead, of course. She looked deflated, bony and wraith-like as if the skeleton inside her had become more pronounced in death. Her pale skin was speckled with blood. It was even clotted in her hair. And that wasn't too surprising because it looked as if a bomb had gone off inside her, tearing her open from crotch to belly in a dark gash. She sat in a pool of blood. It was splashed up the wall behind her. It even dripped from the ceiling.

Ramona turned away, trying to keep her stomach down.

In a flash that made her head fill with sharp blades of pain, she knew what had happened and she saw it in all its grisly detail. She had to lean up against the doorjamb so she did not pitch straight over.

It came out of her, she thought numbly. *What she carried, the seed that was planted in her and blossomed, it came out of her...no, it chewed its way out of her and she was awake through it all. At least, until the shock and trauma and agony made her pass out.*

Ramona leaned there, what was in the room reaching out to her, striking her in waves of formless black evil. She could barely catch her breath.

(THIS IS WHAT HAPPENS TO CITY SLUTS)

In her head, it echoed and echoed. The pain was unbearable, each word like a razor dragged across her gray matter, slitting her open and making her bleed. *"Please,"* she heard herself say.

(THEY COME TO STOKES, OUR PERFECT TOWN, AND SPREAD THEIR DISEASE WITH THEIR FILTHY CONTAMINATED DIRTY PARTS)

Ramona was down on her knees now. It felt like each word landed with physical force, with impact. Her head felt like it was a bag being worked by a fighter. *Boom-boom, bang-bang.* She was fighting to stay conscious, but Mother Crow was winning. And who was she to stand up against something that could cheat death and re-create an entire town from smoking black ash and gutted ruin?

(THE DIRTY CHINK, TWO-DOLLAR GOOK WHORE, ASKING FOR IT)

"No, no, no, no," Ramona moaned. *"Oh please, please, no more…"*

(BEGGING FOR IT, JUST BEGGING FOR IT, AND SHE GOT IT)

"Shut up!"

(SHE SCREAMED WHEN HE IMPALED HER, WHEN HE RUPTURED THE FOREIGN CUNT AND MADE HER BLEED LIKE HER KIND ALWAYS BLEED IN THE END! SHE SQUEALED AND CRIED OUT AND HE KEPT RAMMING, SPLITTING HER OPEN AND MAKING THE HOT RED FOULNESS WITHIN HER RUN BETWEEN HER LEGS!!!)

Ramona felt anger rising in her and it canceled out the fear and made the pain subside. And she knew it was her only true weapon, the only weapon anyone had in the conformist, meat-grinder, police state of Stokes: free will. Mother Crow could not abide it. She did not like men who thought they were her better and she did not like loose-tongued women who thought they were her equal. People needed to know their place and she had no truck with those that didn't. Questionable morals or independent thinking were enough to get you ejected from the prison camp of Stokes in the old days and now such things were enough to condemn you. And the judge, jury, and executioner were one in the same: a bitter, frustrated, sour-souled, acid-tongued old spinster that no man had ever touched. So since she did not have a man to run and belittle and control with an iron fist, she forced her affections on the town and ran the people like cattle.

"FUCK YOU!" Ramona screamed at her. "FUCK YOU, YOU VICIOUS, FRIGID OLD TWAT! FUCK YOU *AND* FUCK STOKES!"

The house shook and Ramona thought it would come down around her such was the pure wrath of Mother Crow. Nothing hurt worse than the truth. Nothing could possibly cut deeper. And no wound bled as much or refused to be cauterized. There was thunder in the streets and the stench of roasted flesh and burning hair. It cycled through the house in a hot, gagging stink.

When it was gone, Ramona stood there with the light on Soo-Lee while Mother Crow's hate and rage made the town tremble outside the walls of the house. Soo-Lee was like an old pipe that had burst and gushed blood in an ensanguined flood. A dear person with a dear, understanding heart and her death was made ugly and brutal by the old hag.

Ramona would make that evil bitch pay for it.

There were no two ways about that.

It was at that moment that she heard something under the bedframe. A scratching sound like the claws of a rat. But it was no rat. She put the light over there and saw glittering black eyes like those of a Raggedy Ann doll staring out at her.

"So there you are," she said in a beaten voice.

It shifted under there, a darkly evil pygmy-like form that the light could not adequately reveal and maybe that was a good thing. Illumination gleamed off its shoe-button eyes and teeth. Its claws ticked against the floor. Ramona stepped closer to the bed frame, not wanting to see it…but something in her *demanding* that she look upon it like some freak in a sideshow jar. The terror building in her was nearly enough to make her faint dead away.

"Show yourself," she said, her voice sounding determined yet weak.

The thing rustled in the shadows. It made a wet sucking

TIM CURRAN

sound. "*Eeee, eeee, eeee,*" it said with a shrill little voice that went right up her spine. It sounded like a stepped-upon mouse.

She kicked the bed and it scampered away, faster than her light seemed to be able to track it. It ran across Soo-Lee's corpse and splashed through her blood, its nails ticking along like those of a cat that could not retract its claws. The light caught its toothsome grin and a shiny, bulb-like, embryonic head with trailing hair on one side that looked like seaweed.

It thinks you're playing with it, Ramona thought.

The very idea was twisted and horrible, yet she was certain of it. Maybe Mother Crow had thought it all into being, the rape and the pregnancy and the birth, but now that it was alive, it *really* was alive and had a child's sense of play.

It was grotesque to the extreme.

Ramona tried to follow it with her light and it scuttled across the floor, to the left, then the right, then she lost it and felt it slide between her ankles with a hideous weight. *Oh, Christ.* Something told her that such a horror needed to be destroyed, that letting it survive was practically a sin…but she didn't know if she was up to it. The idea of getting close to it made a hot liquid madness run in her mind.

She heard a squeaking noise.

She swung the light around.

It was jumping up and down on the bedsprings, flying five or six feet in the air and then coming back down to repeat it again. It was malformed, lumpy, and squirming like a fetal rat. It leaped off the bed and waited there like it wanted her to try it, too. Ramona was simultaneously filled with horror and pity. She put the light right in its face and it squealed like it had been scalded. It did not like the light as she supposed things like it never did. Its face was wrinkled and deeply seamed, its eyes rolling blank gray balls. When it squealed, its jaws yawned wide and she saw it had two teeth. Each long, sharp, and tusk-like. One on the bottom jaw and one on the upper. Both were stained pink from what it had chewed through to be born. She likened them to the egg teeth of baby birds.

It hid from the light, turning its back to her and she saw protuberant, knobby bones straining against membranous flesh.

It was shivering. As she stepped closer to it, gripping the Ray-O-Vac like a club now, it skidded across the floor, making that same *eeeee, eeeee, eeeeeeee* sort of sound that was tinny and strident.

Ramona went after it and it leaped through the air straight at her face.

She dodged it, but just barely. Even so, its flesh brushed against her cheek and it felt cold and slimy like a dead carp. It struck the wall, but did not fall. It hung there, claws embedded in the plaster. It was breathing very heavily now. As she stepped closer to it, it squeaked and trembled like it was frightened and a glop of pink jelly dropped from its hindquarters as if it had shit itself out of fear.

This was too much.

She was going to leave. Maybe that was wrong and maybe it was even unethical somehow, but she couldn't take any more of this. Her revulsion for the thing was simply too great and if it touched her again, she was going to really lose it.

It craned its head around and looked at her, flashing her a grin of juicy pink gums, its two spike-like incisors looking lethal, made for tearing out jugulars. Its doll eyes watched her, shining and reflective, filled with a naïve idiocy that made her heart ache even as goose bumps broke out over the backs of her arms. She couldn't get past the idea that it was really not a living thing at all, but some horrible prop or loathsome toy.

It thumped its knees against the wall repeatedly. It wanted her to come after it again. It wanted her to try and catch it. Play, it was all just play…yet, she had seen its teeth and claws and they were the sort of things that could play you right to death.

"*Eeeeeee?*" it squeaked.

"No," she said. "No play. I don't have time"

It snapped its teeth at her, drumming itself against the wall. It made a hissing sound like a snake. Long ribbons of drool hung from its mouth. "*Eeeeeeee!*" it squeaked again, but this time there was a definite note of anger and impatience in the shrilling little voice.

Nearly mad with terror, the flashlight shaking in her hand, Ramona backed away toward the door. The hellish little moppet watched her with gleaming eyes. It climbed up the wall, digging in its claws, leaving gaping holes in the plaster.

"*EEEEEEE!*" it shrieked at her. "*EEEEEEE!*"

She wanted to toss the flashlight and cover her ears with her hands because the sound it made completely unnerved her and made a scream loosen in her throat. Sweat ran down her face and the trusty Ray-O-Vac jiggled in her hand. It was up near the ceiling now, hanging there like some mutant simian horror. It closed its mouth and puckered its swollen lips into something like a suckering kiss. Maybe she had lost her mind, but she sensed that it had a certain affection for her. It hung by one claw-hand now, swinging back and forth.

I don't have a mommy now, Ramona. I want you to be my mommy and my playmate and at night I'll curl up next to you and I'll never let go. And when I'm hungry, I'll fasten my mouth to your tit and suck the blood right out of you. You can scream all you want, but once I get my teeth in, you'll never pry me loose!

Those words ran through her head, all inflected with that piercing elfin voice. Fuck this. She went for the door. She couldn't take it anymore. The light splashed over Soo-Lee's gutted corpse and this time she did scream.

The little beast got very excited. It mimicked her scream with a perfectly awful "*EEEEEEEEE!*" and jumped up at the ceiling, again digging its claws in and crossing it quickly like a kid on the monkey bars. Ramona dashed for the door and it slammed shut in her face. She felt claws like the thorns of rose stems tear open her cheek and she fell back, swinging at the little monster with her light. But it was too fast, it dodged away into the darkness and she swung around in a drunken circle with the light, trying to find it. A blur swept past her face with a hot rancid wind and she cried out.

"GET AWAY FROM ME!" she shouted.

But that only delighted the creature and it squealed right back at her, bounding across the floor and nearly knocking the legs out from under her. When she thought she had found it with the light, it was suddenly somewhere else, making her spin around wildly, trying to pinpoint it as a crazy sort of vertigo whirled in her head.

Breathless, dizzy, her face wet with sweat, she saw it on the ceiling, then the walls, then she lost it completely right before its dead weight dropped onto her shoulder and she felt its hot breath against her neck. She dropped the light and reached up to grab it, seizing it in her fists. Its flesh seemed to crawl under her hands and waves of disgust swept through her.

"NO!" she cried as it pressed its monstrous, bloated face into her own, grinning with child-like glee, its carnivore fangs darting out and nipping the end of her nose.

Cold sweat flooded her body, and she went absolutely feral with panic and rage. She peeled it from her and threw it as hard as she could, hearing it strike the wall with a meaty slap. She grabbed up the flashlight and put the beam on it. It was squatted there on the floor, making a perfectly frightful mewling sound. Its head was wet with what had to be blood and she soon saw why. She had injured it. Maybe it *was* alive, but it was still a degenerate hybrid of human tissue and mannequin and its skin was more like a shell. Its head had cracked open like that of a baby doll upon impact with the wall, a piece of its cranium lay at its feet.

Its gray eyes glistened as it looked at her. Its mouth opened and let out an angry roar. Bleeding and broken, it was now an animal and it would fight to survive. It launched itself at her and she knocked it aside with the flashlight. It barely hit the floor before she was kicking and stomping it with everything she had, determined to destroy it. Painfully, mewling, it skittered across the floor, damaged and cracked open, trailing bleeding springs and fleshy stuffing, clockwork gears and a smear of tissue.

"*Eeeeeee,*" it squeaked in a perfectly pitiful little voice. "*Eeeeeeeee-eeee…*"

As Ramona watched, filled with revulsion and remorse, it half crawled and half hopped over to the corpse of its mother. It gripped the splayed thighs, trying to force itself back up into her where, perhaps, it saw safety and security from the big bad world. The slopping sound and gushing fluids as it tried to tunnel into Soo-Lee were too much.

Ramona ran over there, moaning in her throat. The beast

looked up at her accusingly right before she kicked its head off its shoulders. For the longest time she stood there, feeling strangely exhilarated and guilty. But one look at Soo-Lee's blood-spattered face was enough to cure her of the latter. For a few seconds there was a gentle whirring from inside the moppet's trembling body, then it ceased and there was only silence, huge and enveloping.

She moved away toward the door, opening it and stumbling down the corridor. She found the stairs and went down them on rubbery legs, barely able to hold herself up, not properly categorizing what she was feeling at that moment. It seemed to be some unbelievable combination of grief, guilt, and relief. When she got outside, she distanced herself from the house and made it out into the park, where she collapsed on her knees.

She clicked off the light and breathed in and out.

I killed it, she thought. *Yes, I certainly killed it.*

And though she felt that was a necessary thing, it did not make her feel any better because, in its own way, the creature had been a living thing and it had been a child.

After a time, Ramona climbed to her feet and started east again.

48

When Chazz again opened his eyes, he was spread-eagled in midair, hanging twenty feet off the ground in some huge shadowy chamber. He could see skylights far above and pale moonlight washed down over him. He was naked and felt a chill against his skin.

His most immediate thought was: *If I'm dead, how can I feel the cold?*

Which meant that he wasn't dead at all. His last memory was Lady PegLeg holding him up by the ankles like a newborn in a room that looked like a Victorian dissection theater. He remembered the bulbous woman. He remembered Lady Pegleg squeezing his balls…then nothing. Just a blank gray sameness. A sleep without dreams.

With a shudder he tried to reach down between his legs to see if everything was still there, but he couldn't move his arm. In fact, he couldn't move either arm nor his legs or even his body. The best he could do was to crane his head a bit. He was tied-up, roped up in the air in that immense moon-washed room.

Panic washed over him. He was a strong guy, but even he was not strong enough to breaks the bonds that held him. "SOMEBODY!" he shouted out. "SOMEBODY HELP ME! I'M TRAPPED!"

His voice echoed and died, and he wondered if it was such a good idea to be calling out and drawing attention to himself. He was quiet after that, flexing his muscles and making his body move as much as it could, but all that did was make him dangle slightly back and forth. And it was then, as he craned his head, he saw that there were no ropes or cords binding him. No, he was not roped, he was *stuck*. He was adhered to something that he could not break free from.

What the fuck?

What the fuck indeed, because the moonlight showed him that which he did not want to see. He was in a web. He was in a great web of spun silk that was anchored by strands to the walls and the ceiling high above. Disturbing images paraded through his head of the guy in *The Incredible Shrinking Man* fighting the immense house spider for dominance in his diminutive world. Except in this case, he knew with rising hysteria, it was not a spider as such but the thing he called the Spider *Mother*.

Unable to control himself as he went hot and cold, sweating and fighting and straining, he put up an almost superhuman attempt to break free, crying out, sobbing and screaming and finally whimpering.

None of it did him any good.

He had been naïve to think that death and dismemberment at the hands of Lady Pegleg was the worst possible thing. Now he would know true terror and true horror.

Clip-clop, clip-clop, clip-clop.

His breath would barely come now. He inhaled and exhaled in short, spiky bursts. His flesh was crawling from his belly right up to his throat, his scalp tingling and running with perspiration. She was coming now. She had secreted herself in some dark corner or funnel web and now she was coming. Now that he was awake, it would begin.

Clip-clop, clip-clop, clip-clop.

Louder now. Her hundred legs were rapping against the floor below as she returned to her web and the fat, juicy fly that waited for her there. He fought even more frantically now as she approached, wondering in some insane way if flies heard such sounds as spiders bore down upon them with slavering jaws.

CLIP-CLOP! CLIP-CLOP! CLIP-CLOP!

She was nearing the wall now for her climb up to the web and he knew if he didn't break free, it was over. There would be no more head-games with Lady Pegleg, no more Stokes, no more anything. The life he had known before would end in the most macabre and grisly way and he actually saw it as panic and madness and absolute dread fused inside of him. In a white thunderbolt that split open with a flash of light, he saw his life. His shitty, desperate childhood and his sadistic stepmother, the dark confines of the closet, the beatings and burnings and threats and hatred. He saw all of that and then saw it lifted like a veil before his eyes as he was a teenager and he got big and fast and strong and excelled at athletics. And that's what it had always been about. Not rushing for the winning touchdown or banging the ball out of the park or jumping higher or finishing faster…no, that was all candy glaze, it was superficial…what it was *really* about was putting on the speed so he could run as fast and far away from his horrendous childhood as possible. It was the black specter that haunted him. It was the thing in the darkness with upraised claws. It was the shadow that forever reached out for him.

And now here in this awful place, it was not only a spider thrown together out of doll parts that threatened him, but the darkness of his childhood coming at last to get him, to choke the life out of him and smother him with his own secret terror.

CLIPCLOPCLIPCLOPCLIPCLOPCLIPCLOP!!!

She was coming up the wall now and there couldn't possibly be a God above because he or she would have stopped this. No, there was no supernatural father figure up in the sky because if there truly was, all those kids wouldn't have died in the concentration camps or starved to death or been kidnapped and beaten and raped and molested and murdered. There was no God, only chaos. God was created because people needed something to believe in, something that would convince them they weren't meaningless crawling insects and that there really was some fairy tale wonderland beyond the pale of death and not a formless void without end.

Chazz laughed at these realizations, these truths and certainties that had come to him here in his final hour. They could have enriched him and empowered him and sculpted him into a decent, caring person had they come before but they had never been able to break through the wall of fear, arrogance, and frustration that he had built around himself.

"I KNOW NOW!" he cried out. "I REALLY HONESTLY KNOW NOW!"

But by then the Spider Mother had mounted her web and the entire network trembled with oscillating waves, the individual strands sounding like plucked violin strings as she neared him. *Plink-plink, plunk-plunk-plink.* He saw then that he was not alone in the web. It was strung with dozens and dozens of well-gnawed, well-juiced, and well-stripped carcasses of men, women, and children. He could smell their viscid death-stink and it was like maggoty carrion was rubbed in his face.

The gossamer cables of the web were shaking badly now and he could feel the freezing shadow of the spider horror approaching him, knowing it was the embodiment of man's primal fears, the seed of the fear of the unknown. This was it.

And then it was hovering over him, an immense abstract sculpture knitted together out of mannequin legs and doll arms and puppet heads, bones and sheaths of silk and dripping spider spit. It whirred and clicked and hissed. Death vapors blew out of its many black mouths that puckered open and closed, ropy tangles of saliva falling from them into his face and burning, God, *searing* like acid and Chazz screamed as he felt the tissues of his chin and cheeks dissolving.

I won't go out like this! a voice in his mind bellered. *I will not die like this! I...REFUSE!*

The agony of it all made him give one last Herculean effort, and he managed to get one hand free that he tore at the Spider Mother with, batting aside crawling snakes of silk and tearing open clusters of bulging egg sacs that burst like water balloons, spilling jellied slime over him.

Still, he fought.

He wrenched a grasping doll arm out of its socket, shattered a grinning puppet face and pummeled the Spider Mother until his knuckles bled. She had pushed a dozen hollow-eyed mannequin faces out at him and he punched them, smashing his fist into them, knocking some back, cracking others open and making them open their hinged jaws and scream at him. He was hurting her; he knew that. She was screeching and mewling and shaking.

If only it's enough...

He kept at it, completely out of his head, until his knuckles broke and the skin was sheared from them. And the only thing that really stopped him was the crowding faces that opened their black, dripping mouths and sprayed him with sticky threads of silk that were very much like Silly String. They netted his face and webbed his bloody, broken hand. They were wet and elastic and burning, their tensile strength unbelievable.

She had him.

He had hurt her, but now she had him and he was helpless. One of the mannequin faces hinged open like a clamshell. A fleshy proboscis emerged, horridly phallic and pulsing. The end of it puckered open like a tiny mouth and a surgically fine black needle emerged. She jabbed it into his throat and, as she did so, other mouths produced similar proboscises and likewise jabbed him. Numbed by toxins, Chazz hung there limply as the Spider Mother began to suck his blood with a perfectly ghastly sound of children sucking milk through straws. She siphoned off enough to take the fight out of him and by then he was flaccid and partially cocooned, whimpering out of fright and madness.

"Now, Mr. Man," she said in a dozen smooth, silky, and blatantly sensual voices. *"You've been promised to others and it's my job to dole out your good parts."*

The mannequin heads parted like a sea and a set of mandibles emerged like a set of gigantic scissors. They were chitinous things, snipping open and closed, their inside edges set with razor blades. The Spider Mother took what Lady Pegleg and the bulbous woman wanted first: his manhood. They darted in and snipped his balls and cock free and Chazz screamed with a high, wailing sound that was amplified in the huge chamber, echoing and coming back at him. His breath came in great gurgling, pained gasps as he screamed and screamed again.

There must have been an audience down there somewhere because he heard what seemed hundreds of voices moan with pleasure: *OOOOOOOOOHHHHHH....*

The Spider Mother was throbbing with ecstasy by that point, her mouths blowing out hot plumes of steam and things inside her—gears and motors, cogs and red-hot bearings—whirring and whining and squealing.

Chazz was still crying out, though his strength was fast ebbing. As the blood gushed from between his legs, countless swollen pink tongues emerged from the spider's underside and greedily lapped it up. Still, he continued to thrash in his silken harness, mouth shrieking and head snapping from side to side, his eyes bulging like they were going to blow from their sockets.

She snipped off his left arm and then his right.

AAAAAAAAAHHHHHHHHH, moaned the voices.

By then he was fading fast, hearing the voices and his own screams and feeling his life draining away as she nipped and licked him, drilling him with stingers and opening him with glistening, busy mouth parts like sheaths of surgical knives.

The last thing she took was his still-beating heart, ripping it from his chest like a bulb from black soil, holding its pumping, bloody mass up for all to see before dropping it below to anxious outstretched hands.

By then, Chazz knew no more.

49

Ramona stood on the road, staring up at the factory on the hill and a deep chill settled into her bones. Even if she hadn't known that this was the evil core of Stokes, she would have felt it. The factory brooded atop the hill like a poison mushroom, seeping toxic juices that blighted the countryside and filled the town below with venom. This was it. This was the malignancy that needed to be cut out, torn up by the roots and burned to ash. The nucleus of the tumor itself and she was about to drive right into it like a hot needle.

She was not unexpected.

She knew that much.

Mother Crow did not want her here. In fact, she feared it as Ramona herself feared the idea of coming in the first place. That was what they had in common: fear *and* rage. Because they both stood ready to fight to the death and neither would back down.

This was endgame.

Resolutely then, Ramona started up the drive to the factory.

And things began to change just as they had in the park. Reality was warping, unzipping itself and she smelled smoke. Yes, the thick, pungent smoke of the burning town. She heard something like a muffled explosion and the factory ahead of her literally split right open, gushing flames and huge rolling clouds of ash.

It started here. The fire started here at the factory and swept down into the town. That's what happened.

There was no way she could know that, but the certainty remained: it had started here and she was seeing it. Regardless of what Mrs. McGuiness said, it had not started in the town. It had started right here.

The sky above was lit by a red glare, and waves of heat rolled down at her as the trees to either side of the road burst into flame. The field was burning and the factory was engulfed in tongues of flame, and she could hear people screaming. She looked behind her and watched the town down there burn. It was an amazing conflagration and nothing was spared. It looked like a bonfire. She turned her gaze back to the factory. It was broken and mangled, immense walls of flame rising into the night. There was another explosion and then another from its blazing guts and things rained from the sky: slats of burning wood, smoldering bricks, and fiery bits of metal. The factory was giving up its ghost, and this is what it vomited up in its death throes.

The heat was enough to roast her, but Ramona pushed on, untouched by any of it. She stepped through smoldering ash four inches deep, moving around pieces of the burning factory, parting sheets of churning smoke. The factory erupted again and more debris rained down into the fields of cinders. She thought they were parts of corpses, but they were not corpses but doll parts and mannequin parts. She saw grinning melted faces and blackened heads, limbs and bodies. Things welded together by the heat, human-shaped armatures whose plastic and wax flesh was bubbling and oozing free. It all continued to burn and she realized the screaming she heard was not that of people, but from the dolls themselves...their charred and blistered mouths were crying out into the night, rising in a single wavering note of agony.

But dolls can't scream. Mannequins and puppets can't know pain, a voice of reason informed her. *But I'm hearing it. I'm hearing something.*

Then...it all faded, and it was daylight many years later, and the factory was in ruins around her. Why was she being shown this? But there were no answers, so she quit asking questions and let it happen, soaking it all up. The remains were scattered everywhere like bones in a field after a great battle. Bricks were caught in the tangled grass, crumbling walls of them and teetering cairns from which saplings grew. Great crawling shadows were cast by the looming skeleton of the factory itself, gathering in dark pockets and nighted hollows. A spooky, pervasive silence shivered in the air. She could hear a creak of metal in the wind somewhere, maybe an old rain gutter or a loose piece of tin.

Two smokestacks still stood, rising from the blackened wreckage like fleshless fingers, one straight and tall, the other leaning to the side like it might tip over at any time. Crows held court atop them, spreading their wings and cawing. Scrub brush had grown up everywhere, heaps of debris becoming hills of wild weeds and devil grass. She heard creatures scurrying about, birds calling out.

The closer she got to the factory, the more wreckage there was.

More bricks and rotted planks and old smoke-blackened timbers, but also rusty machine parts, girders, conduits and iron piping in which swallows nested. She stepped around the remains of a third smokestack that had fallen and was netted by weeds. Huge gears rose from the earth like the backs of fossil saurians. The factory had fallen into itself, filling vast pits and cellarholds below in junk heaps of twisted iron, collapsed walls, and a multitude of tiles that reminded her of flakes of skin.

And yet again, she had to wonder, *why am I being shown this?*

But the answer was obvious now. Mother Crow had shown her the fire and its aftermath as if to pound into her head that whatever had lived (or existed) in the factory was long gone now. The fire had neutered it and made it harmless. It was all just a memory now and the entire area was a graveyard. There was no danger here. Ramona should go back into the town. That's where the real threat was.

But Ramona, of course, wasn't buying it.

She wasn't buying any of it.

Approaching the hulk of the factory and stepping into its black shadow, she could almost hear it sigh with displeasure.

She opened the door and went in.

Because it was time.

50

Where are you going, doll-face? And what are you going to do when you get there? said a voice of scraping metal. *Do you know who you'll see and what they will say to you?*

Creep pressed himself to the wall of this place that could not be but was real enough to touch. He had been escaping a doll thing down a black corridor that should have led into the hub, as he thought of it, but did not lead there...unless it had and he was there because who really knew and nothing made a lick of sense anyway.

He waited, thinking, *I should escape it before it finds me.*

But escape where? That was the question. The voice was inside his head, yes, but it was also in front of him and behind him and to all sides, it seemed.

Don't you worry and don't you fret, little doll-face, because you ain't seen nothin' yet, the voice said, giggling.

That's when the lights started coming on. Not good clean electric lights, of course, but wavering orange-yellow lights like those of huge antique tapers. The sort that threw greasy shadows and created pockets of writhing darkness. But light was light and Creep was content with anything he could get. The corridor was more along the lines of a circular industrial tunnel, he saw now, set with aluminum conduits bolted to the walls that must have held electric lines or steam piping, something of that sort, heavy ducts overhead.

Not knowing what else to do, he moved on and soon the tunnel widened and he began to see...at first he did not know what they were only that there were many of them crowded along the walls. He looked closer to all sides and saw that they were molds, casting molds of the sort that were used to thermoform plastic parts. They were all hinged like clamshells, standing open. He saw molds for hands and feet, legs and torsos, arms and heads, a variety of faces all carefully machined or carved from aluminum. They looked like death mask impressions. He saw others, molds taller than he was, that were full-body molds—one section had a perfect hollow of a mannequin back and the other that closed over it, a hollow of the mannequin front. When the thing was closed, hot plastic or some other material would be injected into it and, when it cooled, it could be opened and there would be a perfect life-size doll.

As he walked along, he saw dozens of these.

Some for men, others for women and even children. Looking at them and thinking about what they might turn out, Creep began to shiver, and then he began to sweat. Though he was hot and feverish, the sweat that rolled down his face was cool to the touch. It had a foul, yellow smell to it that sickened him. This was the odor of the human machine poisoned out by the bile of its own fright, dementia, and horror. This is the stuff that ran from you, he knew, when all hope was gone and you were fundamentally fucked in every conceivable way. Men who walked to the gallows or the electric chair probably sweated out corruption like that. He had never smelled anything like it before and he supposed most people only did once—right before they died.

C'mon, doll-face, stop thinking. You're no good at it. And, besides, you're almost there, you're getting real close to who you came to meet.

The voice kept taunting him, but Creep stumbled on blindly, obediently. He saw no reason now to argue his fate or try to run from it. Who he had been his entire life, he was not now. He would go where the voice suggested and he would see what waited there, because there really was no alternative.

As he walked and the molds became more numerous, piled against one another in heaps until he could no longer see the walls themselves, he heard the voice telling him how close he was. Then, he saw the owner of the voice. Even though he trembled with terror, he was not really surprised.

Danielle was hanging from the wall.

Not really Danielle, but the same horror he'd seen on the
TV at that house, Danielle remade as a doll—a pallid and naked
thing, her limbs swiveled at the joints, her smallish breasts like
pert mounds with nipples that were shiny pearls. The gash
between her legs seemed to throb with vitality, swollen and juicy
like a ripe peach. Her flesh was textured burlap, formfitting, but
not lying on what was below quite right as if she were a snake
gradually sloughing its skin. Her chest rose and fell as if she
really needed to breathe.

Look at me, doll-face, she said, her hinged jaw mocking speech.
As I am, you will soon be.

Her blonde hair was lustrous and shining, but like a wig it
seemed to be coming loose from the white scalp beneath, shifting
off to the side. One eye was a black pit, the other gleamed like
a moonstone, opalescent and milky. It was recessed from the
masklike face, blank yet hideously alive.

Creep thought of running. It was purely instinctive, but it
was the only thing he could think of doing.

No, no, not now, the Danielle-thing hissed. *Not when you've
come so far.*

It writhed on the hook that suspended it, straight waxen
lips pulling back from tiny teeth that were like jagged kernels
of corn. She kept squirming, something inside her wriggling
obscenely like a Slinky in a sock. If he did not obey her, Creep
knew, she would climb down and show him exactly what was
beneath her skin. Maybe she would make him touch it and he
did not want that, oh God, anything but that.

Go see who waits for you, doll-face, Danielle said, but by then, he
was already doing so. Tears spilled from his eyes and his teeth
chattered, his hands shaking so badly he had to press them to
his sides to hold them still. His eyes felt dry and scratchy, but he
did not dare blink. In the blink of an eye the most malign things
could happen in this place.

Go, doll-face, show her what you're made of...she'll like that.

"No!" he hollered, some last fragment of free will and
survival instinct kicking up its heels inside him. "I won't go
and there's nothing you can do that will make me!"

He felt good saying that. Hell, he felt empowered

and determined and resilient in the face of this god-awful nightmare…but he was still walking forward. Maybe there was a last struggling fragment of defiance in his mind, but nobody had told his body about it and onward it went to keep a meeting with revelation and doom.

The perfectly disturbing part about it all, was that he could not stop.

His body would not respond. His somatic nervous system had been hijacked and he was no longer in charge of his own body. He was just a rider now like a man on a bus. He no longer had control…yet, he could speak, he could move his lips, his head, his arms, but he could not stop the forward progression of his feet.

It was insane.

Desperate now, he slapped himself in the face with one hand after the other until his cheeks were red and burning, until pain and confusion made tears run. But none of it shocked him out of it and there didn't seem to be a damn thing he could do about that.

There comes a time, the Danielle-thing informed him, *when all choices are made for us and happy we are for it.*

Creep had a powerful need to tell her to shut the fuck up because she wasn't even human anymore. She hadn't been much before, but she was even less now and he wanted to find a nice five-pound ball-peen hammer and smash her to pieces. God, it was crazy, but the idea of pulverizing her was sexually exciting… not that any of that really mattered because he was still moving down the tunnel to his fate and the realization of that made everything else seem pretty damn insignificant.

The tunnel was gradually widening.

And it was getting warm.

Creep was perspiring freely now. Some of that was fear and anxiety, but not all of it. The heat was palpable, rising a few degrees at a time. The air felt hot in his throat, difficult to breathe. It was about then, as sweat began to drip off the end of his nose, that he heard a rushing/roaring sound like hot water gurgling through a high-pressure pipe and the entire tunnel began to quake. The rushing noise got louder. The tunnel felt like it was in motion.

What the fuck?

Now it was filling with a churning white steam like the sort of thing that a whistling teakettle blows out. It came on in a hissing, rolling cloud. And even if Creep had been able to turn and flee, he would never have escaped it. The steam hit him, engulfed him, and the pain of being seared was instantaneous. He hit the floor and bounced off the walls, hurting and gagging, but knowing that as painful as it was, it was not lethal.

The steam was not enough to kill him.

He heard a thrumming sound and something came out of the tunnel, which had grown quite large now. Whatever it was—and he could see very little of it—it came charging out at him like a phantom from the fog, grim and hulking and horribly industrial, bringing heat and noise and the hot pig iron smell of a foundry. It was a machine becoming flesh or flesh becoming machine. A deranged biomechanical thing that was assembled from yellowed rungs and knobs of bone that protruded from a riveted shell of discolored canvas-like skins, a machine of corpses and wriggling doll parts set with hissing vacuum lines and bulging pneumatic hoses, a great steel bear trap of a mouth that was a 5,000-psi cutting ram.

And above it, like a hag broken on a wheel, he saw a mummy with whipping white hair, a living death mask grinning and cackling.

These were the things Creep thought he saw as it seized him and pulled him into itself, as his hands and feet were impaled by spiked drive chains that carried him into a core of boiling smoke where an immense buzz-saw split him from his crotch to the crown of his head in a gushing baptism of his own blood and meat.

51

Lex heard Chazz's final death-scream, though he did not know who it was. The scream echoed and faded, but there was no doubt which direction it came from and that was exactly where he went: to seek its source. He felt his way along the walls, knowing that at any moment a pair of gnarled puppet hands might reach out for him, but he didn't think they would. Not just yet. He was being drawn into this place to meet the puppet master and he would not be denied that.

He made it to the hub, which was partially lit by moonlight streaming in through skylights some three stories above. He couldn't see too much as his eyes adjusted. Just enough to see lots of gleaming machinery and to recognize that the hub was like a cylinder that went up and up. It was an immense chamber and he knew it was the puppet master's lair. There was a hot, charnel stench in the air that was sickening.

Now pale blue phosphorescence began to illuminate his surroundings.

The walls were set with a veritable industrialized maze of tubing and dirty gray conduits, metal ductwork and what looked like spiraled ribs jutting forth that seemed to be in slow clockwise and counterclockwise motion like gears of some sort…and gears they indeed were because he saw that he was in the heart of what seemed to be a clock. It was insane, but he was seeing it. How much was real and how much was subjective, he couldn't be sure. He only knew that he was inside the puppet master now.

Stokes was a physical reality she or *it* had created, an idealized homage to a town that probably never really existed in the first place, at least not in the way Lex had seen it tonight.

The town was a physical projection of psychic or mental energy, but the factory…well, that was the flesh and blood of the puppet master. If the town was its mind, then this was its body…and this chamber was its heart.

A clock.

Why not? The doll people seemed to operate in some way or another like clockwork toys, so why not the puppet master as well?

Sighing among the eerie and abnormal grandeur of it all, Lex shook his head. He could sit here and speculate for hours, but the truth, the real truth of all this would probably be denied to him. He had come for a reason and he had to see that through.

Yet…this place was fascinating. A living machine. The spiraling ribs that made up the walls were rotating slowly but constantly, kept in perpetual motion by the immense mainspring and swinging collection of pendulums high above, which in turn moved the immense toothed escape wheels of the clock train, pinions, levers, and ratcheting mechanisms. Minute wheels and hour wheels were in precise calibration, keeping the biorhythms of the machine in perfect balance. And everywhere, the elaborate gear trains clicking and grinding and meshing—driver gears and worm gears and spur gears. Like the anatomy of a flesh-and-blood organism, none of it ever stopped, ever rested, ever even slightly varied in sequence or the result would be total chaos and the end of the machine that powered Stokes and the puppet master who lorded over all.

Destroy it, Lex thought, *and you destroy the puppet master.*

He edged farther into the room, stepping over tangled electrical lines and steam hoses that moved against one another with sliding, slithery sounds like mating pythons. He ducked beneath revolving cylinders and around hydraulic rams, his ears humming with the clanking of gear boxes, red-hot bearings, spiked drive chains, and thrumming generator shafts. He kept moving, but moving carefully because it was a dangerous place, a surreal nightmare of a factory in which everything slammed and hissed and whirred, hungry toothed and razored chains anxious to pull the unwary beneath presses where they could be processed properly. High-voltage lines sparked, vats bubbled, steam pissed out through cracks in hoses, and great jagged hooks swung through the air, seeking flesh to impale.

The heat of it all was nearly unbearable. A mist of oil and grease rained in the air that was clogged with smoke and nearly unbreathable. Beyond the odors of lubricants, hot iron, wax and melted plastic, there was a darker odor, an ever-present slaughterhouse stench of well-marbled meat, blood and marrow and burnt hair.

Then he saw the machine.

Maybe it was what he had been looking for the entire time.

But was it real? Was any of this real? Yes, it all had physical dimensions and all of it could slash you open, crush you, scald you, electrocute you, or boil the skin from your bones, but that did not make it real.

And the machine not twenty feet from him could not possibly be real.

It was forty feet long at least, machined out of some black metal that was knobbed and ribbed, gaping with chasms and spiraling protrusions. At the back end of it he saw men, women, and children lined up like stock. One by one, they gave themselves to the machine and grinding spiked wheels pierced their hands and fed them into its labyrinthine depths. Through mesh fine as wires, he could see spinning saws slicing them open and dragging the bloodied halves into a boiling vat where they were rendered to a superheated liquid that was fed by transparent arteries into a great aluminum press that smoldered and whined with gouts of escaping gas. The mold was cooled and when it opened at the other end with billowing clouds of steam, a doll person stepped out and joined ranks of other synthetic people that stood around like gape-jawed mummies in a Mexican catacomb.

Lex blinked his eyes again and again.

He didn't believe for a moment that this was how they were made, but something wanted him to and he had to fight against an impulse to join the others at the feeder end.

It was then he looked straight up through dissipating clouds of hot vapor and saw an immense web up there, a spider's web, but made of some pink silk that looked oddly like needle-thin sections of human skin. A man was crucified up there. He was dismembered, but all parts of his anatomy were arranged in comparative relation to one another.

Lex knew it was Chazz.

And as some immense spidery horror of wriggling doll parts hovered over the dismembered man and jabbed him with needles, he was certain of it. He could even hear his voice: *"God...God...God...help me...oh please let me die..."*

Lex was speechless, struck dumb by such an atrocity.

At least, until his own mouth opened and he heard his voice say, "You're being pulled into this...you're making this dark fantasy real...you're getting weak..."

Yes, he blinked it away and concentrated and it was only then that he noticed something that had escaped him thus far—everything in the factory maze was connected with gossamer web-like filaments. Every piece of machinery, every gear, wheel, and press was connected to something that was coming out of the darkness now, racing out of it, an immense black shape connected to what seemed millions of white filaments like a gruesome puppet with a thousand strings.

It was time to meet the master of the maze.

52

Close now, so goddamn close.

Ramona was nearing the axis of chaos and she could feel the dark magnetism of it pulling her in just as it simultaneously tried to force her away. She was afraid of it and it was afraid of her, only she did not know why and she feared she would die before she found out. In the distance there were the loud industrious sounds of a foundry—clanking and gnashing, snapping and popping, metal grinding against metal and an ever-present hissing of hot gases.

The corridor would lead her there.

Step by step, she was closer.

Thoughts scurried through her head, things she did not want to be thinking about but kept sprouting like weeds nonetheless. This night had been endless. It might have been going on for hours or days now. Time had lost all meaning here in the devil's playground. She knew the fate of Soo-Lee, and Creep was probably dead, too. Same for Danielle. But she wondered about Lex. She even wondered about Chazz. She still had feelings for him—struggling, fleeting things though they were—and she wondered if he was still alive.

But a voice in her head said simply, *No. He was physically strong but mentally weak and morally corrupt. Once you stripped away his muscles and good looks, there wasn't anything beneath but a frightened whiny little boy and you know it. Easy prey for Mother Crow.*

Ramona wasn't going to think about him anymore.

He was gone. He had to be gone.

And what they had had been gone even longer.

She scanned the corridor with her light. She was heading in the right direction; her instincts assured her of this. The floor was messy, unlike the rest of the town. Did that mean anything? Where was the precision, the sterility, the obsessive neatness you saw in the streets? Underfoot was a carpet of leaves, cigarette butts, candy wrappers, metal shavings, wood splinters, and an extremely aged water-stained copy of *Playboy*. There were gray doors set in the walls. One said PRODUCTION SUPERVISOR and another PLANT MANAGER. Something brown and crusty like old shit had been rubbed on them. Maybe it was blood.

At the very end there was a large six-paneled oak door. Very elegant compared to the others. It was shiny, well-waxed and polished. It gleamed like a table in a Pledge commercial. There was a plaque on the door. It read:

MOTHER CROW
PRESIDENT

Ramona knew it probably hadn't said anything like that back in 1960 or the decades preceding. But there it was, black letters emblazoned on a gleaming brass plaque. MOTHER CROW, PRESIDENT. She was struck by the absurdity of it. Could it possibly have said something like that back in the day? Was the old lady that crazy, that arrogant, that full of herself? But the answer to that was obvious. The hag thought she owned the town. She had cursed the fleeing workers when the orders dried up at the factory. She had fucking *survived* death and created this sideshow.

Yes, the old lady had certainly been that crazy, that arrogant, and that full of herself. Typical despot. Typical tyrant. Typical matriarch of a fallen dynasty. MOTHER CROW, PRESIDENT. It was enough to make you fucking puke. In fact, it was enough to—

Wait.

It didn't say *Mother* Crow now. It said something else:
RAMONA CROW,
PRESIDENT

That made Ramona take a step or two backward. A sick joke perpetrated by a sick mind. She realized then that the old lady could have insulted her, her mother, her entire family and

Ramona would have shrugged it off. But this was more than an insult, it was disturbing. It was like having the old hag cackling in her ear with her sour old lady breath.

"Stop it," Ramona said.

But the plaque persisted: RAMONA CROW, PRESIDENT.

"FUCK YOU!"

RAMONA CROW, PRESIDENT AND CEO, it now said.

"STOP IT!"

RAMONA CROW, MAKER AND UNMAKER, CREATOR AND DESTROYER.

She rubbed her fists against her eyes to make it go away, but it would not go away. Mother Crow had found a weak nerve and she was going to work it, nip it, pluck it, yank on it. And the pain was nearly physical, but more so it created a building misery in Ramona, a bottomless grief, a black chasm of despair.

Do it, she ordered herself.

She moved quickly down the hallway to the door. That's how you did it in this place: if something scared you or filled you with anguish, you charged it dead on. She gripped the doorknob and threw it open. She took a step into the room, expecting some austere and utilitarian sort of office, something harsh and puritanical to fit in with the mechanistic mind of Mother Crow, but instead she found a workshop.

There were tables heaped with mannequin parts, of course. But by that point, Ramona was not really frightened of them. You could only see so many snakes before they lost their shock value.

You lie, God, how you lie.

She studied the racks of tools and instruments on the pegboards along the walls. They were hung with gleaming probes, long silver needles, loops of sutures and catgut, clamps and saws and knives of every description. Spools of wire and exotic looking pulleys sidled up to bone screws and forceps, ball sockets and swivels, iron rods and gears. Another pegboard held faces, eyeless and jawless, things of wood and plastic and wax waiting to be fixed to some dire living machinery. There was a wall of eyeballs pinned to a corkboard. They were in every color. She expected them to watch her, to follow her like eyes in old paintings, but they were only glass orbs. A fire hose was coiled on the wall, next to it an axe painted red.

The accoutrements of firefighting would of course be prevalent here in Mother Crow's reimagining of this place, Ramona knew.

There was a pull string dangling from the ceiling and she pulled it, half expecting to see a dozen ghoulish marionettes drop down in a jerking dance macabre, but the only thing that happened was that a light came on. It was an old-fashioned thing with a funnel-shaped shade that directed the light downward. It seemed to create more shadows than it dispelled. It lit up the contents of the table, but beyond its illumination was like the edge of the known universe where formless night things hopped and crawled in bleak nonexistence.

There was a door at the far end of the room and that's where she was going.

She made it a few feet before she bumped into something hanging from the ceiling that she was certain had not been there a moment before. She gasped, shining her light around and whatever it was—her mind had a quick flash image of an articulated Halloween skeleton—dropped to the floor with a clattering noise.

Breathing hard now, wary, she put her light on it.

It was Creep.

Not the real Creep, but a doll version of him that had fallen apart when it struck the floor. There was his torso, a detached arm, a detached hand, an eyeball that had rolled across the floor. He was just a heap of parts. His head had no hair, his cranium was seamed like the monster in an old Frankenstein movie (for the ease of brain transplants, perhaps).

"They only got you because you let them," Ramona found herself saying. "You didn't fight, Creep. You went with what they offered. You looked for an easy way out. I'm sorry."

The parts began to tremble, then to rattle.

They were alive and part of her had suspected as much. The heap that was Creep began to sluggishly crawl across the floor in a loose jumble, and Ramona heard a high tittering in the back of her head like the insane laughter of a madwoman locked in an attic room. She had seen worse…yet, this collection of abstract humanity was like white ice cracking open inside her. She was dancing precariously on the edge of a full-blown nervous breakdown. The most alarming part was not the clattering progress of the parts or the thumping roll of the head itself, but the eyeball that rolled behind and the foot that hopped along in pursuit. As demented as it was, had it been a cartoon, it might have offered some morbid comedy.

But there was nothing funny about that heap of disjointed parts.

And there was nothing remotely amusing about how they began to stir in a whirlwind, jumping and rattling and spinning in the air before striking the floor again…then putting themselves together in proper order. Like a child stacking blocks, the Creep thing assembled itself. When it was finished, it stood there stiffly like a window dummy, swaying slightly back and forth.

Then it began to breathe in and out, chest rising and falling.

Something like a black leech slid between the lips and licked them. There was a tearing sound and a single eye winked open with a puff of dust. It looked over at Ramona with barely concealed lust.

"*Dolly, dolly, dolly,*" the Creep puppet said. The voice was his…nearly, but with a dry, rasping caliber to it like a rusty nail head scraped over concrete. "*My dolly's name is Ramona and with her I shall play.*"

Click-clacking, it stepped in her direction, reaching out with white fingers lacking nails. Bits of them flaked off like loose plaster. The flaccid penis between the legs rose up, hard as a tent stake. It was throbbing. As Creep stood there, breathing harder and faster, a gout of drool ran from his lips to his chin. And his wooden penis—if wood it was—became positively engorged until it was as large as the Ray-O-Vac in Ramona's hand. The head was pink and shiny, except it wasn't a human glans but a pulsating baby doll head whose pink, blubbery lips opened and said, "*Ma-ma, ma-ma, ma-ma,*" in a squeaking doll voice.

Ramona was shaking all over.

Madness scratched inside her skull and she had the urge to

laugh hysterically. Was this horror or humor or both or neither and why was she shaking uncontrollably and gooseflesh crawling up her spine and down the back of her arms?

Creep stepped forward and there was no doubt what was on his agenda, which, of course, was the agenda of Mother Crow: what better way to debase, defile, and destroy Ramona than to have her violated by a fucking puppet? It had worked wonders with Soo-Lee.

Ramona wanted to step back, but she faced her fears even though it felt like her guts were crawling with slinking white worms that were sliding up into her chest. Creep reached out for her and she batted his hand aside with the flashlight. His mouth split into a grimace and he clawed out at her, but she was faster. She brought the cylinder of her trusty Ray-O-Vac around in an arc and struck him dead in the face.

He did not go down.

In fact, all he did was swing back and forth as if held aloft by strings she could not see. He swung in her direction and his fingers scraped along her breast. She smashed him with the light again and he swung away, picking up momentum to come swinging back, his leering mouth seeming to say, *You silly twat, I can play this game all night. Back and forth, back and forth I go. You'll get tired and when you get tired, I'll move in closer because you're my fuck toy and I'm going to treat you like a fuck toy, my sweet little dolly.*

The thing was, Ramona could hear his voice inside her head, each word seeming to gain volume.

She smashed him again as he got his hands in her hair and yanked out a strand. She batted him away and he swung away into the darkness and faster, it seemed, than the light could track him. He was getting the entire room worked up. All the parts were beginning to wriggle. They wanted to get off tables and free themselves from hooks.

She ducked under him and he giggled with a piercing, gleeful sound. He swung back around, fixing her with his single glaring eyeball, which seemed to be bulging from the socket like a duck egg.

She sidestepped him and felt the head of his penis brush her arm, the baby doll mouth now lined with teeth like fishhooks that drew blood. They were chattering with a dead, hollow sound like a skull in a catacomb. *Clickety-clickety-clickety-clickety.* Gravity should have ground him to a halt or at least slowed him a bit, but it did neither. The Creep puppet began to move faster and faster with slicing pendulum strokes, zipping past her. She couldn't get out of his way fast enough. His fingers clawed her. The head of his bulbous, bright red penis nipped at her. The needling teeth chattered and with such volume she thought she would lose her mind.

CLICKETY-CLICKETY-CLICKETY-CLICKETY-CLICKETY-CLICKETY!

When he came around again, he knocked the Ray-O-Vac out of her hand and it rolled under the table, going out. There was no time to retrieve it. He would have had her the moment she tried. Now it was just the two of them and that circle of light concentrated on the moving doll parts on the table. She could hear him giggling in the surrounding darkness, but she could not see him. The door wasn't far away, but she knew she'd never make it...not without a rider mounting her from behind.

The Creep puppet came out of the darkness with a swooping sound like an owl seeking a mouse. His penis was standing hard and perversely bloated, streaking at her like a surface-to-air missile. She dodged past him and he disappeared into the darkness, giggling. Panicking, she dashed for the door and he struck out at her like a shark coming out of the depths, his fingers tearing her shirt up the back and scraping slivers of skin free.

When he came at her again, she sidestepped him, then knocked the light aside so it swung back and forth, disorienting her and hopefully him. He came after her and crashed into a pegboard. He made a growling sound and came again, but when he did, Ramona jumped out at him with the fire axe in both hands. Before he could slow his descent, the axe was in flight. It caught him in the head, splitting his face wide and his puppet body immediately struck the floor, its invisible wires sheared.

Ramona, axe held to strike, bore down on him.

Creep reassembled himself. It was like watching a film run

in reverse. He was standing between her and the door and she planned on going right through him, but she never got the chance. As Creep stepped out to meet her, the door behind him flew open...then blew right off its hinges, taking a good section of the wall with it.

Even Creep hadn't been expecting this.

What stepped through the hole in the wall was the apex horror: Frankendoll.

It was back.

A hideous, gargantuan mass of writhing doll flesh that throbbed and pulsated, roiling and grotesquely alive. It stepped forward on a dozen legs, a multitude of mannequin and puppet faces screaming and crying out in death agonies. Ramona recognized the new additions: Soo-Lee, Chazz, and Danielle.

Now it wanted Creep.

If a puppet could look frightened, he did. He tried to shamble forward and a brace of arms shot forward like greased pistons, fists and claws tearing into him, raking him apart with hooked nails. The Creep puppet cried out as it was pulled apart and ingested, assimilated into the mass like a corpse fed into a wood chipper. He sank away and then his white face pressed back out, joining the other ghost faces that hung from the creature's chest like swollen polyps.

Still clutching the axe, Ramona made a mad dive for her flashlight.

Face your fears. Overcome them, a voice instructed her. *Do not empower them.*

But looking up at the howling, shrieking, grinning faces of Frankendoll, it was not so easy. They looked like fetish masks carved from teak and pitted driftwood, eye sockets gouged deep into blackness, mouths cut into jagged sawtoothed holes, noses hacked into the triangular hollows of skulls. They reminded her of the leering faces of Japanese temple demons. Some were whole, others split apart by the birth of yet another head, still others had divided like cells. And for every complete head, there was a cluster of fetal, unformed knobs sprouting around it. Some with mewling mouths and others with a single eye, and some that were nothing but toothy hungry chasms.

"It's our Ramona come back to us," a choir of voices sang, discordant and moaning, squeaking and shrilling like the pipes of a poorly tuned church organ. *"Bring her to us. A place has been prepared, let our queen reign from high above."*

As if proof of that, two mannequin heads at the very apex of the creature parted to show Ramona the place of honor and glory her head would decorate.

Think! she commanded herself. *There's got to be a way out of this! There's got to be a way to fight!*

But the fight was nearly gone from her.

She just didn't have much left.

Frankendoll stood there, its glistening jellied flesh shifting with a near-constant osmotic motion, tissue draining away and filling hollows, leaving gaping crevices in its wake that revealed mainsprings, skeletal armatures, and whirring gears. Heads migrated and changed positions. It made slopping, juicy sounds, its many fused torsos expanding and deflating like soap bubbles. Ramona was reminded of the plastic army men her brother had played with. How one day, he dumped lighter fluid on them, claiming they had been nuked, and lit them up. What was left after the flames died out, a molten magma of melted bodies and jutting limbs and oozing faces, looked pretty much like what she was looking at it. Except this thing was viscidly alive, pulsing and pink and breathing, an elastic conglomeration of dolls, puppets, and mannequins trapped in a communal tar pit of seething, bubbling doll meat.

"I'm going to kill you," she said, trying to channel all the hate and frustration and rage that had haunted her ever since this nightmare began. "I'm going to hack you to pieces."

She said this calmly, but authoritatively. At first, it was all lie and bluff, but then steadily her anger began to rise and she knew if she could not put this horror down, then she could not possibly face what lay ahead.

"NO, RAMONA! YOU MUST NOT DO THAT!" the voices told her.

She stepped forward, burning with rage.

Frankendoll took a few wary steps away, bumping into a table and overturning it.

Click-clack, click-clack, click-clack, went its many drumming feet.

It was unsure now. The balance of power had shifted and Ramona could feel it in the air like a breath of heat surrounding her, pulling her in, making her its own...a spark, a blazing coal that would set tinder to burning and bring down a great forest of dark, twisting dread.

"Poor, poor Ramona. See how alone she is, how alone she has always been. Never able to trust and never able to forgive even herself. Always confused and miserable and burnt black to her core," the voices taunted. *"See how small she is, pretty, pretty, but small and weak and filled with a void of hot wind lacking substance."*

Yes, she was being taunted and her buttons were being pushed, quite expertly at that. Mother Crow knew what lived in the mind of her enemies, she knew how to squeeze out every last drop of their terror, self-loathing, and secret angst like foul gray water from a sponge. Images of Chazz filled her head. He was an asshole, a bastard, a user and abuser...yet, *yet,* she blamed herself because her manic OCD could not accept the fact that she had not fucked up something somewhere, a dropped word, a missed clue, a skein of misery that she had not followed it its source.

Click-clack, click-clack, click-clack.

Frankendoll was closing in on her even as her own mind was closing up like a bivalve as she drowned in a sea of self-doubt and guilt that filled her with indecision that became weakness that weighed her down and made her unsure of who she was and even what she was.

"The poor dear, always so alone. She's needed to become part of something bigger than herself and now she will," the voices said, more to themselves than to her. *"We'll love her, we'll protect her, we'll let her join us."*

"But I won't," she managed, wanting to believe it but unsure now.

Certain that the hot air was bled from her, Frankendoll came after her like the monster in its namesake film—a barbarian of hate and destruction. It flipped tables aside and crushed wriggling doll parts beneath its step, knocking shelves free and tearing pegboards from the walls, bearing down on her with absolute fury.

And in that moment of vulnerability as her life hung in the balance—and an unspeakable fate—she brought up the axe and charged and Frankendoll met her on neutral ground amongst the wreckage it had created. The mouths yawned wide and screamed with an outpouring of rage. Dozens of new doll faces opened like blossoming flowers and hands reached out, clawed and deadly hands, and she saw Chazz's disfigured doll face opening with the teeth of an ogre to peel her face free.

The axe landed.

It struck the monster square in the chest, splitting open two heads and cleaving into the mass beneath, which splintered with a loud cracking like deadwood or a crushed human rib cage. Bits of Frankendoll dropped away, a limb here and a head there. A viscous gout of hot yellow fluid erupted from the wound, burning Ramona's face and sizzling as it struck the floor. The many agonized mouths screamed their displeasure.

And Ramona kept chopping and chopping as hands scratched her face and struck her, tearing out handfuls of hair and ripping her shirt open, busily trying to get at the flesh beneath to pull it apart and assimilate it. A million red globular eyes pushed out of the mass, a million scraping gray fingers clutched at her, and the brace of heads atop the creature's shoulders opened wide and expelled a gurgling white vomit that had the consistency of rice. Ramona fought and it fought. They tore and thrashed and clawed at one another. Limbs flew and heads dropped and then the axe was wrenched from her hands and she was drawn closer to the pulsating mass, dozens of worming black tongues erupting like eels from deep sea caves to lick her eyes from their sockets.

But she did not give in.

Soaked with its vomit and its burning yellow blood that continued to squirt free in noisome loops, she was pressed up against the revolting tumescent flesh of the thing as it tried to bury her alive in itself, in its hot plastic skin, the gummy infected soup of its tissue, which even then webbed over her and snaked around her in waxy, sodden ropes.

Still, she fought.

She tore at the mass of Frankendoll, digging into it, tearing out its flesh in spongy cobs and pulpous clots as its discharge flooded over her and engulfed her and she felt its many hands pulling at her limbs, making ready to dismember her and add her biology to its morbid collection. But it was also at that moment that she heard something throbbing inside and knew it must be its heart. Machines did not have hearts, but this thing was not exactly a machine anymore than it was a living thing, more of a biomechanical interface.

With her last ounce of strength, she plunged her hands deep into it, tearing her knuckles on gears and cogs and spinning wheels and felt her hands grip a fleshy beating mass that felt about the size and general shape of a football. She yanked with everything she had and tore it out by the coiling roots, falling back with it, free of the monstrosity that wailed and screamed, blistering and dissolving and swimming in a fountain of its own doll waste.

She held the heart of the thing over her head.

"NO! NO! NO! NO! NO!" the voices boomed, seeming to make the room shake. Vessels shattered, and the walls cracked open and dust was shaken from the ceiling overhead.

The heart was enormously slimy, dangling with fibrous pink tendrils that coiled and snapped. It was like some rotten, swollen black tomato pulsing in her hands.

THUMP-THUMP! THUMP-THUMP! THUMP-THUMP!

She tried to rend it with her fingers but it was rubbery and slick, palpitating wildly with what seemed conflicting arrhythmic beats as if it was trying to jump free.

THUMP-THUMP!   *THUMP-THUMP!*
THUMPATHUMPATHUMPA THUMP—

As the hissing, bubbling mass of Frankendoll came at her, she threw the heart to the floor and picked up the axe. The voices screamed one last time before the blade came down and bisected the quivering muscle. It exploded like an overfilled water balloon. It erupted with an explosion of yellow juice that flooded over the floor and Frankendoll screamed, coming after Ramona again, but staggering and clumsy, smashing into things and tripping over wreckage. She grabbed up her Ray-O-Vac and axe and went through the hole it had made where the door had once been.

It followed, but not for long.

It tripped over ribbons of its own flesh and sloughing limbs, leaving smears of tissue on the walls that squirmed with fingers and mashed faces as it put out clouds of boiling fumes and its flesh went liquid and pooled on the floor.

And then she was out of range of its death throes and before her, the hub and who she had come to meet.

53

L ex had seconds.

Amid the deadly clockwork that was the surreal machinery of the puppet master's mind, he knew that the only way to stop all this was to stop the machine itself. It had to be unplugged, yanked out by the roots like a parasitic weed or its wheels would never stop turning. It was the only way. It was the only possible way.

As he felt the puppet master coming for him, he searched for something, anything that could be used to start smashing things.

There had to be something.

Then he saw there was.

A huge four-foot torque wrench that had to weight thirty pounds. It would have been child's play for Chazz to swing something like that around, but for Lex, who had always been a thin, wiry guy who could never put on weight regardless of how much junk food he swallowed, it was like swinging an immense battle axe.

He gripped it, liking the feel and heft of it.

Without hesitation, he brought it up over his head and swung it at the first thing he saw—a gearbox. He thought he heard a cry from above him as the housing broke free and then he was certain of it as the wrench landed again, smashing several gears and upsetting their calibration, making them grind and spew flakes of metal and sparks.

At that precise moment, the siren started up again.

Here, at ground zero, it was like an air raid siren, deafening and blaring, so goddamn unbelievably loud that he couldn't hear anything else. He gave the gearbox another whack for good measure, then he turned and brought the wrench down on a metal conduit that immediately crumbled and hissed with escaping steam. Just these two small blows seemed like nothing in comparison to the immensity of the machine around him... but it was felt. Something around him shifted. The factory trembled. Its delicate instrumentation was being attacked. He was an invading virus that would infect the body.

That's when the puppet master revealed itself.

It had been hiding, creeping about, rushing out, then retreating as if it were confused, but it was not confused now. There was nothing left to do but fight and fight it would. It came out to meet the intruder in a dark, amorphous shape that seemed to be constantly in flux as if it couldn't decide what it was.

And Lex couldn't decide either.

Something inside him demanded that he flee, but something else, something much stronger and inflexible, told him to stand his ground.

Face it. Look it in the eye and show no fear. Expose it for the weakling it is.

Which was great in theory. But as it came out to get him like a spider rushing out to snatch an insect, everything inside him went to rubber. The first thing he thought he saw was something like an immense sheet metal press with teeth. Then something more along the lines of a slinking mammoth demon worm encased in the chitinous black shell of a millipede that screamed in the voices of flayed children. It showed him a hundred mouths, then a thousand globular red eyes veined with black, and finally descending talons like shards of glass that had come to eviscerate him.

Don't even blink. Do not look away.

Hefting the heavy wrench in his hands, he felt positively impotent against this thing that circled around him, a horrendous industrialized and mechanistic centipede suspended off the ground by its puppet strings of white tendrils. They were like a million-million wire-fine fiber optic cables, so many that they formed sheaths and braids, growing out of the beast and cradling it in a cocoon of cobwebs whose origins were high, high above.

It looked down at him with seeking red eyes, which were

not only horribly profuse but horribly intricate in design, like spinning gyroscopes, multi-lensed and multifaceted like the compound eyes of meat flies. The great undulant, vermiform body was a geometrically complex machine that pumped out hissing spirals of steam, trailing compression hoses and high-voltage lines like looping entrails. Its flexing shell looked like it was more metal than flesh or perhaps flesh becoming metal. Like the walls of the clockwork chamber itself, it was set with knobs and crevices and meshing gears, all of it seeming to be in constant industrious motion, spinning and linking and turning. And as it got closer to him, he dared blink and saw that it was composed not just of machine parts and flesh in some unnatural synchronicity, but of interlinked mannequins welded into some loathsome congregation of the damned. Eyeless and screaming, they reached out with thousands of thrashing arms and fingers.

And high above at the end of the corkscrewing neck, he looked into the face of the puppet master...and it was female. There was no mistaking that. The face of the old woman he had seen in the house, the one stitching up the dead boy. Maybe it wasn't exactly human any longer, but he saw that it had once been so. She or it had trailing straw-dry hair like luminous white worms, the fissured face of a petrified corpse, blank eyes like the buttons of greasy toadstools, and puckered gums set with what seemed to be the whirring teeth of chains. A dire machine of hate and retribution now, but once, *once*, she had been a living woman and not a crawling malevolence.

As it came for him, he held up his wrench, more than a little aware of the pitiful threat he presented in the face of this immense chimera that had been birthed from the black womb of the factory.

54

"LEX!" Ramona cried when she saw him facing off against something that her mind could not even begin to categorize. "*LEX!*"

The thing that had been coming for him paused, its segments flexing and gnashing. It hovered there, bleeding steam and breathing out smoke, drops of fluid dripping from its underside.

Now it turned and started in her direction.

Its appearance made her take a step back and she tripped over a drainage pipe and went promptly on her ass, but she did not let go of the flashlight or her axe.

It's Mother Crow, Ramona! She's coming to get you!

But what she saw in that dizzying, hallucinogenic moment was not Mother Crow or the mutant mechanism she indeed had become, a hybrid of flesh and iron, but hordes of doll people stiff-walking in her direction. They were white-faced mannequins in black cloaks, evil clown puppets sprouting writhing red hair like wriggling rubber worms, blow-up dolls and marionettes with vicious sucking mouths, fanged moppets and razor-wielding baby dolls, kewpies with too many limbs and nightmare Raggedy Anns brandishing meat cleavers. Some dark toy chest had been opened, and out they came to maim and mutilate.

Leading the pack was something like a wizened, corpse-faced hag in a ragged gray gunnysack dress that hobbled on a pegleg. Her face was a sutured gray bag that looked like it had been peeled from a corpse in sections, then stitched back together in a living pelt. Her eyes were huge gaping holes, her mouth shriveled back from gums and teeth. Ramona saw she carried a giggling mannequin head in one hand, swinging it back and forth by lustrous black hair, and there was no doubt it was Soo-Lee.

"RAMONA!" a voice shouted. "RAMONA! SNAP OUT OF IT!"

It might have ended there but for the voice.

She blinked her eyes and cleared her head and saw that Lex was busy. He was in action. He had some great wrench in his hand and he was smashing it into the machinery and tearing hoses from couplings. With each blow, she noticed, there were fewer doll people and the factory itself seemed to tremble with rage or pain and possibly both.

By then, the pegleg woman was closing in. There was blood running from her empty eye sockets and more of it misting from her stitched mouth. It ran down the leathery mask of her face. Her gait was more uneven than ever, determined but drunken. She reached up a withered claw and Ramona saw three fingers drop from it.

She was damaged.

This whole place was damaged.

Lex was killing it.

"DESTROY IT ALL!" he cried out. "WRECK IT! TRASH IT! BREAK IT!"

But Ramona already knew that. Mother Crow was the machine and the machine was Mother Crow. They existed in some abhorrent, deranged symbiosis and one could not live without the other. Each blow struck to the machinery was a blow struck to her.

The pegleg woman was mere feet away by the time Ramona found her feet. The stitching of her face was coming apart and blood that was dark like runny ink spilled freely from numerous gaps and tears. Howling, she clawed out at Ramona with bloodstained fingers, but Ramona easily sidestepped the foundering automaton.

"*Cunt!*" the woman growled with a guttural sound. "*Interfering do-gooding cunt! I HAD HIM AND I'LL HAVE YOU! DO YOU HEAR ME?*"

One of her hands grabbed Ramona's wrist and it was burning hot as if she was blazing inside. Puffs of smoke were beginning to churn from every orifice and split seam. Ramona yanked her arm free and three of the pegleg woman's fingers came away with it.

She was beginning to crumble, to decay and dissolute.

Ramona brought the axe around in a savage arc and the blade sheared right into the woman's face, which cracked open like a snail shell, something moist and pink inside drawing away from the intrusion of light. She stumbled back, tripped over her own peg and hit the floor with a cloud of dust and fragments, a viscid yellow ooze draining from her ruined head.

She moved no more.

The axe still in her hand, Ramona swung it again, shearing a couple of hydraulic lines that gurgled out copious amounts of red blood. It wasn't possible, but she saw it spill over the tops of her shoes. She smashed a control panel and sheared the couplings of a huge spring, then gashed open a power box that went with a blinding blue flash that should have knocked her on her ass but didn't.

Lex was in a wild frenzy, doing the same thing.

They were winning.

They were winning, by God.

The factory around them was sputtering and grinding, things clanging that should have moved with oiled smoothness. There was a groaning of metal fatigue and the sound of leaking fluid. The air was hot and stinking, everything backlit by an irregular flickering like a dying fluorescent.

This was the pivotal moment.

55

Mother Crow came charging out of the shadows making a screeching, squealing sound like a grinder biting into steel plating. She pushed out a rolling mist of red steam, jerking and thrashing on her scores of puppet strings. She made a clanking noise like machinery, a sibilance of boiling vapors, and a repellent slithering sound that, to Lex's overheated imagination, reminded him of immense, bloated leeches intertwining.

Now, at this final hour, the terror inside him was deep and shivery. How could they possibly stand against her? How could they hope to overwhelm a biomechanical monster driven by pure deranged supernatural wrath? It seemed they were beaten on every front.

The creature was going for Ramona.

And somehow, someway, he knew that she had been its target all along. Not him. Not any of the others. They were throwaways, stock characters, spear-carriers. The real center of power was Ramona and if she could not be usurped here and now, it would end for this horrible twisted monstrosity that—

Mother Crow, a voice said to him quite calmly. *Her name is Mother Crow.*

It sounded like Ramona's voice, as if she had spoken right next to his ear.

As it bore down on her, another voice—his own—informed him, *Stand and fight! Fight for Ramona! If she can't win, you can't either! So fight! Goddammit, fight!*

Yes, that was thing, and nothing else mattered and maybe it never had.

Ramona waited for Mother Crow and there did not seem to be even a momentary twinge of fear or apprehension on her face.

"COME AND GET ME, YOU OLD FUCKING HAG!" she shouted. "YOU DRIED-UP OLD BAG OF HAY! I'M RIGHT HERE! YOU NEVER HAD ANY POWER! YOU NEVER HAD ANYTHING! YOU WERE *AFRAID! AFRAID OF BEING ALONE! AFRAID OF NOT BEING ABLE TO PULL THE STRINGS AND MAKE YOUR WORKERS DANCE!*"

Mother Crow shuddered with rage, roaring and growling.

As the bulk of her passed overhead, Lex swung his wrench and shattered a brace of mannequin arms that reached for him. But that wasn't enough and he knew it. The witch would merely regenerate herself. He had to destroy this place. *Habitat destruction.* That was the key. He went wild at that point, swinging his wrench and bashing pipes and valves and amplifiers. He saw a massive worm gear set in the wall and went at it like a berserker, pounding it until the chain slipped its cogs and there was a scream of tortured metal, an explosion of fiery blue sparks, and the factory itself seemed to cry out in agony.

(NO! NO! NO! I CANNOT DIE!)

He could hear Mother Crow's screaming, tortured voice in his head. It seemed to be coming from some distant plain of suffering, gathering strength like a tempest, and driving right into his skull, punching through his thoughts.

The chain whirred and sparked, throwing out black smoke that smelled like burning oil and industrial sludge, and then it came right off its cogs, swinging like a boomerang and nearly taking Lex's head right off. It clanged to the floor, its heavy iron teeth stripping a junction box off the wall in an explosion of discharged electricity.

It was like some kind of devastating chain reaction.

The driver gears and clock wheels lost their balance and the mainspring lost its tension, and there was a great high-pitched squeal from above as chains and pinions came loose, tearing apart the machinery and ripping vacuum lines and steam piping free as they fell. The great pendulums above were out of calibration like everything else, wobbling and gonging as they smashed into one another. One of them broke free of its housing and sheared through the great spider's web above...

and the spider that clung there. Both came crashing down, the pendulum impaling a machine, belts and rotors flying up into the air like shrapnel as bearings superheated and melted and relays went with a blinding white flash, oil and diesel fuel igniting and sending up a mushrooming curtain of flame. The spider itself crashed amongst the wreckage, bursting into a million writhing doll parts upon impact that were swallowed by the blaze.

And again, Mother Crow's voice pounded through his head.

(MY CHILDREN! MY CHILDREN! MURDERING MY CHILDREN!)

There was a searing stink in the air, a burnt smell of blown fuses and melted rubber, fatigued metal and hot ozone. The entire complex was coming apart.

"NOW YOU'LL BE ALONE WITH WHAT YOU MADE!" Ramona taunted her. "YOU BELONG ALONE! YOU NEVER HAD ANYONE! YOU'RE DRY! YOU'RE BARREN! NO ONE EVER LOVED YOU AND NO ONE COULD STAND THE SIGHT OF YOU, YOU FUCKING OLD MAID! OLD BAT! *VIRGIN!*"

Mother Crow's worming bulk struck the floor as her tendrils snapped and burned. She towered above Ramona, sizzling and smoking, an acrid steam pouring from her that stank like burning corpses. Her body was melting and popping, mannequin faces screaming out their agony and limbs liquefying like hot tallow. She struck the floor and then rose up again, glued to it by millions of oozing strings of hot plastic.

(I REFUSE TO DIE!)

Lex dropped to one knee, the fury of the beast's words like a hive of bees in his head droning full blast. He let out a cry, feeling the true intensity of her mind as it pierced his own. She could have turned his brain to sauce if she wanted to and if it hadn't have been for Ramona, she probably would have.

Her image blurred in his eyes and then blurred again and he saw...he saw her head become a great clock face that had to be twenty feet or more in circumference. Instead of hour and minute hands there was a corpse-like husk crucified to it, a thing of bones and rags and whipping white hair: the physical remains of Mother Crow. Her face was ravaged and worm-holed, the parchment-dry skin suckered to the leering skull beneath like papier mache. Dozens of lines and hoses were plugged into the mummy as if she were the central brain box, all of them slinking and trembling like tentacles. Whatever still haunted those bones was a flat and blatant evil, a swollen parasite with a noxious, polluted mind. Even in death, the mummy's death mask was hitched in a scowl of unearthly hate.

Ramona threw what looked to be an aluminum barreled flashlight right at it and caught it dead-on, the skull breaking apart like a vase and there was an eruption of white light.

She kept at it, swinging the axe and chopping into the beast, cleaving mannequin parts loose that struck the floor, some melting and others struggling with stolen life that was fading fast now.

The clock face was gone then and there was some gruesome hybrid of a woman's head and a centipede that screamed in agony, thrashing back and forth, side to side. As Lex hit it with his wrench, it slapped him aside and he hit the floor, blood streaming from a torn gash in his forehead. As the threshing mandibles of the head—which looked oddly like jagged ice tongs—reached down for Ramona, she let out a wild and resounding rebel yell and buried the blade of her axe right into the thing's face, which split open and gushed ribbons of yellow slime.

Crippled and blind, Mother Crow half-crawled and half dragged herself out of harm's way, but Ramona kept after her.

WHACK! went the axe.

WHACK! WHACK! WHACK!

Lex got to his feet, pipes and machinery crashing all around him as the chamber came apart. He swung the big wrench into Mother Crow overhanded again and again, smashing the chittering plating that held her together, hot fluid shooting into the air and blistering his face.

(I WILL I WILL I WILL NOT CEASE!)

But she no longer had a choice, he knew. Even her deathless, energetic mind could not survive the total disruption of its environment. She was nearly vanquished and only her raging ego kept her going by that point.

She crept away like a stepped-upon spider, broken and crumpled, great sections of her falling away and revealing the unnatural struggling machinery within that was enclosed in a welded steel armature that resembled some abstract skeleton. She was crippled badly, her dying screams steadily losing volume and becoming a shrill whining that itself dissolved into something like a sobbing and mewling. Severed compression lines and hydraulic hoses trailed behind her like slit arteries, gushing black fluid in gurgling pools.

Ramona charged in and brought the axe down on the remains of the cleaved head and it broke apart, a discharge of opaque blood squirting up into the air. Burning and sparking with high-voltage arcs, barely moving, the remains of Mother Crow were engulfed in flames, crackling and collapsing.

And by then, the entire place was on fire.

56

Ramona grabbed Lex by the hand and towed him out of the burning wreckage, navigating among heaped debris as everything came apart now that there was nothing to hold it together, no psychic atomic fission of an undead mind. Glass shattered and walls fell. Churning steam and roiling clouds of black smoke filled the air. Shards of metal flew. Electrical lines discharged their final volts as fuse boxes exploded one after the other.

They barely made it out of there before the real destruction began.

They ran across the courtyard, through the burning grasses until they reached the verge of the road, coughing on the gathering fumes. Below them, the town; before them, the factory in its death throes. It did not go easily the way an ordinary building might. There was too much sentient wrath and malevolence in every plank and nailhead. It had soaked up evil like a sponge and evil did not die easily.

The ground rumbled and shook, immense cracks opening up to all sides as if the earth was made of glass. The looming structure of the factory itself was burning, shuddering on its foundation, putting out an orange blaze that lit the dark sky and great rolling clouds of black soot that hung above it in a pall. There was a pained groaning sort of sound and one of the walls fell in and then another, gigantic flames rising up in red spikes. Everything was coming apart in there, shattering and snapping and incinerating. The sound of voices screaming echoed into the night in an eerie sibilance, rising in volume. The fire began to spread in all directions.

"That's how it happened," Ramona said as she watched it

all. "The townspeople...they came up here and they torched this place. It was arson. They had to break the spell of Mother Crow, they had to sever the hold she had on them so they burned the factory with her in it. And the fire spread. It took everything."

Lex drew a hand across his smudged face. "It swept from here right down into the town itself and burned it flat."

Though the fire blazed hot and they could feel the heat blowing out at them in waves, they stood and watched, knowing they were right in its path. Something wasn't quite over and they would not leave until it was.

The blazing structure trembled and shook. Even though it was falling apart, the glowing heat seemed to weld it together into a terrible black life force that refused death. There was a groaning, buckling sound as it became a living entity that fought for survival. They could see glaring red eyes like fireballs staring out at them as it tried to rise up like a blackened skeleton trying to pull itself free of a plague pit. It seemed like it was actually going to do it. A weird thrumming noise came from it and the world began to roll with shockwaves as some critical mass approached like a nuclear core going critical.

"RUN!" Ramona cried out, making for the road.

She didn't know what was going to happen, but something inside her knew that when it happened, it would be devastating beyond belief like Hiroshima at ground zero.

She saw Lex running and stumbling down the road back down toward the town. He turned back once and called out something to her, but she could not hear what it was.

Behind her there was a roaring eruption of pure energy and she was trapped in the center of chaos. It felt like millions of blades of light punched into her, lifting her up and throwing her through the air with crushing force. She was kicked into the deepest, darkest well within herself and then sucked back out to be launched with incredible velocity through screaming cosmic blackness.

No...no...please...

Whether it was her mind or her body that was in flight, she didn't know. Perhaps both and neither. She was fired like a bullet through red vistas and green dimensions, cycled through time and space and matter, it seemed, particulated into shrieking dust that howled through skull-white anti-worlds and then into an immense outer blackness that was darker than anything the world had known or ever could know.

When it ended, she was crawling through the blackened ruins of Stokes, mindless and whimpering, her entire body stiff and hurting, a monstrous headache throbbing in her skull.

"*Lex?*" she heard her sobbing voice cry. "*Oh...Lex, where are you?*"

Covered in cinders, burned by hot ashes, she pulled her sooty, pain-wracked body through a warped doorway, coughing on the thick smoke that blew through the jigsaw of streets like a gritty ground fog. The house or building or whatever in the hell it was, was still smoldering. She hastily tore her shirt off and pressed it over her mouth so she would not asphyxiate.

Stairs.

The air might be better up there.

On her hands and knees, she climbed them, breathing hard, her muscles bunched and tense, an odd numbness in her limbs as if she had been stunned like a cow. Upstairs, it was warm, but the air was easier to breathe. She found a doorway and crawled through it, pushing it shut behind her.

She waited there, knees drawn up to her bare chest, leaning against the door, unable to even stand and find a chair. Her exhaustion was complete. Shaking in the darkness, she surrendered to it. For minutes or hours, she did not know.

"*Ramona? Ramona?*"

A voice was calling out to her and at first she did not recognize it, but slowly she remembered where she was and who the voice must belong to. She moved a bit, thumping her shoulder against the door.

"Ramona?" Lex called out.

Yes, she thought. *I'm here.*

He was outside the door now, pounding on it with his knuckles, calling her name. She could hear him breathing, the desperation just beneath his words. His voice was like that of a little boy who was holding back tears.

"Ramona?"

Her throat felt so very dry she could barely speak. She shifted, cocking her head, a strand of dark hair falling over her eyes that could no longer see. A crooked grin split open her white, flaking face as her hinged fingers reached for the doorknob. *"Is that you, doll-face?"* she said.

ABOUT THE AUTHOR

Tim Curran is the author of the novels *Skin Medicine, Hive, Dead Sea, Resurrection, Hag Night, Skull Moon, The Devil Next Door, Doll Face, Afterburn, House of Skin,* and *Biohazard.* His short stories have been collected in *Bone Marrow Stew* and *Zombie Pulp.* His novellas include *The Underdwelling, The Corpse King, Puppet Graveyard, Worm, and Blackout.* His short stories have appeared in such magazines as *City Slab, Flesh&Blood, Book of Dark Wisdom,* and *Inhuman,* as well as anthologies such as *Shadows Over Main Street, Eulogies III,* and *October Dreams* II. His fiction has been translated into German, Japanese, Spanish, and Italian. Find him on Facebook at:

https://www.facebook.com/tim.curran.77

Curious about other Crossroad Press books?
Stop by our site:
http://store.crossroadpress.com
We offer quality writing
in digital, audio, and print formats.

Enter the code FIRSTBOOK
to get 20% off your first order from our store!
Stop by today!

Made in the USA
Las Vegas, NV
05 December 2021

36206421R00154